WINTERCHILL

WINTERCHILL
Ernest J. Finney

WILLIAM MORROW AND COMPANY, INC.
New York

Library of Congress Cataloging-in-Publication Data

Finney, Ernest J.
    Winterchill : a novel.

    I. Title. II. Title: Winter chill.
PS3556.I499W56   1989   813'.54   88-13573
ISBN 0-688-08305-6

Printed in the United States of America

First Edition

1   2   3   4   5   6   7   8   9   10

BOOK DESIGN BY NICOLA MAZZELLA

For Nan

CONTENTS

WINTER CHILL: a period of cold weather during the dormant season necessary for normal fruit set and growth in the following growing season.

BIRDS LANDING
1972–1979

I was out waiting by the mailbox and I heard James coming. It seemed like it was colder than it should have been for November, frost on the ground as even as white paint. When the pickup stopped I hopped into the back. The boys were sitting in front with James, and Elmo was already at the club. I eased myself a space, careful not to break any of the heads off the decoys sacked up all around me. It was warmer on the bottom; I could feel the wooden shapes of the mallards digging into my sides as I closed my eyes.

While I unloaded the sacks and took them to the skiffs, James and the boys went over and got some coffee. The sky was still black dark, except for where the blaze of the open fire shot up flame and sparks as high as any of the stars. When I finished the sacks I started in on the sports gear, carefully, making sure I didn't drop anything, especially the leather gun cases. When I was done, Elmo handed me a tin cup of coffee and I got closer to the fire, but not so close I'd melt my rubber boots. When they started filling their flasks from the bottles on the table I slipped past and through the side door into the kitchen. There were plenty of biscuits left and I filled the pockets of my jacket before I could hear anyone coming and got back outside.

Mr. Conlin started calling out the names and their blind numbers. He knew what he was doing. The poor shots got James or one of the boys or even his son Mickey Conlin: all of them knew how to say, "It must be yours; I never got off a shot." Everyone got a limit, or as many ducks as he wanted. Especially Mr. Conlin's best investors. But he kept Elmo for himself to call.

Mr. Conlin and his friends all stood together. You could almost tell who had the most money by how loud they talked. "Well, I'm ready any time you are, Conlin."

"Hold your horses. It's too dark to go out there." And the laughing. The sports laughed at anything. "You never shot a triple in your life." Some doubled over, holding their sides. Mickey was making sure everyone had more coffee and bourbon, moving among them with the coffee pot and a bottle.

James and the boys stood by themselves. With their hoods up they looked like three large bears, probably bigger than any of the bears I'd seen in the magazines. Elmo, over by the liquor table slipping a bottle under his leather jacket, didn't look like a bear. Didn't look like anything. He was too thin and stooped; it was hard even recognizing him unless he was turned facing you. It was only when you saw James, who was nine or ten years older, standing beside Elmo that you noticed the resemblance. They had the same sharp long nose, cleft chin, same shape of the head, but Elmo looked used up, as if he'd been the same size as James but then had shrunk and shriveled. They were brothers. The boys were James's sons. I didn't belong to anyone here.

Virginia, Mr. Conlin's daughter, finally came out. Down the club stairs two at a time. "Did I keep you?" she asked. No one complained. She was perfect. She was as interesting to look at as a wood duck. The longer you saw her the better it made you feel. She had a good word for everyone. Pulled my cap down over my eyes as she passed, going to the boat. "Hey Gerald," she said.

"Watch it," Mickey said, walking behind her, "you'll have to wash your hands." Some laughed. It didn't bother me. Mickey was a pissant even if he was her brother. I steadied the boat while she stepped down. We were going to have to hurry. The darkness was cracking. "Remember the limit," Mr. Conlin shouted before he sat down in the stern.

"Come on, Conlin, we came here for a shoot," someone called.

Mickey yelled out, his hands cupped, "We have four spare licenses to fill. And if that son of a bitch of a warden shows up, he'll wish he looked the other way." Some of them cheered.

Elmo rowed. I could tell in the dark as well as at noon where we were. We passed the place last summer where I found the muskrat nest near number seven blind. Like miniature pigs they were, stuffed down in a last year's red-winged blackbird's nest. I waded back in the tules to hang them up again. We spent weeks in the summer cutting the tules, repairing the blinds, keeping the water open enough to bring the ducks down. Hours stooping low and grabbing fistfuls of tules just above the mud and slashing them loose, then stacking them in the skiffs to haul away to burn on the levees. My hands turned as clean as they ever got and that layer of skin peeled away and I was cleaner yet. August was the busy time of the year when the plums had to be picked, but working in the ponds had to be done for Mr. Conlin. He owned the whole marsh now. He owned all the way to the road on one side and the river on the other side: wheat fields, plums, nectarine and apricot orchards; six square miles, James said once.

James and Elmo had about a hundred acres left from what their grandfather had left them. They worked for Mr. Conlin when they had the chance. During the winter they made more money at the club then they did at farming in the summer. But it was never enough. I was never in the main house that James or Greta didn't say, "What are we going to do now?" The bank was after them or someone else was dunning them. But that didn't stop James from buying a new pickup for himself or a new boat. Elmo couldn't get enough credit for that. But he could go on a two-week wingding that would end him up in the county drunk tank or drying out somewhere. James would always get him out.

Number three blind was in the best place, and with Elmo calling they'd get their pick of ducks. Mr. Conlin had his brazier going and a blanket around his shoulders the minute he settled himself. He didn't like the cold. The blind was built out of planks, like a small cow stall in a barn, but up on stilts. Virginia had her side fixed like a kitchen: nails to hang her shot gun and heavy jacket and hat; a cushion for the bench she sat on in front of a small folding table where she played cribbage with Elmo and heated her tea on a small burner. "We still got room for a couch," he'd tell her.

I had to hurry and set out the decoys. All I had to do was what Elmo told me: take them out of the sack, one at a time, making sure the line was attached to the next one and they set right in the water. Sometimes the piece of lead we nailed to the bottom for balance came loose and the decoy would list. I'd bang the nail back in against the oarlock. By the feel of them I could tell who had carved them or if they were store bought. James's were perfect; they looked more like ducks than real ones do. He'd spend a day painting one of them: he'd put the white ring around a mallard's neck and the green in a teal's wing. James and Elmo's father's were smaller than usual, and he made his out of one piece of wood, head and body. He used fruitwood, which was too heavy, and they sat low in the water. James wanted to throw them away but Elmo said they brought us luck. James and Elmo's father's father used to make them like they did where he originally came from, but there were only a few of them left. You could tell those ones because he'd taken two pieces of wood, hollowed out the middle, and glued them together before he shaped them. They rode high in the water and looked like they were getting ready to raise off. Elmo's didn't even look like decoys. They were big, almost the size of brant. And their heads and necks could be pointed anywhere, standing straight up like a fence post, parked sleeping under a wing, stretched out feeding. Openmouthed and quacking, even. They got broken easily. And I took pains too. He'd carve a mallard's head on a sprig's body and paint it all gray. He once made a canvasback with a head on each end. James hid it somewhere in the barn so Mr. Conlin or Mickey wouldn't see it. Neither of the boys, Tommy or Gary, carved. Before I lost my knife, I'd done seven. I had them under my bed. I hadn't shown them to anyone yet.

When I was finished it was light enough to see the whole raft of decoys. They hung together like they were visiting. I sculled the boat out of sight but close enough to the blind to hear. I would rather be by myself in a boat than cooped up in one of those small blinds. I kept my eyes peeled but my face down. They could see anything; ducks are clever when they're in the air. I ate some biscuits, wishing I'd soaked the faces in the skillet full of bacon fat. I must have dozed, because Elmo was calling. I stayed like I was, not moving, even though I'd pulled tules over the boat: those birds would see me and shy. By inches I moved my head so my eye was able to see up. It was yellow light of morning now but the flight was too far away to hear. He kept calling. I could almost feel the sound of those wings starting to slow, hesitate. I could believe those stories James told of the skies black with ducks, so many they would block out the sun. Now they came in single Vs and Ws and you had to know what you were doing. Things had to be just right before they'd come down. They'd pass over the whole country now if they didn't get tired and hungry. The flight started to turn, come back.

I'd seen him do it lots of times when it was just the three of us in the blind: Virginia in her green high-school sweater crouched down holding her sixteen gauge; Elmo bent over, his eyes closed as if he were asleep or praying. He used just his hands, taking deep breaths, then letting them out as if streams of ducks were coming out of his throat. I'd close my eyes too. It was like you were a sprig too; it filled you up, tossed you and made you listen. You had to call back, extend your neck to listen for the next sound. Then glide down lower, all the other ducks following behind.

Elmo would stop. The leader would get frantic and drop faster, calling, calling. Then Elmo would start in again, bring the ducks right over the blind, guiding them. Their wings automatically jutted out to brake; their legs came down limp. Sinking. Hovering. Then Virginia would raise up and let fly. "My own magic voice," she would say, rubbing Elmo's neck, after. He'd wink at me as I loaded up her shotgun again.

There must have been a dozen guns blazing off and on all morning, the spent shot coming down like hard rain on the surface of the pond, the ducks smashing against the water with a splash and then floating there like pieces of colored cloth. It was busy for me, keeping low, out of sight, but getting around to all the places the ducks drifted to and chasing down the cripples. That was a chore. I used my pole to whack them on the head when they tried to hide and got too far in the tules. Some just swam around in circles, crazy; others sat quiet on the water and let me pick them up.

I did like Elmo showed me, sat down, put them between my knees, put my fist around their necks and yanked. Sometimes they weren't hurt bad, just a broken wing or an eye shot out. If I could feel the shot under the down, I could squeeze it out. Some I couldn't find anything wrong with. It was as if, from the surprise at not finding what they were looking for, they weren't able to leave. They'd light in the water and stay put through all the noise and confusion. Wild ducks who had never been shot at before did that. Sometimes they were dead and never were hit. I put some of the live ones in a sack, when I was sure no one would see me. They never made a sound, never moved. They knew. The dead ones I pitched in the stern.

Through the morning I took four loads of ducks back to the dock. The flights were coming less and less as the sun rose up. There was still some morning mist left from the night when I went back for the fifth time. The sun wasn't hot enough yet. Some of the shooters were talking out loud now. One yelled, "Conlin, let's go back for lunch; I've had enough." "I second the motion," someone else yelled. Mr. Conlin blew the whistle and I heard the shells flying out as they were ejected.

Mickey made me stop at his blind to take him back. There was nothing I could do. James had their boat hauling ducks in. I kept as far away from him as I could. He sat on the bow point, and instead of sculling I poled from the stern. The other two sports sat in the middle. He didn't say anything until I poled past two teal that were floating. Without missing a stroke I grabbed them up. "Now you see why we don't use dogs. We got Gerald, here. He's as good as any retriever you could find. There won't be a downed bird left around here when he's through." The sports looked me over, and I began to feel sweat on my upper lip.

I knew Mickey would give me at least a five-dollar bill for helping, no matter what he said. Some of the other sports would give me something; a box of shells, used boots, a jacket, money. Showing off. I cracked a hen mallard who thought I didn't see her hiding with the decoys, then got it in position and flipped it in the air and it landed in the boat. "See, he's good. Does he come back in the boat and shake water on you? Get you wet? No sir. He's better than a blue-ribbon retriever. Then, on the other hand, he's got a propensity to smell worse than one." Everyone laughed. I kept poling.

I went back for Mr. Conlin. He yelled at me for not taking him in first. I went in as fast as I could. Most everyone else was there. I held the boat steady for them to get out, Mr. Conlin, Elmo, and Virginia, then helped the boys and James separate the ducks for the pictures. Teal, six rows; mallards, four; and pintails, almost one and a half. Virginia had shot the first snow goose of the season. They were all lined out, hundreds of them, and the sports were swigging beer and talking and starting to form up behind them.

I began hauling the gear up to the club and stashing it by the fireplace in the lounge. I liked the way it looked, knotty-pine walls and ceiling, with the big stone fireplace at one end. Long tables with benches down the middle for eating and playing cards. Soft chairs. The floor was so polished it seemed impossible anyone walked on it. On shelves along one wall, flying, sitting as if they were still alive, were the stuffed ducks. I could remember handling some of them. On the other wall were the small framed photos of the sports and kills.

Greta saw me as I went by the kitchen and waved me in. She cut me a wedge of lunchtime apple pie and I put it all in my mouth in two bites. While I was chewing she stuffed my pockets full of bananas and oranges for the boys. Then I hurried back out before Mickey noticed.

When I saw the warden's green pickup I wanted to run. Mickey was talking to him to one side, and everyone else was milling around. Virginia had Mr. Conlin by one arm and was talking to him. No one was taking pictures or standing anywhere near the ducks. I went down and picked up two more gun cases and a wooden box of shells that hadn't been used. I heard Mickey say, "You're new, I guess. You know who these people are? They're from the city. That one over there," and he pointed with his thumb "is the governor's brother. We bring them here, invite them down so they can shoot some ducks, that's all, and you're going to embarrass everyone?" The warden said something I didn't hear.

I took the load in but hurried back out. The warden was counting the birds on the ground and writing in his notebook. Mr. Conlin broke away from Virginia and rushed over to the warden. Gave him a little push on his chest to get his attention. "Who in the hell do you think you are? You're trespassing. Get the hell off my land." The warden kept counting. "You no good son of a bitch," Mr. Conlin yelled. The warden got red-faced but didn't back down. Virginia went and tried to pull Mr. Conlin away. Then Greta rang the dinner bell and everyone hurried up the steps to the club.

Going down the steps of the school bus, I could see Elmo. He was just fishing a decoy out of his drum of linseed oil. He always soaked them before he painted them so the water wouldn't get to them so fast. I put my books down on his front steps to help. "No, no," he said, "you'll get all greasy." He'd been drinking since the weekend shoot. "You've been keeping yourself squared away?" I nodded, tucking in my shirt in back. "Doing your work, too?"

"I'm ahead."

"I don't want to have to go up there any more. And talk to Mrs. Ross," he added.

"You won't have to."

"Go change and we'll paint some of these things." I hurried down the path to the house. The toothpick I propped up against the front door was still up. I checked her bedroom, going upstairs to the attic. But she hadn't come back. I changed, hanging my trousers folded at the crease, putting my shirt over the top. She hadn't been back in three months, more than that. It was before school. I missed her. At night, hearing her come home, I knew all the sounds. The screen door bang, the front door. Putting her heavy purse on the table. The floor against her heels. I stopped listening if there was someone with her. I'd practice my calls in my head. I asked Elmo once what he was telling them when he called. "I don't know, just what comes to mind. What they want to hear, like the rest of us." I put on my old overalls, then my rubber boots. I knew how I was going to kill Mickey. I heard him talking to someone in a blind once, when she was here and she went up to the club to help. "Keeps the hunters happy, services them and the locals." I knew who he was talking about. I knew all about it. Her and Mickey. Her and Elmo. Even Mr. Conlin and some of the sports. It didn't bother me. This summer she took off with a bartender from where she was working. Greta invited me to stay up with them but I didn't want to. My mother sent money and that kept James quiet.

I went around back with an armful of salted crackers, just to look at my herd, as Elmo called them. There had to be a couple of hundred cripples at least. A few from last season but most from this one. I kept them in the old pheasant pens that James had built for one of his schemes once. I had water running in there, and it was good and muddy. I didn't have to feed them much grain. I let them loose in the field and they ate up the grass like a lawn mower'd passed. They came to me like chickens, and I crumbled some of the crackers for them. I'd clipped their wing feathers, but it wasn't necessary. They knew what it was like outside in the marsh. I herded them into the pens like sheep at night.

We painted the decoys. Elmo was no good at it; he didn't have any system. He put too much paint on and it ran. He never let one color dry enough before he put on the next. He stopped after a couple and lit a cigarette. He always wiped his mouth with a rag after he had a drink from the bottle he kept by his chair. And he watched me, working back and forth between a dozen drake mallards, keeping the paint stirred and the lids on until I needed the color. I asked to borrow his knife to whittle down a high place on the slope of a head. He never liked me to make any changes on his decoys unless they were absolutely necessary. He started fishing around in his pocket and came up with my own knife. "Will this do?" he asked, holding it out. "I meant to give it back to you before, but it slipped my mind."

I took the knife. It had cost me, because it was handmade and bone-handled. I'd sent away for it from an ad in a magazine. I'd thought Elmo was going to keep it. He had been sitting right where he was now when the superintendent brought me back. He got up out of the chair when the superintendent asked, "You his father?"

"What happened?"

The superintendent was getting so excited, talked so fast, it was hard to understand what he was saying. "He broke some eighth-grader's jaw and tried to stab three others. With this." He took out my knife. "He's to stay out until I see both his parents up at the school." The superintendent was almost yelling. "Mrs. Ross says he's not at his grade level either." He took a few steps away and yelled, "I couldn't get hold of a deputy or I'd have had him taken into town." He was almost to his car when he turned for the last time. "He needs to learn about personal hygiene, too."

After he drove off Elmo asked me, "What do you have to say for yourself?"

"Nothing," I told him. From the first day of school they had me where they wanted me. The eighth-graders. I don't know why. But they could no more help hitting me than I could help getting a split lip or a bloody nose. They were going to flush my head in the urinal because I had crusted ears. They chased me at recess. Flipped dried snot at me. Finally I made a plan. I made sure they saw me go into the lavoratory after lunch, a place I never went anymore, no matter how bad I had to pee. I jumped up on a sink and unloosened the adjusting nut so the door swung free. I waited, just like you do for a teal to come down. The door opened a little, then a little more. I could picture his head between the edge of the door and the doorjamb. Then I ran from across the room and hit the door with my whole body. Ducks don't shriek like that. I was trapped, too, something I didn't plan. But I had my knife.

"Well, you ready for some supper?" Elmo said, weighing my knife the superintendent had given him in the palm of his hand. I didn't want to go up to the house. "Greta's got two panfuls of ducks; you know what you're missing." It made me hungry just thinking about roast duck. Sitting in the kitchen, just eating until I was so full I had to unloosen the top button of my pants and my shirt too, James and the boys eating meatloaf or pork chops, anything but duck, because they said it tasted of fish. "You ought to eat, there's no use hiding," Elmo said. I still shook my head. "You better come, Gerald." When he used my name, I got up and got my jacket.

We walked. James, Greta, and the boys lived in the old farmhouse three miles up the road, where Elmo and James were raised. Elmo lived in the foreman's house. And my mother and I lived in the hand's house behind Elmo's, except there wasn't much farm left and no one except me for the foreman to tell what to do, anyway. When James liked me I was a shirttail cousin and he told stories about himself and my father, who used to be the foreman. "That man could do anything, fertilize, graft; I never had to hire anyone but pickers. Fix machinery, they never made any motor Claude couldn't get running. He was a natural farmer. Born to it." When things weren't going too good, my father was an ingrate who had left six or seven years ago for no reason. I didn't remember him. Elmo never made any comment but Greta told me once it was because after James took over the farm from his grandfather they had argued. "About what?" I'd asked her. "It doesn't take much with either James or Elmo," she said. He was supposed to send for us, but he never did. We never heard from him again. We came and went but mostly we just stayed because there was nowhere else to go. And then Mr. Conlin built his club.

They knew. James just sat there with his hat pulled down, eating. Didn't say anything. I got two small teal down, eating slow. No one said a word until James yelled, "You're going into a foster home. You're not staying here. I should have thrown you both out a long time ago." Greta liked ducks too, and both she and Elmo kept eating. They had heard this before, too. "I was out talking to Mickey on the road and the superintendent stopped and told us. What was I supposed to do? You're not my kid. You're not my responsibility either. It's not worth twenty-five bucks a month, I'll tell you that. And why can't you take a bath, change your clothes once in a while?" The boys both laughed.

"What do you think about me going up and talking to your teacher when things cool down?" Elmo asked as we walked back. I'd had Mrs. Ross last year and this year and I'd have her in the sixth grade next year if I was still going there. Up until the trouble, I'd spent most of my time planning, drawing ducks and geese in my books, and waiting for noon-time so I could eat the lunch Greta packed me. Two big cars passed us on the road, going toward the club, filled with sports for next morning's shoot. How was I ever going to get in one of those shiny cars? I dusted them off sometimes at the club. You could see yourself in the paint. When no one was looking I'd rest the side of my face on the warm hood. "What do you say?" Elmo asked. "It can't hurt," I told him.

When I went back it was wearing new clothes, with a shower before I put them on and a shower the night before. I didn't just stand there and let the water hit me until it ran cold. I soaped and scrubbed, soaped and scrubbed. I was cleaner than anybody else in the whole world. No one said a word. They left me alone. Two weeks after I was back Mrs. Ross called me in and said I was behind again. I had stopped drawing and listened now and worked at my desk. And I worked at home. And I was ready for her. I gave her a hundred and sixteen pages of answers to all the problems in my math book. Then I took more out of my folder, a hundred and forty-two pages of answers out of my geography book. I straightened the edge of the papers against the top of her desk and laid them in front of her. She looked through them. "You've done all the work," she finally said. "What are you going to do during math period?"

"You'll have to give me the sixth-grade book."

"What about catching up in your reading?"

"I'm going to do that next. Elmo said that I could do it this way," I added.

"He did?" she said. Because she was listening and interested I told her the rest.

"I'm going to work my way right out of this place. I'm going to do all the books until I'm in high school. And then I'm going to do the same thing there," I told her. "I'm going to know it all; then we'll see."

That was seven weeks and two days ago, that long that I didn't have my knife, I was shaving down the top of a bill when Mr. Conlin and Mickey drove by and stopped at the gate but didn't get out. "You seen James?" Mickey called out. Elmo didn't answer. "Elmo," Mickey called, louder, "you seen James?" He just sat, smoking. Mickey drove on in his new car, leaving the raised dust to come down. Elmo wasn't talking to James either. Not since James had gone into town to the justice court for Mickey and taken the blame for all those extra ducks. As if he could shoot them all. Paid with a seven-hundred-dollar check signed by Mr. Conlin, and they confiscated his twelve-gauge Iver Johnson. I never asked what kind of gun Mr. Conlin bought him back. Elmo took another sip, then wiped his mouth, closed his eyes, but he wasn't asleep.

When Elmo was drinking you had to be careful. Even when he was sober there was no telling what he'd do. It made my stomach churn, thinking about what could happen. Not just the attacks. Once up at the house I saw him have one. After dinner we were all talking—he was as sober as he ever got—and we could hear rain on the roof, when thunder clapped right over the house and the lights dimmed for an instant. He made a kind of sound like he couldn't breathe and rose to his feet. Then he yelled something and jumped behind the couch against the wall. He wouldn't come out. Greta started crying. James kept saying Elmo, Elmo, kneeling on the couch, looking behind. Elmo stopped making the noise but he wouldn't come out. I stayed upstairs with the boys and heard them trying to get him out until I fell asleep.

I had to admit to myself that even with a coat of paint Elmo's decoys didn't look much better. But the ducks didn't seem to mind. One time I put just his out, just to see. Didn't make any difference; it was a good shoot. The boys drove by, coming home from practice, and waved, and I waved back. Elmo told me once I could be as well off as they were if I'd use my head. People out of state were already phoning up at the house, presidents of colleges where they wanted them to play football. They were strong. I saw them lift Elmo's car off the ground and carry it into the barn and lock it in there so Elmo wouldn't drive. They were going to make a lot of money, James said. He liked to count the scholarship offers out loud to Mickey. Just like Mickey always wanted to tell us about some deal he was promoting and how much money he was going to get. Out of James's hearing Mickey would go on to say that the only smart thing James ever did was marry Greta who was six three, and have the boys, who were the only cash crop he'd ever been successful at raising. If, he'd add, if their knees didn't get broken up in college they'd be worth some money in the pros.

I looked over at Elmo, dozing. No matter what seemed to happen, nothing really changed here. We all just kept doing the exact same thing we did before. Like those ducks, they just kept coming down, no matter what they saw. As long as someone called them. I put the lids on the paint cans and stuck the brushes in the fruit jar of turpentine.

I left Elmo on the porch and went up to my room. I promised myself I'd do twenty pages. I had to keep moving. I lay on my bed looking up at my pictures. I'd cut out every duck I'd ever seen in a magazine and tacked them up. I couldn't imagine any of them in the ponds. Broken. Floating. I looked at the page I'd torn out of Virginia's high-school yearbook she'd left at the club one time. Smiling down while she played tennis. Sitting at the student council. Then the chocolate cake tacked next to her pictures. Full size, on a yellow plate. It made me sleepy, watching it there on the wall. Virginia had told me once in the blind that she could remember Elmo coming to stay with them when she was a little girl. He must have been in the boat; he never allowed anyone to go over the past if he could help it. Mickey Conlin was his age; I would have guessed a lot younger. That was when Mr. Conlin leased land from Elmo's grandfather. I couldn't imagine him staying in that house of theirs in the city. He pointed it out to me once when we took a load of birds to sell to the big hotels— we got four bits for the smaller teal and a dollar, dollar and a quarter for mallards and sprig. He took me by that house and we parked across the street. He took a sip and wiped his mouth. "There she is," he said. It was big, not as big as the hotels we were just at, but big enough, three stories, with yellow and white striped awnings on the windows. It made even the club look small. "I could move in there if I wanted," he said. I didn't laugh. I knew what Mickey said about Elmo. Not where he could hear it, yet. And Mr. Conlin didn't like it when Elmo decided he wasn't going to call for him. He'd taken the boat back and left him and his friends stranded a couple of times. And I couldn't imagine his wife ever welcoming him now. I'd never met her or even seen her but from what Virginia said she thought the whole club business was a waste of time.

"You hungry?" Elmo called up from the door. "Let's go." I hurried down. He must have snoozed. He looked better now. When he was on the outs with James we ate at his place. He cooked whatever was handy in a black number ten cast-iron frying pan. For dinner we had something like seven or eight eggs with a big can of spaghetti on top. He divided the pan across the middle. My half he put in a plate; his he ate out of the pan. It was good with hard bread and coffee. After, we took turns dipping out half a spoon of Greta's grape jam, then half a spoonful of peanut butter, for dessert.

"I was thinking of going into town," he said, taking his first sip from the bottle, casual. I knew the check he got from the government was already gone because it was almost the end of the month. He gave some of it to Greta for eating up there, like I did. He and James owed everyone in town. James wouldn't go in; he'd send Greta. Not Elmo. He'd go and dare them to say something. I'd spent all my ready cash on my new clothes. If I didn't give him some money, I knew what he might do. We had gone through this before. I had my cash reserve, and I went to get the whole twenty-five dollars. There was no taking chances with Elmo. He didn't count himself, like even James or Mickey did. He just did what he wanted, no matter what anyone else thought or did.

When I handed him the money he didn't bother to count it, and he knew it was all I had. But he felt he had to say something. "Do your homework," he said. Sometimes he said, "Get an education; they can't take that away from you." Mickey had a degree from upstate. How many years did all those dentists and doctors that came here to shoot have in college? But Mr. Conlin only had a third-grade education before he had to go to work. It made it hard to estimate a plan. Once I asked Elmo how come he'd never got one. We were up at the club; after cutting all day, we'd stop in. Mickey might be up there, if he'd had an argument with his wife. Mr. Conlin, never. Virginia, if she knew Mickey wasn't there and Elmo was. He just sat there thinking over what I'd asked. Mickey was mixing drinks this time, arguing with James over who had the tougher training, the Marine Corps or the para-troopers. "I got sidetracked," he finally said. I knew what he meant. He'd been married. They drafted him into the army. I saw the clipping that Greta had from the town paper. It didn't say what happened to his wife. But he'd got hurt. And we were all glad to have him back.

I was doing my work when I heard his car start up. Then it moved off across the gravel apron and onto the dirt road. It was a relief to know I didn't have to be wary. At least, not until he came back. I put my empty cigar box where I kept my money back in its spot under the rafter. I could have moved down to the bedroom now, but this attic was better, more places to hide things. And James couldn't see that I kept the light on all night. Without going to the window, I knew Elmo had left on every light in the foreman's house and the barn, and the old floodlight system in the pheasants' pens too. The ducks would like that, probably think they were south of the border. They were more worry than they were worth. I calmed myself by laying back and looking at my cake. It was soothing and I knew I could go up and taste it if I needed to.

When I got off the bus Friday I could see Elmo. He'd come back. As I walked toward his place I could hear that laugh. He was running around stiff-legged in the grass, laugh-ing and hooting, chasing something with a broom. I got closer but stayed ready to pretend I hadn't seen him, was just pass-ing by. He'd been gone since Monday. Then he caught it, a bull snake about three, four feet long. He picked it up behind the head and held it close to his face, eye to eye, as the big thick body whipped like blades in a windmill. I got back out of sight before he saw me. I didn't like snakes.

I heard James's pickup coming past on the road. If I didn't like snakes, James was terrified. If he just heard a rumor that one had ever passed where he was standing he'd be gone.

Elmo really started laughing when he heard the pickup and ran to get into his car, carrying the snake. He got it turned around and going down the road toward James. As he passed, Elmo tossed the snake through the open window of James's truck. James came out of there along with the door when the two hinges snapped off. His truck kept going and took out a hundred feet of fence and two Friar plum trees. Elmo stopped and got out of his car and James was on him, knocked him down and hit him a couple, but that didn't stop Elmo from laughing. He kept saying, "You should have seen your face."

Saturday morning I was out waiting by the mailboxes. I knew Elmo was watching. When James stopped, he didn't come out. And at the club, Mickey wanted me to go with him. "Stinkpot. I'll take you." There was nothing I could do. Elmo wasn't there. I went with Mickey and two fat men to number four blind. They must have been important; it was a good blind and bigger than most, and their equipment was the best. Mickey never let up. "Don't get downwind of him," he told the sports as I rowed them out. James and the boys, they didn't just keep on. Mickey did. Don't go in the club. Don't touch the cars. Don't hang around the food. But he was cutting his own throat as far as I was concerned.

I called, brought those ducks down; they were lined up ten deep to see what was taking place in that blind. But the sports couldn't hit anything. Even Mickey wasn't doing any good. They were blaming me, their guns, the ammo, the ducks, and each other for getting in the way. It started lightening up and the ducks stopped moving so much. But I was still bringing them in. A stray came over, high; I got him turned around and interested. We exchanged greetings and salutations, mentioned mutual friends and acquaintances, then had a complete weather report, as Elmo would say. That sprig came down I swear within two feet of the blind. One of the fat sports raised up and emptied his shotgun. Point blank. Missed. He took the shotgun by the barrel and smashed the stock

against the four-by-four frame of the blind. Broke it off and
then swung the barrel out into the pond. I heard the splash.
"Get me out of here," he yelled. "I'm through with hunting.
That goddamned gun."
    I took them all back. When Mickey was getting out he
said, "You can have it if you can find it." He thought it was
impossible or he'd never have said that, because he tried to
buy it from me later. That sport could have thrown his gun in
that marsh anywhere and I would have got it. It was like
finding food on your plate for me. I went back and took off my
clothes and started diving, cold or not. Elmo would know
where to order a new stock. Then I'd have one of the most
expensive custom-made guns in the whole world. I knew it
was only the start, too. I went under again, feeling with my
finger tips in the soft bottom mud of the pond. I was going to
have the best of everything.

    A week after that, Elmo surprised me when I called out,
"You coming with us, Elmo?" by his porch. He came out. His
face was still swollen up and there were scabs on one side of
his jaw. And he was on the Tokay now. I'd never seen him go
this long before. The boys walked up and we all took the
shortcut to the orchard. We had to start pruning the plums.
James took the ladders around on the road with the flatbed.
James and Elmo still wouldn't say a word to each other. But
they'd work together and get the job done. And they never
included the boys or me in their argument. Elmo was the best
when it came to the orchards. You could say that for him. He
knew the trees. Each one. Could tell you when it was planted
and how many lugs it had produced the year before. He could
take a tree that should have been pulled up, graft on new
branches, prune it just so, and it would come back good
enough to keep. James would kid him that he had names for
them. But he'd shake his head and say no sir. We were walk-

ing along: I was still carrying Elmo's old Mossberg pump; the
new gun stock hadn't come yet. The boys had their guns too,
of course. Elmo was carrying a stick and the quart of Tokay.
The boys were walking on the rim of the ditch. They looked
like giants from where I was, down below. Geese are where
you find them. A pair took off right under our noses and we
let go. It happened so fast I didn't remember bringing up the
stock to my cheek. It was like an explosion.

Gary emptied his gun first, and only the female was still
going, and he was yelling, "Break her wing, her wing." It was
too late. The female crumpled. If we could have crippled her,
then staked her out in the field, she would have brought them
down. She would have called and they would have come,
whole flights of geese. They'd sail down like clouds and try to
land next to her. It was too late for that. Gary picked up the
honker by the feet and held her out at arm's length. Its head
almost touched the path. I turned back to yell to Elmo, "Good
eating tonight" but he was on the ground. I went back running. He had dropped to the black dirt face down. His body
was flat but his hands, elbows, and knees were digging him
into the soft dirt. He was burying himself. I tried to turn him
over, yelling, "Elmo, Elmo." Tommy ran to get James.
"Elmo." He stopped when I got him tipped on his side. His
face was covered with mud and when I scraped it off I saw his
mouth was filled with dirt. I reached in with my finger and
tried to get it out. White foam was coming out around the
corners of his lips and he had wet himself. The worst was the
gray was gone from his eyes, and they wouldn't close. I had to
put my hand over them so I couldn't see them.

He was supposed to come back after six months but it
went on, seven, eight, then a year. Then the spring again. He
wrote Greta, and she would read me parts he put in for me.
Keep the lid on his barrel of linseed oil so the rain didn't get

in, and things like that. It didn't seem like the same place without him. In fact it wasn't. James pulled up all the orchards and planted Christmas trees, and leased what was left to Mr. Conlin to flood for the club. The boys went to school somewhere back east and never came home but at Christmas time. They sent me a jersey once and a photo of them in their football uniforms, each holding a girl's leg by the ankle while she balanced on their shoulder pads.

Virginia stopped once, after they'd taken him to the veterans' hospital. She went up and visited Elmo practically every week. She'd brought me some boxes of magazines, *National Geographic* and *Smithsonian*. She didn't know how busy I was doing those extra pages of work. I'd finished Reading and Science and was halfway through the next book of math. There were two cardboard boxes and she wanted to carry one into the house. I wouldn't let her. It wasn't because the place was dirty. I had not only got interested in cleaning myself— I showered before I went to bed and in the morning too, changed my underclothes and socks once a day and was thinking about twice a day if I could get more socks, and my trousers and shirt every Monday morning—but the house was cleaner than Greta's. I scrubbed the wooden floor where the linoleum was gone with a brush all the way up the stairs to my room in the attic. After I cleaned the stove I never used it if I could help it. Same with the shower and the toilet. I'd go over to the foreman's house or piss through the hooked screen door out back when I didn't want to go out in the dark.

She wouldn't take no for an answer. After she set her box on the table she looked around. The place was clean. My mother's bedroom: I'd found an old key and locked the door shut and I never went in there. "Where's your bedroom?" I pointed to the ceiling. She was up the stairs before I could stop her. My room was the cleanest. She looked at each of the pictures of the ducks. I must have had every kind there was in the world. Some were so fanciful they looked like flowers. She didn't say anything about the pictures I had of her, just moved her head past them to the cake as if they weren't there.

"Why the chocolate cake?" she asked, looking closer at it. "Is it your favorite?"

"I like them. Sometimes Greta makes one for my birthday," I added.

"That's why you put it up there?" She turned to look at me. I looked down. "Tell me, Gerald, I really want to know."

I told her. "Before I go to sleep, I check off the ducks. Then I come to the cake." I tried to explain. "The cake makes me feel better. No matter what's happened to me that day, I feel better. It makes me remember the last time I had one. It is my favorite of everything. When I have to, I get up and go to the picture and lick it and the taste comes back just as if I had a mouthful of cake. I can taste it."

"Show me," she said. I didn't care. I went over to the chocolate cake and closed my eyes. She had to stoop, but she went over and did it too.

Elmo came back when I was just getting ready to leave the eighth grade and go to high school in town. Same laugh. But no drinking. None whatsoever. I walked him up to eat at Greta's. Showed him my herd. James knew about them now and never said anything. They ate all the weeds; mustard never had a chance. He never had to disk. All Elmo could say was wow. All the pens were full. The overflow swarmed around us like a rainbow. I'd even got a couple dozen honkers now, and some canvasback that hardly ever came to this marsh. I should have thinned some of the hens out. They were breeding and there were ducklings everywhere. When James had found out he'd said I had more ducks here than they got in a season now at the club. Elmo watched the ducks like he'd never seen one before.

He wouldn't go to the club. Both Mr. Conlin and Mickey stopped by. He let me use his seasoned wood to carve decoys but didn't want any part of making them himself. Not interested even in looking at my expensive custom shotgun. He sat on the porch. Smoking. Tapping his shoe. It was only when Virginia'd come by, driving her car behind the barn, that he'd ever start returning a little like he used to be. Imitating Greta: "It's Miss Conlin," jump up, dust off a porch chair for her. "My, aren't you pretty today," then yell out to me, "Get the china, get the silver, Miss Conlin's here." We'd laugh. They'd go into the house while I worked on the decoys.

There was as much to do as always but he didn't help. He sat on the porch. He acted like he'd never been here before. Where the old orchards had been across the road were the Christmas trees. Acres of green. The damned things could grow eighteen inches, two feet in a year if you poured the water to them. And James and I did. We rigged up a sprinkler system that nearly drowned them. It was like growing a three-mile-thick wall: we couldn't even see the marsh anymore. James was going to make some money; people were going to come from the city to cut their own tree.

I don't know what set him off but he started drinking. Not heavy. Easy at first. Off and on. He had one spell. James tried to get him to go back to the hospital. "I'm never going back there," Elmo said.

"They should never have let him out the first time," James told Greta. "Not until he was cured." Virginia would come and get him and take him on long rides. She was in her first year of college. She gave me a book with nothing but decoys in it. Pages. Colored photos. Elmo wouldn't look at it with me.

I bought him a battery for his old car and we worked on it until we got it started. He wouldn't concentrate. He'd ask, "Where's my five-eighths?" It would be hanging from the nail where it always was. Right in front of him. I'd handed it to him a few minutes before. I rebuilt the carburetor, because he was taking forever. He had showed me how the last time.

The first time he took the car to town he smashed it up and broke his leg. He stumped around with a cast, drinking more now. It was like before, nothing was going to stop. Wings locked. He brought this down on all of us. I told him that when he was complaining of the pain in his leg. "I can't sleep," he said.

I stopped carving. "Whose fault is that?" I asked him.

He stopped rocking back and forth. Gave me one of his grins. "You're going to start in too, Gerald?"

"We never broke your leg, Elmo."

He started laughing then. Kept laughing, slapping his thigh. Tears came down his cheeks. I wished I hadn't said that. And I got up and backed away. I could still hear him laughing from up in my room in the attic.

Cutting, it was James and me in the ponds that summer. The boys stayed where they were. Elmo sat on his chair on the porch. We couldn't do it all. We had to hire some help from town; it was too much for us. Mickey paid them. He'd take out a big roll of hundreds and ask James what he thought we were worth. Wearing his yellow golfing pants and matching shirt. He looked like a streak of chickenshit. It was all I could do not to laugh at him. I had grown some, enough to fit into the boys' clothes after Greta cut them down. He didn't give me so much trouble, but he tried. "Get the gear in the boats. Move it. Did you hear me? Where are you going? Hey!" I'd leave, walk home. Or one time: "What are you doing in here?" I was reading in the club dining room, waiting for Greta to get done for a ride home. "Go out and sit on the stairs. Did you hear me?" I just kept reading, not even excited.

Coming home, I always stopped if Elmo was out on the porch, no matter how tired I was. He wanted to give me a lot of advice now. "Leave the women alone; there's plenty of time for that," he'd start out. "Get your education." We both laughed at that. I was getting one faster than anyone. "Don't go in the army, no matter what happens, don't go." Another time he told me, "Put out one of your eyes." He paused, took a sip and wiped his mouth, considering. "They still might take you; better yet, cut off your forefingers so you can't shoot. Just don't go." He took another long sip.

We couldn't talk Elmo into coming with us to watch the boys play the only time this year they'd be on the coast. He would not go. James and Greta were more excited than I was. We were going, two days and one night in a motel. I fed the herd and left everything clean and tidy in the house. I gave Elmo all the money I had. I knew James had the free tickets already and I could sleep in the back of the car if I had to. When I handed over the money he wanted to shake my hand. When I was down the stairs and ready to go he wanted to shake again. With that smile.

It was a time. The boys moved around the field like a locomotive and a coal car. They knocked people down. When they went down it was like uprooting big trees. We went in the locker room after and it was like being among movie monsters. The boys took us out to eat and we sat there for hours, talking and ordering things when we felt like we had enough room. I must have had four or five different kinds of chocolate cake. The school picked up the bill, so I didn't hold back.

We stopped at the house first to let Greta out, and James noticed his pickup was gone. I never thought anything about it. James drove me back to my place. When he slowed and then slammed on his brakes I didn't understand what was happening because I was half dozing. James jumped out and was running. In the headlights I saw the old John Deere we used to use in the orchard. I could see where it had made a swathe with the gangplow through the Christmas trees. But they were too thick for the tractor, and it was over on its side. I got out fast. James was yelling, "Elmo, Elmo, where are you?" I ran for the pens. The lights were on and there were the three or four dozens of ducklings left, but the rest were gone. Disappeared as if they had taken flight. Elmo wasn't in his house. I went back to the pens again. Trotted out into the field where they fed. They were gone. In some city hotel by now. Dead. Roasting in the ovens. Then I was running again for the house. I could tell he'd been there but I still took the stairs two at a time. He'd found my custom shotgun. It wasn't there. On the table where I did my work he'd written on a piece of lined paper, You know how it is. Your friend, Elmo. Greta drove up and was yelling to James, "Mr. Conlin's on the phone; he wants to know if Virginia is here. She's been gone since yesterday."

James came over after looking through the barn with Greta. She yelled up, "Come stay with us." But I couldn't then.

When they left I sat back on the bed for a long time. I wasn't tired any more. I didn't want to go to sleep. Sometime during the night I got up to look at the pictures close up. Then I started tearing up the pictures of the ducks. Then Virginia. And finally the chocolate cake.

I didn't catch the bus the next day but stayed in front, working on the decoys. I fixed the neck of one of Elmo's; it was stretched back, head tucked under its wing, like it was asleep, so the neck made a kind of handle. I glued and clamped it where it was cracked. Then I started sorting the ones that needed paint. James came by a couple of times. "You missed the school bus?" he said, acting surprised, and left me my lunch. The second time I asked him, "When do you think he'll come back?" But I was beginning to dread it the more I thought about it. "Your guess is as good as mine," he said, and he sat down and started stirring the paint for me. My back was to the road and I was thinking about painting the sleeping decoy when Mickey drove up. I didn't know who it was until he reached around and grabbed me by my shirtfront and yanked me to my feet.

"Where are they?" he yelled. "Where's my sister?" I could feel the spray of his spit against my face. At first I didn't understand. He started shaking me back and forth, yelling, "You know, you know," still holding me by the shirt. Then he started hitting me with his fist.

James was yelling back. "Get off my land. Get the hell off, Mickey."

Mickey stopped. "Your land." He was out of breath, but spoke even. Reasonable. "We can take the rest any time we like. Any time."

I brought the decoy around as hard as I could and caught Mickey in the face. He went down on one knee, still holding my shirtfront. But I got my knife out and knew from before, from a long time ago, where I was going to sink the blade. Just below the ear hole in the fat of his neck. James grabbed my arms and held them to my sides. There was blood streaming from the cut on Mickey's forehead and he let go and backed away.

"All right," he said. "If that's what you want. Two can play that game." He got into his car and drove off.

Because it was easier on everybody, I moved up to the main house. The boys were gone. My mother had stopped sending the money the year before. But they still wanted me. I'd be able to help more and be more handy. Greta said she missed cooking for a crowd, for the boys. She didn't go up to the club any more. None of us did. She let James and me pick our favorite meal at least once a week, and she'd have it on the table for us. Anything.

We were busy, not only when the customers came out to

buy, from Thanksgiving to Christmas, but all the time. Pulling up thousands of cutoff stumps when the ground was dry enough, planting new trees. We sold seventeen hundred trees one weekend before Christmas last year. It turned out that the customers didn't like to get down on their knees to cut them off: "I'll take that one," they'd say, and James would always ask, "You're sure? You can't change your mind when it's cut. That's it." They'd nod, already having second thoughts, and I'd get my saw and whack it down before they had a chance to change after all. James made so much money we had to go to the bank in town that night to deposit it. Two brown paper sacks full.

I never saw her, but we heard Virginia came back. Nothing else. Months later, Elmo wrote. Just a short note. That was about the same time the club was put up for sale. He wrote again, off and on. I could tell when a letter came because Greta's eyes were red from crying. She never read me anything from the letters. And I never asked. I think James went up north to see Elmo a couple of times, but he never said. Greta must have written him too, because when I was ready to graduate from high school he sent me a package.

The handwriting looked like his. I opened the wrapping. First, taped to the top of the box, was a stack of worn dollar bills, seventeen, my age. Inside, wrapped in a torn T-shirt with ELMO stenciled on the neckband was a decoy. At first I thought it was painted dark because it was a mud hen. It was hard to see; Greta never turned on the kitchen light until the sun was nearly down. With the light on, I saw it wasn't a coot. It had first been painted all black or a dark blue. Then red over that, but it didn't cover well. Then there were a lot of paint drips all over. Mostly red, but some white.

I would have sworn the body was a mallard, even with the head so out of proportion. It was too large by half, and the bill was too short. The head was just too thick. The longer I looked at it the more confused I got. Merganser's head with a sprig body. Green wing teal body with a honker head. I kept looking.

When James came in he looked it over, holding it up to the light bulb. The bill was open; it looked like there were sharp teeth, dripped white, but the black-blue-red paint showed through. He turned it around and around. The eyes had been gouged out, just holes. He didn't have any glass ones like we used. He'd tried to fill the cavities with drips of red paint. Finally James shook his head and gave up and handed it back to me.

When I went to bed I put Elmo's present on top of the dresser. I was reading when I happened to look up. The decoy was smiling at me in that light. It was Elmo. It was his head. I got up and looked closer, not touching it. I counted the drips from the paint brush when he tried to make the eyes see. They spotted his face.

My first thought was to go tell James and Greta. The decoy was Elmo. Instead I got the wrapping with his address. I wrote him a letter thanking him for the present. Telling him I missed him. I wrote on and on. Pages. Things he knew about from before, and my plans. I asked him to come back.

He never came down.

TWO SPOTS
1949–1950

I heard the yelling but by the time I got there my father was just glaring at the two of them. I recognized the older boy from before. James Clark. He was taller than I was now. The other one, eight or nine, was ready to cry. He was holding the loaf of bread in one hand and the open jackknife in the other; the mustard jar and baloney were in the crook of his arm. James had half a dozen sandwiches made up and ready to pass through the half-rolled-down window of our car. Delores and the twins had disappeared down behind the smeared glass.

"This is my grandfather's road," James Clark said.

"You're missing the point," my father said, appearing calm, if you didn't notice the red in the back of his neck, and his clenched fists. "I'll feed my own kids. I don't need you boys to do that for me." He was trying to speak in his normal voice now. He could go for years without raising his voice. He hardly talked at all, Joyce used to say when she first came to live with us.

"It was lunchtime," James said. Then old Mr. Clark came up out of breath, just as the little boy started bawling. Just bellering. Loud enough for all three kids to raise up and see who got hit.

"Elmo," old Mr. Clark yelled louder. "Get up to the house." He didn't move until James Clark turned him and gave him a little shove. Then he went off. You could hear him for a long way.

Old Mr. Clark cleared his throat and spit before saying, "Neither of us is making any money this way, Mr. Seidmeyer." My father didn't move, didn't answer. But his hands were flat in his back pockets. "Come on, James, let's get back to work."

"But," James started out.

His grandfather cut him off. "Don't stick your nose in other people's business. Get a move on now. They need plums in the packing shed."

My father went back into the orchard. I waited until the Clarks had disappeared, then unlocked the car door. The kids were pretending they were asleep down on the floorboard below the front seat. There was a cooler of water, a box of graham crackers, their toys. My oldest comic books, all torn up, their pages scattered over the back seat like leaves. I tickled the bottom of Delores's foot until she jerked away, but didn't laugh, and opened an eye. "Greta, we didn't ask them."

"I know that. It's almost dinner time; you be good." And I emptied out my dress pockets, the best ripe elephant-heart plums I'd found all morning, onto the seat before going back to the trees.

I didn't mind plums. Raspberries were worse. Tomatoes. Though you don't have to drag around a heavy ladder. Apricots are the very best tree fruit. They smell so good and taste better. You can keep the pits in your mouth and not have to get down for a drink for hours. They pop right off the branch when your fingers reach for them, no twisting or pulling hard. It's like you just have to raise your arms into a big Y and let the cots roll down them into the bucket without lifting a finger. Another thing, apricot trees are small once you get inside, so you don't need a ladder. You can take your time and sight the best ones to eat. I just leave them for last, hanging there like hot pieces of sunlight, until I've picked the tree clean. I used to put my face up close to them then and snap them off with my teeth and suck the seed out and swallow them down, one two three. Joyce caught me once and started laughing. I almost swallowed the pits. I came down and all she was able to say was, "Don't tell me, don't tell me, I don't want to know," before she started laughing again.

She was almost pretty then. But she wasn't regularly unless you knew her. She'd had acne and had pits and scars you could see in the dark. She let me feel them once and they were like the outside of an orange. She was kind of fat, and bleached her hair platinum blond. She'd plucked her eyebrows until they didn't come back and used eyebrow pencil when she remembered. People looked when she came into a room but she didn't seem to mind. I was happy to let her go first so no one would see me.

You have to hand it to Joyce, she fit right in. I never thought she could. We've had a lot of reverses the last few years. I saw a woman cross herself when my father passed by, back in the place we came from. But it was never his fault. My mother burned up in our house my father had just rewired. All the dairy cows had to be destroyed because of Bang's disease. The bank foreclosed on our pastureland when we couldn't pay. My brother Lyman was killed. I was listening when one of his friends came home from the army. They were talking, drinking the morning coffee I'd brought in, and my father was barefoot, I could see his white foot against the blue linoleum floor through the crack in the door, when my father asked how it happened. The sergeant started almost in a whisper but got louder and louder. "He didn't have to go first. I said 'Let's keep moving' and he jumped up first. It was only a matter of time before the mortars would have found us.

They had the ravine covered. He started running. Three or four hit close. I got back up and ran. Thirty yards up the ravine I saw him there, kneeling. He had his arms around a boulder like he was hugging it." The sergeant took a deep breath through his mouth before finishing. "But his head was gone." I ran out the back into the yard but there wasn't anything I could do to make those words go away.

"What's wrong with you; come on down." Joyce was pulling away at my pants leg. "I'm hungry, so you must be twice as much." She kidded me about my size. I didn't mind it coming from her. She could get my father to smile, and he had got out of the habit by the time he met her. Our luck began to change then too. Delores and the twins came along, his second family, which helped. We had a nest egg. Not enough to buy anything, but getting close. The trailer and the car were almost new. He had a pickup he bought last week off someone, out of the paper. It needed new rings, but we were working on it. Joyce was the kind of person that could straighten a messy room in a second and always say the right things. When I told her about those boys going to feed the kids she just laughed. "They didn't mean anything by it. They just didn't know we eat late."

When we found my father he wouldn't come down. He had to finish the whole tree before he'd stop. "Come on, it's time to eat," Joyce said.

"I'll be with you."

"Now that fruit won't spoil. And the Clarks can afford it if it does." She talked and pulled on his cuff at the same time. He came down. He didn't like to, but he did.

She spread out a blanket and we had our picnic. That's what she called it, not dinner, picnic, when we were too far away from the trailer. She had everything ready from the night before. Sandwiches, pork and beans or potato salad, deviled eggs sometimes, and Kool-Aid. Cookies. We always had them. She made them every night, no matter how tired she was. The kids sat there waiting behind their plates like soldiers, twins almost two and a half, Delores three and a half. They had better manners than a lot of adults I'd seen.

That was because of Joyce again. She had the patience. We all learned from her. She told me what was going to happen with my body and I didn't get taken by surprise. It wasn't the same as the school nurse telling us something in Health with the boys sent out. I never believed anything they told us in school.

Joyce would say, "Wear some jeans under your dress; it's more comfortable." I did and she was right. And I didn't have to worry about people looking up under me when I picked. "Braid your hair. The best style is when you're comfortable." I did that too. It was cooler.

She wasn't perfect by a long shot but on the other hand neither was I. I mouthed back to her and she slapped me in a restaurant once. It sounded like a shot. My father was embarrassed. I think his face was redder than mine. We all just sat there without moving until people around us started eating again. It was hard. I could remember my mother so easy. Like Lyman. But she always said she was the mother of all four of us. And I came to like to hear it, too.

It's hard going back to work after eating. It's not natural. I don't think a person's body can churn all that up as easy as if you were laying down resting, letting the stomach do its work. I told that to my father once and he just smiled, thought it was funny. "We won't always be doing this kind of work. Just until we get enough money to buy a business."

"What kind?" I'd say.

"Not anything to do with cows." We'd discussed it pretty often.

"No fruit trees." After I'd say that, Joyce would always add, "Nothing to do with laundries. Or restaurants." It was kind of up in the air right now.

* * *

Too much dust in a plum orchard, I can say that too. Between dragging those heavy ladders around and the tractor hauling the bin trailers it gets so you can hardly see what you're doing up there. Not that it really matters. Those plums can't get away. We'd been here at the Clark's before: last year, year before last. That was the first time we came this far north after we left the dairy. They gave us a place to park our trailer near the packing shed. Treated us as well as can be expected, as my father said, for people with no current address. We'd laugh at that, too. My father had done this as a boy, so he knew the ropes pretty well. But he didn't like working for someone else. I didn't blame him. You got the wages and they got the profit. But the Clarks made it easy on everyone. Didn't hang around with their hands on their hips watching over your working; just left you alone. Old Mr. Clark ran things. Mr. Clark mostly kept out of sight. The older boy James worked right along with us, bringing us bins to empty our buckets in.

They lived in the big house up on the road. Screened porch, two story, doodads under the eaves, and the biggest trumpet vine I'd ever seen, growing around half the porch posts. Each time we passed by one of them would be out with a hose watering it down to cool the house. Big lawn, we never ever had a garden in that amount of ground at the dairy, and a metal fence with points like an arrow around the whole thing.

My father would phone from town, ask old Mr. Clark if the fruit was ready. Then we'd go out, stop at the house. My father'd go in, cleaning his feet on the mat, and the big white door would shut. We'd all wait in the car and after a while he'd come back out with the keys to the generator shed and we'd pull the trailer out to the orchard. Other people would start arriving in the next few days for the plum season.

I never liked coming back here. I always felt it was like we were watching a race and then all of a sudden we had to join in the running. It was the way they drove each other. All the yelling. Carrying on. From the top of a plum tree once I saw Mr. Clark shove the oldest boy almost off his feet. He was screaming at him. The grandfather had to put a stop to it. He was the biggest of them all; I had to look up at him. Mr. Clark was half a head shorter and had gone to fat. Each generation was shorter: James Clark was shorter by a couple inches than his father, but almost square. The youngest one, Elmo, looked stooped, like a little old man.

No one would want to watch them when they carried on. Everyone turned away. No snide looks. No half smiles from anyone. I felt like you could catch what they had if you watched. They mostly took it out on themselves or the equipment. If something would break on the John Deere they'd start hitting the whole machine with a sledgehammer. Tools, they threw them more than they used them. But no cussing. Never. I overheard someone telling my father once that one time years ago the grandfather had an argument over a contract with a fruit broker and let the whole crop rot on the trees. There were other stories too.

That family never rested. When we were done, all cleaned up, over with supper and ready for bed, they'd be doing things in the orchard in the dark. We could hear the tractors and the pickups, yelling, banging. "What could they be doing out there now?" Joyce would ask. My father just shook his head.

We'd been picking at the Clark's for over a month. Friar plums now. It was going fast. My father kept what was owed us written in a little green covered book that stayed in his front shirt pocket. He put rubber bands around the cover to keep it closed. Keep everyone honest, he'd say. We'd all look at it at night when he wrote the new figures down. That kept me going sometimes, thinking of the money. Not always. And not for long, either. I was up the ladder, thinking about the green book and that I could pick almost twice as many boxes as Joyce, not as many as my father yet but more than some of the men here, when I heard the tractor pulling the bin trailer go by. I could see through the rising dust the Clark boy driving. Then Joyce was calling "Eddie, Eddie." I came down fast. She had my father's hands and he was on the ground covered with squashed plums. They had come out of his bucket when the ladder was yanked out from under him when the bin trailer hooked one of the legs.

Old Mr. Clark came running. I didn't get close. The plums looked like blood. He started yelling at the boy to phone for an ambulance and James took off running. My father was conscious, talking to Joyce, who kneeled beside him, listening. I backed off and went to the car and got the kids out, let them run and stretch their legs. I didn't want to think of what was going to happen next. We never had any luck. Just when I thought things had changed. We were right back where we started from. I had used up all my hope.

I stayed with the kids while Joyce went into town in the ambulance, fed and bathed them and put them to bed. She never came back that night, and I got them up and put them in the car and got my ladder the next morning. I never saw the Clarks. I just kept picking.

Joyce came back about eleven, climbed up the ladder and sat in the tree. Her eyes were red; that was the closest I'd ever seen her cry. We hugged each other until she could get her breath. His back was broken and one lung was punctured when his ribs hit the metal edges of the bin. I just listened. There was nothing I could do to change what she was saying. He had to be taken to a specialist. She was going with him. Her sister was going to take the kids. And I was to stay here. I was numb. All last night I kept thinking of the worst things. But I hadn't thought of staying here. At first I thought she

meant in the trailer. Then she explained to me it was with the
Clarks. I was to stay with them until she came for me.

"No I'm not," I said. "I'm coming with you."

"You can't."

"I can go with the kids."

"There's no room; she's got her own family plus our kids
and her mother-in-law's there too. You've got to stay here.
There's a cook up there at the house. You can help her out."

I wasn't going to cry. I wasn't.

"It's the only thing we can do now."

I helped Joyce get things packed. Kissed them all
good-bye. Waved as they drove off. She was in a hurry. Went
back and cleaned up, rebraided my hair. Straightened the
trailer. And finally just sat there in a chair. Waiting. It was
almost supper time before I heard the car. The car door. The
footsteps on the plank. Then the knock.

"What next? The floor's swept."

"Peel those carrots," Mrs. Budge said and turned back to
the big stove. I peeled as fast as I could, the dirty orange skins
flying until they covered the whole porcelain sink. She banged
the pots against the stove top as if it wouldn't sit still. Mum-
bling. Stamping her foot, raising it like a horse and driving it
back down when something didn't go right. She was so short
I could look down on the top of her head when she passed by.
She had big freckles on her scalp where her gray hair was
thinning. She didn't have a good word in her. For anybody.
"If they don't like it they can lump it. Five o'clock sharp my
tail end. Now slice them up, those carrots don't fit into the pot
that size and they sure won't cut themselves."

At a quarter to five she really started hopping, getting
bowls out to put the hot food in, stamping her foot and yelling
for me to set the table. I could do that. I made it as perfect as
I could, even got most of the forks and knives to match by the

time I heard them coming. Mrs. Budge had worked herself up to where she was clacking her false teeth so hard they slipped out of her mouth and she had to catch them with her lips and suck them back in. But the hot food was on the table: steaming bowls of white gravy, mashed potatoes, carrots. A platter of pork chops and biscuits. Apple sauce. When they came into the kitchen Mrs. Budge turned her back on the stove and faced them with two balled-up pot holders in her fists. I turned back to the sink and started peeling more carrots. I could hear the chairs scrape. But not a word. I peeled. Under my arm I could see Mrs. Budge pursing her lips and watching them.

Old Mr. Clark said, "Another culinary triumph, Mrs. Budge."

"I do my best," Mrs. Budge said.

"And Miss Seidmeyer, would you join us here?" I knew who he was talking to and turned around, but before I could speak, he went on, "Mrs. Budge prefers to dine later. But we would be honored with your company." No one had even started eating yet and they looked at me like one of us was passing by in a car. Mrs. Budge got a plate and banged it down on the table between old Mr. Clark and Elmo. I went over and got another chair and sat down. They passed me the bowls and I took some. I noticed I'd forgot to wipe the carrot skins off my arms, but couldn't then. They started drying as we ate, like old scars.

No one spoke a word. Elmo hooked his boot around the rung of my chair. I kept my head down and ate. We had bowls of raspberry Jell-O with milk for dessert. The center hadn't set, and when Mrs. Budge slammed old Mr. Clark's down it splashed onto his white shirt. He looked at it a long time. Before he could say anything Mrs. Budge said, "The refrigerator doesn't get cold enough. I've told you that before."

"Mrs. Budge," he started out. "We all admire and appreciate your efforts to supply us with sustenance to keep . . ." She mumbled something, threw her two pot holders on the cutting board, and stomped out of the kitchen. Old Mr. Clark scraped the Jell-O off his shirt with his knife and we all went back to eating.

She came down after they were all done eating and had gone outside. I was doing the dishes. "Who do they think they are?" she kept saying as she ate. I didn't break anything, and when I was done I followed her upstairs. "Sleep in there," she told me, pointing to an open bedroom door, and she showed me where the bathroom was. Later on I heard a knock, but I wasn't going to answer it. Finally I removed the chair I had wedged under the knob and opened the door. It was Elmo with a stack of comic books. I thanked him, put the chair back under the knob, and looked through them until I fell asleep.

In the morning Mrs. Budge knocked on the door and yelled, "I could use your help." I got up fast. While she fried bacon and more pork chops, I stamped out the biscuits and peeled and sliced up the potatoes for the skillet.

It was still dark when we sat down to eat. Mrs. Budge leaned her rear against the front of the stove and watched us. Everyone ate a hearty breakfast. I must have had three helpings of gravy and fried potatoes. I could smell the cinnamon buns baking as we ate. "Mrs. Budge, we're out of gravy," old Mr. Clark said, raising the bowl for her to take. There wasn't any more in the pan, and she had to make some. She said things under her breath, banging the skillets on the stove. When she put the gravy bowl down on the table, she remembered the cinnamon buns and yanked the oven door open. The raisins were all burned out of them.

She threw her pot holders into the sink and went out. "Cooks are all sensitive to failure," old Mr. Clark said.

"Well, she must be very sensitive," Mr. Clark said. They didn't laugh but smiled some. I didn't dare do that.

I cleaned up. Elmo stayed to help, standing on a chair to dry and put away. Mrs. Budge came down with several cardboard boxes, then two suitcases. She said with the last load,

"I've taken about all I can. And you can tell your grandfather that," she said to Elmo

Politely, he said, "I will, Mrs. Budge."

"See that you do." She went out with the load to her car, but so she could hear he said, "Cooks are a dime a dozen," and winked. She slammed the screen door so hard it shook the whole house.

I got my ladder and went up a plum tree. It was a safe place. I felt like no one could see me and nothing could happen to me there. I must have done seven or eight trees when I looked down. All four of them were looking up at me. I almost dropped my bucket.

"Miss Seidmeyer, you're not to pick. For now," old Mr. Clark said. "If you're agreeable, we'd like you to do something else. Please come down." He took the bucket out of my hands.

"Would you like to help in the office?" Mr. Clark asked. "Type payroll checks?" I shook my head.

"Can you drive?" old Mr. Clark asked. I nodded. Since I was eight or nine I'd driven our tractor on the dairy.

"If you like, you can go into town to get some parts. Drive the Buick," Mr. Clark said. The others looked at him when he suggested that.

"If you want me to," I said.

The car was light green, with white upholstery. The top had been left down and it was covered with dust. They had to jump start it to get it going while Elmo, James, and I wiped it with rags. I backed it out and with Elmo sitting beside me holding a list we headed for town. I'd never driven a car before, but it was a lot like a tractor.

"James can't drive any more," Elmo told me, "because he knocked your father out of that tree." When the car started smoking and made a terrible burning smell he said, after looking things over, "I think maybe you have the emergency brake on," and pointed to the lever by my knee. He was like his grandfather, always polite. "You might consider turning the windshield wipers off," he said. "It's that button on your right."

The Buick drove easy. Too easy; it wanted to leave the road, it was so light, and we hit the shoulder and sprayed gravel a few times. "May I call you Greta?" Elmo asked, after I swerved to miss a ground squirrel.

"If I can call you Elmo," I answered, and we both started giggling.

The hardware store had more clerks than customers, but they knew their job. I handed over the list to one of them and watched Elmo. He was getting more things and putting them on the counter. Building his own pile: pocket knife, clear glass vase, comic books, and a magnifying glass. When the clerk handed me the pad with everything written up, I signed like Mr. Clark said. The clerk looked at it awhile, then called someone else over. Elmo came up with two pairs of sunglasses.

"Elmo, what's going on here?" the clerk said, and showed him the pad.

"She's with me," he said. He wrote on the slip. I could see I hadn't got Clark right either. I don't know why I thought it was going to be any different.

It took three clerks to carry everything out to the car. We stopped and got a pump and generator for the John Deere and picked up an order of meat at the butcher's. Then we headed back.

It was cooling off for the end of August. We usually left here now to go to the apples. The Clarks picked almost into November because they had the late varieties, but there wasn't enough work for us. Their orchards went on for miles. Driving that green Buick was like sliding down a limb. There was nothing to it. Elmo sat beside me wearing his sunglasses, his short legs straight out. The wind blew my braids back over my shoulders: wearing my new sunglasses I forgot about everything but that good feeling.

We put things away. Elmo asked me, "Can you cook?"
I shook my head. "Joyce cooked."

He sighed. "That's your mother?"

"My stepmother."

"My mother took off," he said, "and she's not coming
back."

I changed the subject. "I know how to make potato salad,"
I said. "If you peel the potatoes, I'll get busy." I boiled six dozen
eggs and cut up the pickles. I knew they would be hungry.

When they came in and washed up we had five big bowls,
four-quart size, of potato salad on the table. Bread, and some
sardines and cheese we found. "Does each one of us get one of
these bowls?" James asked.

"You can take as much as you want," Elmo said. "There's
plenty."

We drove to town nearly every day and tried to time it so
we could eat at the A and W before we went to the stores. We
brought ice back. Pies. A couple dozen hamburgers for lunch.
All the things on the list. We washed the Buick and rubbed on
some chrome polish. Everyone knew Elmo. He just had to
walk into a store and it came alive. I was never given so many
smiles, him holding my hand, leading me in to one place after
another. He bought me presents; I'd find them under my
pillow. An autograph book. Handkerchiefs with violets sewn
on the corner. A comb and brush set. And a heart-shaped
locket and chain.

"No more," I said when I found the locket. "You better
take it back."

"I can't, it's got your name engraved on it. My mother
had one like that."

Before he could start, I said, "You want a chili dog?" I
didn't want him to have to tell me. I knew the story from
people who'd worked there before us. Elmo and James's

mother had left with the driver of a semi who hauled the dried prunes into town. He had a couple of kids himself, but no wife. Mr. Clark had gone crazy. He took all her clothes and cut them up with scissors and threw them out the window into the yard. Dresses, underclothes, socks, everything. Then he poured gas on them. But it started to rain. It took days before everything was burned up. Then he left to kill his wife. He never found her. Came back a couple weeks later. He disappears sometimes even now, takes trips no one knows where. He keeps a revolver on his desk. And I've heard him playing with it at night, the snap snap of the trigger releasing the hammer.

James kept away. Mr. Clark was always busy in his office. Old Mr. Clark kept the place moving along. Elmo and me put the miles on the Buick. I got that car to do anything.

I guess Elmo thought I was his age because he treated me like a kid. Reading to me. He'd come into my bedroom and lay on the bed and start reading a book he liked. I'd lay there with my eyes shut, listening. I enjoyed it. I don't remember anyone having time to do that before. Not my mother. I told Elmo. He was reading and stopped to turn a page, licked his forefinger first. Before he could start I said, "My mother died when our house burned down. She drank port wine and water. A neighbor got me out. My father was hauling hay to make ends meet. It wasn't his fault."

"She smoked in bed," I added. "Caught the mattress a couple of times. Caught her pink chenille robe once." He waited until he was sure I was through, then patted my hand and went on reading out loud.

The next day, driving to town, he said, "I'm sorry about your mother. But at least you know where she is." I was ready, I had the room, and let him tell me.

For supper if we didn't bring anything from the drive-in we all pitched in and cooked our specialty. I got mashed potatoes down to a science, Elmo told me, and could almost get the gravy to taste right. Old Mr. Clark fried. James actually made good biscuits. Elmo peeled for me and set the table. It was one of the few times I ever saw Mr. Clark enjoying himself. He had a salad dressing he liked to make with olive oil, vinegar, and red onions. "Well, ladies and gentlemen, we're cooking again," he'd say.

"We've had some practice," James said. "Once we had three cooks in a month," he told me.

"Mrs. Morton, Ramona, and Sally," Elmo recited.

"They come and go," Mr. Clark said.

"Mostly go," James said.

"My theory is they can't get used to the solitude, alone all day out here on the ranch."

Old Mr. Clark came in with four loaves of frozen bread from the freezer on the porch. "My theory is most cooks are peculiar. Something happens to a person when they see so much meat fried, boiled, and baked. It overcomes their good natures and makes them cantankerous."

"Listen to him," Mr. Clark said. "What do you think, Elmo?"

"I'm going to be a vegetarian." We laughed away.

"If it's all right with you, Miss Seidmeyer, we'll cook for ourselves like this until we get tired of it."

I nodded. "It's all right with me," I said.

"Anything's better than Mrs. Budge," James said. "It got so I could hardly swallow with her watching me eat."

"You did a good job trying," Elmo said. We laughed again.

Old Mr. Clark told stories while we ate. He could go on and on. If he repeated himself Elmo would pipe up, "You've circled that orchard twice before," and he'd laugh at himself. He was the only one besides Elmo that could. The other two just sat there.

He'd always ask me, "You've got everything you need,

now?" They paid me better than I could make picking. I sent it to Joyce by money order. We went to the post office; Elmo did the writing. I was satisfied with living there. When I didn't think of my father.

Day after Labor Day we were at lunch when old Mr. Clark said, "How old did you say you were?"

"Fourteen going on fifteen next March."

Figuring it out, he said, "You'll be going to high school in town with James then."

"I was in the sixth grade last year," I said. Then added, "When I went." Elmo and James were watching me closer now. Mr. Clark kept eating, paying no attention. Old Mr. Clark was going to find out what he wanted to know, like he always did. Before he could go on, I said, "I was thinking I might be going back home." I felt at ease here; I could speak up. It had been a month, over a month, since I moved in.

"Mrs. Seidmeyer never mentioned it last Sunday," he said. He liked having the last word. Joyce phoned at two-thirty every Sunday to talk to me, but he always picked up the phone and spoke first. He was so clever. They all were. I'd heard the talk about the lawsuit. When I went back to the trailer to clean it some of the pickers would ask. Letting me drive the Buick. Mr. Clark's wife's car. Elmo told me. They might be on their best behavior, like he said, but they knew what they were doing. They were all so polite.

"Perhaps you ought to get yourself some clothes, just in case," he said. He had me. I nodded. Elmo patted my arm.

We went to town early because it started getting hot again. James came too, sitting in the back, lying down on the back seat when we reached town. We stopped at the biggest store. Joyce's sister's three girls passed me down their clothes, they were older than me, so I always had enough. And Joyce bought me some if I needed anything more. There were too many clothes in that store. I couldn't decide.

"Try them on," Elmo said. "See how they look." He'd

already bought what he needed. I tried on several dresses. I had to go in the ladies' section because of my legs. It wasn't easy to find something for someone five feet ten and three-eighths inches tall. I still couldn't decide. But I got some underclothes and socks. And a winter sweater for Joyce and two pairs of work gloves for my father.

James was waiting for us and Elmo had me stop at the A and W. James pretended he was asleep and kept down in the back. Some boys parked next to us. They made some remarks. You have to ignore them, Joyce told me. Just words. They have no meaning when some folks use them. But if they try and put their hands on you, then you pay attention. Kick them where it hurts.

When they said it for the third time Elmo stood up on the seat. They didn't know him and made some more remarks about the both of us. I'd lost my appetite and was ready to go. "James," Elmo said. The boys mimicked him: "James. James." James sat up. He didn't open the door but swung his thick leg over the side.

The boys in the Dodge looked. "Say that again," James said. No one said a word. He took a milkshake from their tray, reached in on the driver's side, and poured it down the heater vent. "This is my father's car," one yelled, and they were all out swinging.

James must have been used to this because he gave as good as he got to all four of them until the cops came. Everyone was looking at us. The cops knew the Clarks.

We stopped at a creek and James washed off his face. The blood had stopped coming from his nose but his right eye was shut solid and his knuckles were all barked. At dinner no one mentioned it or asked what had happened. Old Mr. Clark said, "Did you get your wardrobe?"

Elmo answered, "She couldn't decide this trip."

I knew you had to wear dresses, and I had some that fitted me. Tomorrow school started. Later, when I was up in my room, Elmo came in with a box. A white dress with strawberries all over it and red trim. I tried it on. "You look nice," Elmo said.

I went with Elmo. Wearing my new dress. Him holding my hand. Got on the bus. Got off the bus. He took me into the school. Then to the office. He explained everything to the secretary. I didn't listen. Took me down the hall to the seventh-grade room. Stayed right there talking to me until the bell rang. "I'll be back," he told me.

Then it started again. The seating. Questions. Mr. Gilmore wanted to know what reader I was in. The stares. They all knew each other. Then the essay. The funniest thing that happened to me this summer.

Elmo came back, walked right into the room and came over and sat at my desk with me. No one said a word. He had the run of the place. Everyone else was writing away. He started writing too. To him it was like taking another breath. To me it was like flapping my wings and flying to the next plum tree instead of using a ladder. All those little pencil marks turning into words, sentences, pages. I could pick out some. Elmo was telling Mr. Gilmore about the time I ate two banana splits and got the second one free. And they gave me both dishes.

Elmo drifted in and out of the classroom all day. Got me for lunch and recess. And we looked over my spelling workbook when I got my first assignment. And we got out of there and were the first ones on the bus.

It started at dinner, Mr. Clark staring at James while he chewed his food. Not saying anything, yet. James ignored him, kept eating. All of us did. But it felt like the time my father lost his brakes going down the grade hauling the trailer. He maneuvered it around each turn, gearing down, using the emergency brake, with Joyce trying not to scream. No matter what he did we knew what the end was going to be. It took a hundred-year-old sycamore tree to stop us. Grandfather kept on telling stories. "When spring comes we'll take a trip up into the mountains and haul back a load of ladybugs." He had told about this before. I didn't believe him. "Spread them around the orchards and let them eat up the aphids and red spider eggs."

Elmo and I always kept him going. "What kind of net do we use?" I asked him, trying to keep my eyes off Mr. Clark. "No net, Miss Seidmeyer. Shovels. One person holds the gunnysack, the other shovels them in." Before we could ask, he said, "They don't fly away off the shovel either. No sir, they stay right there. They congregate up in the mountains by the creeks. Hybernate under the snow. Millions. Billions. More than you can count. Two-spot and five-spot ladybugs. The ones with two spots on their backs are the best. Remember that, Jim, going up to the Sierras?" Mr. Clark didn't answer. Just went on staring at James. "We used to go every year when I first started out here in the orchard business. Then I missed a couple of years, spraying was easier, and I never went back. But I know they're still there. This spring." He was getting excited, and so was Elmo.

"We'll go, Grandpa, I'll remind you."

"After Easter is the best time; the snow's usually melted by then."

"You can pick them up by the handfuls?" I asked.

"Just like that," and he opened his fingers to show us.

Just then Mr. Clark jumped up. His chair fell over backwards. He leaned toward James, fists clenched. James dropped his fork. "We have a guest," Grandfather said. It was quiet a long time before Mr. Clark straightened up and went out. When we heard the screen door bang Elmo said, "He thinks James has been driving Claude's pickup."

"I haven't," James said.

"We keep our family business to ourselves," old Mr. Clark said. And they both stopped.

It was only a matter of time. On the Wednesday pretest I missed them all. Mr. Gilmore wrote in red on my paper, STUDY. I knew that word and it stayed still for me. Friday's test I got four right. Two on one hand and two on the other. That's all the room I had on my palms because they had to be big, in block letters, or they'd jump on me. I felt sick again. Joyce would have kept me home. Elmo grabbed my workbook on the bus and said, "At least you're improving." I showed him my hands where the ink wouldn't wash off.

That night at the kitchen table we started working on the spelling words. I could write a word a hundred times and still not know how to spell it the hundred and first time. Elmo would just nod and try something else. He knew a lot of tricks. Dessert. You remember the two s's because they mean super sweet. I could see a banana split and remember the other five letters. But not always in order. That was the trouble. The letters played with me, slipping back and forth, upside down, and sometimes right off the page.

He had me try and read too. He listened a long time before he took the book away. Then he read to me, chapter by chapter, out of the South American history. In math the numbers would move but I was able to hold them down long enough with the point of my pencil that my eyes had a chance to see the answer. Old Mr. Clark would come into the kitchen sometimes. I didn't care if he knew, drinking a glass of water at the sink, listening, as Elmo read to me and then asked questions. "What country does Patagonia belong to?" I'd know. Because I could hear all right. But I couldn't get the words out of the book with my own eyes.

By the time I had got seven out of the twenty-five right in spelling, Mr. Clark and James had a knock-down-drag-out fight. I was in the kitchen with Elmo and Grandfather while he fried chicken. We heard the yelling and James came through the door blood running from his mouth and his father after him. Grandfather got in front of Mr. Clark. "Now hold on," he said. I thought he was going to swing on him. They faced each other for a while and Mr. Clark went out the back door. Just the four of us ate dinner that night. I didn't look at James. His eyelashes were wet. No one spoke. I forgot to turn the kitchen light on and it got dark before we finished.

Mr. Gilmore didn't call me lazy like some did but he gave me the same speller the third grade used. It didn't make any difference. I never got over seven right. He never mentioned putting me back. Or putting me in the room with the kids that wet themselves and wouldn't stay quiet and just played all the time.

Elmo never gave up on me. We worked as hard in the new speller as we did in the seventh-grade one. I got so if he'd read the words enough times, in the order that they came, I could see them on the page and copy them like they were in front of me on the test paper. But Mr. Gilmore would change the order during the test and I'd get all balled up.

Once a month they had a spelling bee for the whole school. We'd stand up on either side of the auditorium, girls against boys. Elmo always won. He'd start out fast, spelling a hard one, stop suddenly at the last couple of letters, close his eyes like he was thinking, then finish the word, winking at me. They asked me an easy word. I tried to stop it with my hands but I spit up all over my new dress. Elmo took me to the lavatory to clean up.

By Thanksgiving they still had my father in a body cast. I spoke to him on the phone. He sounded the same. "You OK?" he asked.

"Just fine," I said, "just fine." I was. The picking was over. We'd put the ladders away in the shed. The leaves of the plum trees were turning and falling; they lay on the ground like yellow feathers. There had already been a frost, and it had rained two or three times. All the pickers had left a couple weeks ago. I didn't go to the trailer every day now. It was locked.

In school I was getting good enough in the sewing class to make myself a dress. And a shirt out of the same material for Elmo. For Thanksgiving I didn't cook the turkey but I made the dressing. Everyone was polite during the holiday. James and Mr. Clark still weren't talking to each other. They'd hand bowls of hot food back and forth but nothing else.

During Christmas vacation we went to the drive-in movie. There was a special holiday triple feature Elmo wanted to see. James decided to go too, and sat in the back. I drove, of course. It drizzled but we could still see. The convertible top didn't leak, but it was strange hearing the raindrops while we were watching. James got out after the movie started and brought back popcorn and orange drinks for us. Later he got out again for red-rope licorice when Elmo wanted some. They talked like I wasn't there. "You better be good," Elmo said. "It's almost Christmas. Tell Claude not to dig out when he brings you home." Claude was James's best friend. They played football together.

"Me," James almost yelled back. "I didn't do anything."

"Yes you did, you broke Mr. Seidmeyer's back."

"That was an accident, Greta. Everyone knows that it was."

"I know that, James," I said.

"Stop arguing with Dad, you know how he is."

"I don't start it." They both stopped talking to watch the screen for a while. It was James's senior year. We had never gone to watch him play football. His last game, they gave him the ball in a ceremony. But I watched him sometimes, throwing the shot out by the barn, from my bedroom window. Elmo told me he was better in track than anything else. Watching him, it seemed like he was trying to drive the shotput across the yard into the house.

"You want to arm wrestle, Elmo?" James asked. They both started laughing; it was a joke between them. If they were in the kitchen, Elmo would swing from James's bicep.

Elmo may have been nine or ten years younger, but he was as smart.

"How far did you throw today?" he asked.

"If I keep improving I'm going to beat the state record," James told us. "Each day I get a couple more inches. A foot a week. At that rate I'll be throwing for league records in the first meets. I know I can do it. The shot's the best. I close my eyes when I get down. I've got the weight on my fingertips and I press it as hard as I can against my neck. I pretend I'm a cannon. When I finally let go, I yell as loud as I can, Boom!" He yelled it loud enough in the car that both Elmo and I jumped back from where we had been leaning over the back of the seat. We all laughed. On the way home, we stopped at the A and W. When we drove back we had the radio on and sang along with the Christmas songs, "White Christmas" and all the rest.

I had the most packages under the tree. We opened them one at a time, taking turns. That Elmo. He gave me a ring, birthstone for March. A Parker pen and pencil. A pink sweater made out of angora wool. The Clarks gave me a chemistry set. A powder and perfume set. And a cookbook. Everyone laughed when I opened that. James made me a wooden jewelry box in shop.

James and his father were getting into it again. Arguing. "You never said that," James said.

"You're telling me what I said?"

They kept it up right to the time we sat down to eat dinner that afternoon. Daring each other. Grandfather had held my chair for me and I had just sat down when Mr. Clark backhanded James out of his chair. James got up fast and caught Mr. Clark in the side of the face and he fell against the refrigerator and knocked the cake box off. He hit James against the table and the leg got broke. I tried to grab the turkey, but it slid off onto the floor. Elmo was wailing. Grandfather seemed as stunned as if he'd been hit. It stopped when James got knocked against the edge of the stove and split his eyebrow open. No one made a move for a minute. It had begun so fast, it was as if we had to catch up to what happened. I was still sitting there holding the cranberry-sauce bowl and a spoon from the peas. Elmo was over in the corner sobbing. Grandfather was holding onto the edge of the broken table. Mr. Clark stood absolutely still looking down at James, the blood oozing from his eyebrow, then coming out like a geyser down his face. He went out and we heard him slam the door to the office.

James finally got up and went upstairs. I held Elmo, rocking him until he stopped. Grandfather started picking things up. We got the table fixed and upright and the turkey back on top. Grandfather was joking again. "I didn't think a turkey could fly without feathers." Elmo tried to laugh. His face was swollen and there were still a few tears that rolled down his cheeks and caught on the wings of his nose.

James came down the stairs. He was so loud it sounded like he was dragging a wooden picking ladder behind him. He went right by the kitchen door and out the front, carrying his sport bag. It was coming down hard, filling the rain gutters up and splashing over. Elmo changed into his boots; always neat, he lined his slippers up under his kitchen chair. Grandfather was at the window. "He's going out to the road," he said. I got on my coat and Elmo and I went out.

We could see him up ahead, running; then he'd stop, walk, and then start running again. We tried to catch him but we couldn't. It was only when he got down to the road and crossed it, then stood on the other side, that we got any closer. I didn't understand what he was doing until Elmo yelled out, "He's hitchhiking." He stood there alone, his arm and thumb out, the rain coming down so hard it bounced off the black top. He was pointed to the city, not the town. There were no cars. We never dared cross over but stayed on our side of the road facing him. He ignored us. There was tape and gauze on his cut, but pink blood and water came down the side of his face.

"James, come on home," Elmo called over.

He wouldn't answer at first. Elmo kept yelling over. "I'm never going back," James yelled. "Never."

Elmo yelled back, "We've got turkey. Greta made the dressing, isn't that right, Greta?"

"I made the dressing, James."

"We can play Monopoly after. You can be banker. You're going to make Grandfather sad. He's made Tom and Jerrys for tonight."

"Go home," he told us. "I'm not coming back. Do you understand. I'm not coming back, not any more. I'm going to join the army."

I looked down at Elmo. His mouth was open and his wool cap was soaked down over his eyebrows. Elmo yelled over, "You can't, James, you've got to graduate first. What about track?"

Then I could hear a car coming. We all heard it. It was like we knew what was going to happen next. Elmo was holding my hand so tight it hurt. James kept his big thumb out.

I started yelling across. "The army killed my brother Lyman. Do you want that to happen to you? I'm never going to see him again. Are you going to leave Elmo? You don't want to see him any more?" The sound got closer, the treads picking up the rain and whipping it around the tires until it broke loose against the car body. The car stopped for James. It had its lights on because of the weather. We watched the red taillights disappear in the rain.

No one mentioned James's name any more; it was like he was never there in the first place. We pruned in late January, each of us taking a row. I let Elmo keep up with me so he wouldn't work alone. My father was getting better; he could get into a wheelchair now. Our nest egg was growing with the disability checks, and because we didn't sue, Mr. Clark paid the hospital and gave my father a settlement. When I took the phone one Sunday Joyce said they had found the perfect business. "A motel and frosty-freeze place out on the new interstate. I hope I don't eat up all the profits." We both thought that was funny. "I can hardly wait to see you," Joyce said. "Did you fill out yet?"

"No, I'm still flat as a board." Did we laugh. I missed her the most of all.

Red buds were swelling on the early plums. We worked after school and on the weekends getting ready for the season. For the last couple weeks, Mr. Clark wouldn't come in and eat with us, no matter how much Elmo would knock on his office door and ask. He took to sleeping in there, not going upstairs any more. When he did come out, he'd lock the door behind him. He never talked to us much. It was like he didn't want to know us any more. He'd go away and come back and we wouldn't even know he'd been gone for a couple of days. Elmo could tell by the mileage on his car if he'd been to the city or just to town.

He had put on seventeen hundred miles once when he was gone for a weekend. If he was looking for his wife she must have been out of state. Grandfather kept up like he always did, making jokes of me and Elmo, and himself, of course, like nothing was happening. Telling us it was almost time to head for the mountains to get the ladybugs. I always started laughing at that. I couldn't help it. I'd asked my science teacher. She didn't know anything about it. But he believed it enough to be able to describe it to me and Elmo again and again.

We got home one day from school; it was the first sunny day of the spring. The side boards of the barn were steaming as if they were on fire. Grandfather had gone across to the city to see someone. The screen door was hooked, so we knew Mr. Clark was inside. Elmo reached through the place where the screen was parted from the door and flipped the hook. The front door was locked. I'd never seen it locked. Not even when everyone was gone. There was no reason.

We walked around the house a couple of times. The only window open, and that was only a couple of inches, was the office. We could hear music from the radio, the station that he always had on. Elmo called, "Dad, Dad. Open the door." I called, "Mr. Clark, Mr. Clark, it's us." We knocked on the front door. Banged the screen door, too.

It was Elmo's idea to get the ladder. I got one in the barn and carried it over, holding it away from my dress, not to get it dirty. Elmo went up. Raised the window as far as he could, another six or seven inches, and slid in head first. I went around to the front door.

Waited. I knocked. Then went back around to the window. "Elmo, Elmo," I called, "open the front door." There wasn't a sound. I went back around the front. Then ran back to the ladder and started climbing. I couldn't see into the office because it was dark. There wasn't enough room for me to get through so I took off my shoe and smashed the glass out of the frame, reached through and yanked off the shade.

Elmo was lying curled up on his side in the corner by the door. His eyes were closed so tight his face was wrinkled up like an old man's. Mr. Clark was sitting back in his chair, one hand flat on the desk. The top was covered with blood so red it looked like spilt paint. In the dark, Elmo had crawled right over the puddle. He had it all over.

Before I went back up to live with my father and Joyce, Grandfather took me and Elmo up in the mountains. "I hope it's not too late," he said. "It's almost impossible to know exactly, but this was the time we did it last." But that was before James was born, it turned out, who was eighteen now. They'd let him come back for the funeral. Bigger than ever. In the paratroopers. Wearing spit-shined boots. He showed us how to do it one night.

Elmo was sitting in the middle. He was his old self again. He slept in my room on a porch cot. We'd tell each other stories until one of us went to sleep. Joyce wanted me to take the bus to her sister's when she heard what happened. But I said I wanted to stay until school was out. She let me. "It's your choice," she said. One reason, I was raising my hand to answer questions now in history, science, geography, and math. I knew. Thanks to Elmo. I never let anyone forget it either.

I'd never been in the snow before and Grandfather let us out. Elmo threw a snowball and got it all over my new coat. I picked him up and stuck his head in a snowbank. There were pine trees: piled-up snow would fall off the bent limbs and then they'd shoot up in the air like someone had let loose of them. I found big pinecones, and icicles in the shade.

We got back in the truck and drove on. The road was clear and the sun came out shining. You could almost see the snow melt. Back off the road I could hear the water running underneath it. There were patches of ground, boulders showing. We went down a dirt road and parked by an old wooden bridge without rails that turned out to be the top of an old railroad flatcar. Elmo had to lean down and read me the name, Northern Burlington, before I'd believe it.

Along the creek there wasn't much snow. The water was still high. Small pinecones were caught in back pools. Old Mr. Clark was carrying a half a dozen wet gunnysacks to put the ladybugs in. I carried a big coal shovel. Elmo had two sacks and his camera.

"We'll take them down to the orchards and let them go on the aphids. It'll be a feast." Grandfather kept telling us things like that. I winked at Elmo but didn't say anything. Elmo followed him up the creek. He brought his camera to send a picture to James. I got one of my shoes full of water and took it off to wring out my sock. They went ahead.

I sat down on a boulder to let my sock dry. The sun and sound of the creek made me feel drowsy, like I was falling asleep. And Grandfather telling us: some people can't carry themselves any further. They get too heavy. Too burdened. Before they get crushed they have to leave the rest of us. They get out somehow. Like my mother. I had nodded then with Elmo. But I understood now.

I heard Elmo yelling my name and I started putting on my sock and shoe. "Greta, Greta, come on." He was so excited he couldn't run straight; he was dancing around in circles on his toes on the bank. I ran to meet him. He couldn't even talk clear. I picked him up and ran as fast as I could.

Grandfather was sitting across the creek just looking at them. There were billions. It was different than blossoming plums or wild flowers; they were alive. I got closer, let Elmo go. It was like Grandfather said. Got down on my hands and knees. They were coming out from under the snow into the sunlight. Heaps of them. They covered whole sections of the dirt bank. I stuck my bare arm into the middle of the boil. I felt them start to crawl on me. When I lifted my arm out it was covered thick. They swarmed onto my shoulder and then into my hair. I closed my eyes and felt them on my face. I kept thinking, If this could be, if this could be, anything could happen. Anything was possible. I yelled over to Elmo as I felt them on my cheeks, my chin, "Take a picture, take a picture."

ELEPHANT HEART
1953

Balancing on his toes, he quietly opened the screen door and tiptoed into the living room. It was almost as dark inside as out on the porch. They were watching TV. He stood still in the blue semidarkness. Grandpa hadn't changed, sitting relaxed in his chair, feet up on the ottoman. Elmo was stretched out on the couch; he'd grown some but was still small for his age, must be twelve now. They laughed at something happening on the show. He saw Greta then; her legs were even longer now, calves resting on the coffee table.

He hadn't been back in over three years, not since the funeral. The room looked smaller. Too small. He saw his photo on top of the mantel. That wasn't him, not any more. He looked so young there. He'd got even bigger since then. "Is this the kind of welcome I get?" He said. They all looked around, surprised. Then Elmo got up yelling "James," running full pelt into him. Grandpa was slapping him on the shoulder, shaking hands. Everyone was talking at once. "How come you didn't tell us you were coming?" Grandpa asked.

"I didn't know until the last minute, myself."

"You made staff sergeant." He pointed at the chevrons.

"It was because I was big. I got that from you." They both laughed.

Greta stood in front of the chair she'd been sitting on, her hands behind her back. She must be seventeen or eighteen and still growing, but she looked the same too, the braids, jeans, sweatshirt, those eyes taking everything in. She came over when Elmo quieted down. "Welcome back, James," she said, putting out her hand.

They sat at the kitchen table eating popcorn and drinking glasses of A & W root beer. The room looked the same; it had to, from all the times he'd imagined it. High ceiling, ten feet, must be. White paint coming down to the ribbed wainscot. Who painted it gray? It had been brown. The five windows, six panes to a sash. He closed his eyes to remember what each window faced. The barn, end of the triangle of road, the Red Beaut plum trees, the section of porch, and the garage. He opened his eyes. It was too dark to see if he was right. They were all looking at him. "It's good to be back," he said for the third time. Grandpa was talking about last season: "No price anymore. You can't give them away. Prunes are the only thing that's saving us."

Looking at the windowpanes, he started seeing little pictures of the past: they weren't clear, but he knew who was in them. It was like someone was holding up black-and-white photos across the table. He tried to look away but the pictures moved with his eyes. Him hitting his father. How many times had he seen that one? His father falling against the refrigerator. Slowly getting up, enraged, but looking almost pleased now.

When he had come home for the funeral he'd insisted that they open the casket. "He's not presentable," the mortician said.

"Who's paying?" he'd yelled back. It was the first time he'd seen a dead person. They had stuffed paper towels in the holes where the bullet had gone in and come out. It made him look like he had little wings on the sides of his head. His whiskers had grown since he'd died but his eyes were closed. He was done. It's not my fault, he'd kept thinking. Since then the dead didn't bother him. If he didn't have to look at their faces.

"How many did you shoot, James?" Elmo asked, shaking salt out into his bowl of popcorn. He didn't understand. Elmo repeated the question. James wanted to get up and run. But he couldn't move, he couldn't even groan. He finally lay his head on his arms on the tabletop and closed his eyes, refusing to see anything else or hear anything else.

He slept better in his own bed than he had for a long time. He heard them in the kitchen. They would expect him to go down. He couldn't fit into his old clothes anymore. He ended up wearing a pair of his army khakis and a T-shirt.

They were all busy, Elmo making toast, Greta peeling potatoes, Grandpa frying the ham. He got the plates and started setting the table. "Just like the old days," he said, feeling they were all waiting for him to say something. "Remember Mrs. Budge?" he asked Greta.

"Do I ever. I never eat white gravy without thinking of her."

"How's your folks? Elmo must have written me, but I don't remember."

"I sent you a letter every week for all the time you were gone."

James put his hand around Elmo's neck and squeezed a little. "It was like being home when I read them." Elmo looked pleased. "Now I remember. They bought a motel," James said.

"That's right. I can make beds as fast as I can pick a limb clean." She sounded so sure, so confident.

"Greta's been coming back in the summers to help out," Grandfather said. "She's got your old job, running the packing shed."

James nodded, thinking it wouldn't take much to do better than he did. He saw the first picture and stopped eating. They all stopped too. He wanted to put his head down again. He closed his eyes not to see. He made himself find his toast, groping on his plate, pick it up, and take a bite. Chew. He opened his eyes.

Later Grandfather drove him around the place. It was the same, the perfect rows of plum trees going away from the road until they ran together. He caught a glimpse of Greta driving the John Deere with a trailer load of fruit bins to the packing shed. One of her long braids was swinging across her face. Elmo had his shirt off and was loading boxes of prunes onto a pallet in the drying yard. They passed the foreman's house, the hands' house. They were all empty now. Needed paint. "Looks the same to me," James said.

"It's not," Grandfather said. "The whole county is changing. People are selling out. You remember Claude Knight from high school?"

"Sure, I remember him. How is he?"

"I heard he joined the navy. His folks sold out. Got a good price, I hear."

"Nothing wrong with that."

"No there isn't. The people who bought the place don't know an early Santa Rosa from an Elephant Heart. Don't want to know, either. Probably try to undersell us next season. When I came here I paid thirty-five dollars an acre for the bottom land. They paid six hundred. What's it going to be like in another thirty years?"

James didn't smile but he shook his head. His grandfather always talked like this, was always worried, never satisfied. They could have a bumper crop and he'd think of something to ruin it. I hope it doesn't hail. Look at those thunderheads. Don't borrow trouble, his father used to tell him.

"We don't owe the bank. That's something to remember. Don't borrow. Once you get caught up in using their money to get the next crop, you might as well hand over your deed. You're just working for them then."

"What's that?" James asked, pointing to the Quonset hut. They'd come nearly to the end of the road past the marsh.

"I lease this out, now, down to the river. They put up the Quonset hut for the hunters. Bring them down for duck season. Remember the blinds we had out here? Let the county supervisor come out and shoot, the assessor, all the rest? For free? Now I get paid. *Mr.* Conlin." He emphasized the Mr. "He brings these dentists and doctors out here in droves. He fleeces them, gets them to invest their money. It makes them feel like he-men, I guess, shooting ducks. They get so drunked up I'm surprised they don't kill each other. This is their club, they call it. Elmo and I come down and show them how, sometimes. They don't know their elbow from a box of tacks about hunting."

Grandfather stopped the truck. "Come on, he's here, that's his Lincoln." As they got closer to the Quonset hut, Grandfather lowered his voice a little. "He wears two-tone shoes," he said and started laughing, slapping his hip.

A short fat man came out of the doorway with a boy behind him. He must have heard, James thought, trying not to look at his shoes. "Mr. Conlin, good morning, I want you to meet my grandson, James. Come home on leave from the army." After they all shook hands Grandfather and Mr. Conlin started talking. James looked around. They'd hunted ducks here as long as he could remember. The mosquitoes were bad. If he had his way he'd drain the whole goddamn marsh. Put in some early plums, Queen Rosa or Black Beauts.

Mr. Conlin kept right on talking, even after Grandfather said a couple of times, "We have to get back to work." They backed to the truck and finally got in. Started the engine. He stood at the window smoking his cigar, talking away. His boy was sitting on the steps of the Quonset hut. Grandfather put it in gear. "See you later," he said.

"Tell Elmo we're expecting him to come over to see us sometime."

"I will do that."

"The wife can take the boys over to the zoo, maybe the aquarium. Be good for them. Educational." Grandfather let out on the clutch and the truck moved away. Mr. Conlin yelled, "Nice meeting you, James."

"That man likes to talk," James said.

"That's his business. Talking. If you give people like that enough time, they'll have everything you own. Just by listening to them. They have the answers, the questions, and most of all, the time."

"Elmo want to go over there?"

"Not while Greta's here. He writes her, phones. I put him on the bus a couple of times to go up there to her folks. She came down for Easter week this spring. She's a good girl. Good for Elmo. And she does the work of three people."

"But she's dumb," James said.

"How do you make that out?"

"She can't even read."

"That doesn't mean anything. I thought something was wrong with her eyes at first, and took her into town, but glasses didn't make any difference. I don't know what it is. Elmo saw her report cards. She got an A in algebra and geometry. And she's taking chemistry this year." He didn't say it, but James knew what he was thinking—and that's a hell of a lot further than you got.

"If she can't read, what the hell can she do with herself?"

"I never asked about her plans," Grandfather said.

He'd been home two weeks: two more to go before his leave was up and he'd have to report back. It was almost as if he'd never left. Greta would come in early from the packing shed and make pies in the shells she'd had ready from the night before. She always had some surprise for them. Orange tapioca. He hadn't had any since his mother left. Stewed rhubarb. She even made homemade ice cream one time. Besides roast beef, medium rare, and pork chops and anything else he could think of.

"You can cook," he told her. Her face flushed. "I don't remember you being so good in the kitchen. On the other hand, I don't remember any of us being too good."

"Joyce, her stepmother, is a good cook and she showed her how," Elmo said, getting out the bread and butter.

"I have ten, no, eleven cookbooks of my own," she said.

Before he could stop to think, he said, "Who reads them to you up there at your motel?"

Everyone stopped what they were doing. Greta was slicing a cucumber and she set it and the knife down, then slowly wiped her hands on her apron and walked out of the kitchen. They could hear her going up each of the steps. "You have a big mouth," Elmo said, and he went out too.

"It's like old times," James told his grandfather. It was just the two of them eating dinner. "I didn't mean anything by that," he said.

"I know you didn't," Grandfather said, "but you have to be careful what you say. Some people don't like to be reminded. There's worse things than not reading."

He went upstairs after they'd cleaned up and put all the food away. Knocked on her door. He had heard Elmo talking but that stopped when his knuckles struck the wooden panel. It seemed like a long time before she said, "Come in."

He stepped into the room. She was at the desk with a pencil in her hand. Elmo was sitting on a chair with a book. "I was writing a letter to my parents. Elmo helps me. So they can read it," she said.

"I'm sorry," James said. "I didn't mean to offend you like that." Elmo was watching him.

"I accept your apology," Greta said.

"That's all I wanted to say," he said and backed out of the room.

"We still go into town on Saturday morning?" James asked. He'd been back three weeks now; he felt better about going in. When he'd come back he'd got the bus driver to let him off on the highway so he wouldn't have to stop in town. He couldn't stand the thought of all those people looking at him. Saying hi James, welcome back. Welcome home. He was ready now. Buy some new clothes. He needed a haircut. Shoes.

"We were planning on it. We've been pretty busy, you know," Elmo said.

James was yelling before he knew it. "Who do you think's been hand-loading the semis anyway?" he yelled.

Elmo didn't yell back. "We're going at nine," he said, dipping his toast into his egg yolk, "as soon as Greta's ready."

James could hear the water running and the drain gurgling as it came down the side of the house. She was up there showering, fooling around. He poured himself another cup of coffee. For something to say he asked, "You going in, Grandpa?"

"I think I'll skip it this time. I was in day before yesterday to get a new chain for the hoist. They got all my money that time." Both James and Elmo laughed. Grandfather was a miser. When he was quoted a price in a store, any store, he'd always say, "I know that's the regular price but what's the cost to a preferred customer like me?" He'd do it anywhere, supermarket, gas station, anywhere. Sometimes it worked, too. It used to embarrass James and he'd look away or pretend he didn't hear. Or tell Grandpa he'd meet him at the truck, walk away, when he was waiting in line. Nothing bothered Grandpa: He'd know why he was leaving, too. Back in the truck, he'd always tell about the time in the post office, standing in line

behind the pastor of the Lutheran church, who asked the clerk
for a ministerial discount on three dollars worth of stamps. "If
he had the gall to try that on the United States government, I
decided then and there I ought to have a chance with the
businesses around town. The way prices are." He was a char-
acter, James thought. No wonder the town people thought the
Clarks were strange.

He saw Greta come into the kitchen out of the corner of
his eye, and he finished off his coffee, then stood up, when she
said, "I'm ready." She was wearing a light-green summer
dress. Had she ever worn lipstick before? He'd never noticed.
Her long brown hair was in a bun now. She was maybe three
or four inches shorter than he was, six feet, maybe. She had
on silk stockings and white shoes. A white leather purse was
pressed between her elbow and her side. A gold locket like his
mother used to wear hung around her long neck.

She flushed at his staring. He tried to shift his eyes—
Elmo was looking at him—but they snapped back to Greta.
She was as good-looking as a model. "Let's go," Elmo said.
"We don't have all day."

He followed them out into the garage. The old two-door
Buick convertible still looked like new. They must have put
six coats of wax on it, he thought. He followed Greta as she
opened the door on the driver's side and got in behind the
wheel. He stood there, confused. "Do you want to drive?" she
asked.

"No, no," he said, and hurried around the front of the
car. Elmo had already shut his door. "Get in the back," he told
James. He almost did, swinging his leg up. Then he opened
the door. "Move over, there's room for all of us in front." He
sat down and slide Elmo over next to Greta, then slammed the
door shut.

He kept his eyes off her. No one said a word the whole way
in. He could only see a section of her cheek, with fine pale
down, and sometimes the bun of hair that was coming loose.

He'd never seen so many yellow butterflies this time of year: they fluttered against the windshield like pieces of sunshine but left chalk-like smears where they hit. Elmo kept turning on the windshield spray, then the wipers. It made a bigger mess. James reached over and pushed the button in. Elmo glared at him. He watched the road cut through the round hills.

The barber was new. The one that had cut his hair since he was a kid had retired. He got it cut back down to a half inch in front. Then he went to Penney's and bought a pair of Levi's, cowboy boots, and a Hawaiian shirt, blue with white palm trees, and wore them out of the store. Leaving, he noticed in the window a straw planter's hat with an orange band, and he went back in and bought that, too. He felt funny walking down the street in civilian clothes. No one noticed him; he didn't recognize anyone. He'd been gone almost three and a half years. He had another five months to go. Then he was out. He'd get things moving on the farm. Try safflower, that was big now. He had the water, try cotton. Diversify. There was money in those crops. Pull some of those goddamn plums out. Dairy, maybe.

He passed a drugstore and stopped to look at the racks of paperbacks. He'd almost forgot. His reading material. On the troop ship going over in '50, they had dumped boxes of paperbacks on the deck. He'd been late and all the westerns were gone. He'd picked up a couple that looked good anyhow, women on the covers, and read them. One was a mystery that took place in England. He couldn't put it down. He traded for more. They were the best things he'd ever read. Chief inspectors. Lords. Upstairs maids. Not much shooting. They used their heads. The victims were usually poisoned. The guilty people usually fell into a bog in the end. He often imagined sitting at high tea eating crumpets. Cucumber sandwiches. He was lucky: he found five altogether. He planned to read them slow so they'd last. Knowing he had one in the back pocket somehow made the time go faster in the army.

It was almost twelve; they were supposed to meet in front of the Rexall. He headed that way, taking a shortcut across a parking lot. "James, James, is that you?" He stopped and looked around. "James." Someone was calling him from the back door of the Rio. "It's me, Claude. What's that outfit: it's not Halloween yet, is it?"

"Claude, for Christ sake." They shook hands, and James forgot to let go.

"We got into port night before last. When did you get back?"

"Three weeks ago, about."

"I heard you were in the thick of it."

"You going to buy me a drink or just talk?"

They played liar's dice first and beat the bartender out of four drinks before he refused to play anymore. James started out drinking straight vodka shots with beer chasers. "You should have never quit school," Claude told him. "You could have gone all the way to the state meet with the shot. Any college would have taken you."

"I had better things to do," James said.

They ate cold beef sandwiches and bags of potato chips. With each round, Claude bought them hardboiled eggs and James called out for more dill pickles. Al came in, someone Claude knew better than James. He'd been a couple of years behind them in school. He'd been on the football team with them. They played another game where the person who lost in poker dice paid for the drink, the one who came in second named the drink, and the one with the best hand drank the drink. "Give the paratrooper here," Claude yelled, looking behind the bar at all the old half-filled bottles down below the cash register, "some of the orange stuff there. No, not that, the one next to it." James drank it down. It tasted like syrup. He salted another egg and took a bite.

"I may be slow," Claude said, "but I'm not crazy. I only signed up for three years. I heard you went for four."

"Dumb," James said. "Dumb, what did I know? I thought four years would be four minutes, like high school. But we beat the two-year draft, didn't we?" They both laughed, hard, but James remembered at the time he'd have signed up for a hundred years to get away. Now three and a half seemed like a thousand. He bit into his pickle, getting juice all over his new shirt, and tried to wipe it off with his hand.

"I was a better offense tackle than you were," Al said to James. He could barely remember Al, second or third string behind him. He didn't want to argue. "You were, Al; they should have let you play."

"No he wasn't," Claude said. "He couldn't carry your helmet. You made all league."

"Doesn't matter," James kept saying. "I never liked football. It was just because I was big, that's all." And he thumped himself in the chest with the side of his fist. "I never wanted—" he trailed off, forgetting what he was going to say. "I should have taken algebra," he added.

"Sure, sure, James, roll the dice."

"In a couple of weeks I'm going to join the marines," Al said.

"I'm choosing," Claude said. He yelled to the bartender, "Give us a shot out of that bottle with the worm in it."

They left the bar and sat in a booth in the back in the semidark. The music was soft and the jukebox, made up of ten colored lights, seemed to hover against the back wall like a rainbow. One couple danced. "Remember in 4-H when we grafted nine varieties on the same tree?" Claude said. "My folks sold out. Sold the tree."

"You can stay with me," James said. "We'll do another tree."

"They got a place in town."

Someone bought James a cigar and he tried to keep it lit, striking match after match. The owner came in and sent over a bottle of pink champagne left over from New Year's. Al had

left and Claude was resting his head on the back of the booth
with his eyes closed. A woman wearing his hat was sitting
next to James drinking the champagne and stroking his arm.
"I've got plums," he was telling her, "as much as you want.
Fancy. You could put them in your store." She had said she
was a checker at the new Safeway. "We're picking Friars now,
best there is in the county. Ask anyone. Clark's are quality
plums. That's what our label says." He blew a mouthful of
smoke out and Elmo was there, staring at him. Was it Elmo?

"Come on, James, we've got to go home now. It's late;
we've been looking all over for you." Somehow he got up on
his feet. He didn't seem to weigh anything. It was as if his
whole body had fallen asleep. All but his ears: they hurt as if
they were on fire.

At the door he turned and called back, "Full moon.
Farmer's moon. Planting moon." Greta was out on the sidewalk, waiting. It was too dark. He tried to keep his legs
moving. "My ears hurt. You got my packages, Elmo?"

"I've got them, James."

"Where's my hat?"

"I didn't see any hat, James."

"I better go back."

"Come on, James, the car's around the corner in front of
the Rexall."

He kept moving. He stumbled. Greta took his arm. "Oh
Greta, I don't feel as good as I should."

"You're going to be all right, James."

He stopped. "Did anyone ever tell you what a beautiful
thing you are?"

"Come on, James," Elmo yelled.

"Just answer me. She can answer if she wants. Did they,
Greta?"

"No, James, no one ever has."

"It's true, Greta. Believe me, it's true." He felt dizzy and
grabbed hold of a NO PARKING pole. He got sick. He felt it

coming and tried to hold on. But his hands slid down the pole until his knees hit the cement sidewalk.

It came up again and again. It was like his lifeblood was pouring out of him. He held on. He could feel Greta gripping his shoulder. He felt lighter, smaller. When he opened his eyes he saw the spread of vomit in the streetlight. "Look," he said, "pickles. Look at the pickles."

"You don't chew your food," Elmo said.

He got sick in the back of the car going home. He got sick in the kitchen. In the bathroom. And when he woke up in the morning. He had the dry heaves and only green stuff would come up. When he could, he rolled off the bed and lay on his stomach on the floor. He felt better with his face against the cold linoleum.

"You OK, James?" Grandfather asked.

"I'm fine, just fine."

"Here, take a shot of this. Hair of the dog that bit you." James didn't understand until his grandfather put the whiskey glass next to his mouth; then he was sick again.

When he heard them come in for supper he went down-stairs, but he didn't go into the kitchen. He was afraid of what the smell of food would do to him. He sat in the front room with just the one lamp on. Greta came in. "I made some soup," she said. "I can bring you some."

He remembered it all, everything. "I don't think I'm ready," he said. Not looking at her, he added, "I meant what I said last night, Greta. I remember." He couldn't tell in that light if she'd heard him. When he turned, he couldn't see her face. She stood there on her long legs, one knee slightly bent, not saying a word back.

When he reported in, they put him in charge of a crew mowing lawns and picking up litter. Everyone on his list was a short-timer, ready to get out. They did the work without him having to be after them. He didn't know if he could do that anymore. He wasn't going to give orders if he could help it. He'd found two thick paperbacks in the PX, but he allowed himself to read them only after supper, until lights out. It was getting hard to find ones he hadn't read.

The captain gave him a reenlistment talk. "We want men like you to stay in, make a career of the army." James stood at ease before the officer's desk, looking over his head. "Take advantage of the opportunities. The retirement. In sixteen years—"

"It's because I'm big, isn't it, sir," James interrupted. "That's why you want me to stay."

The captain looked at him a long time before saying, "You can go, Sergeant."

He signed up for a correspondence course in general math and could hardly wait until the books came. Greta had gone back home to start school. Grandfather had taken Elmo to the Conlins in the city: James was supposed to pick him up on Saturday when he got off and take him back to the ranch. He went early, driving the old pickup he'd taken back to the base. The place was easy to find, a half hour from the barracks, overlooking the beach. It was a mansion.

A maid dressed in a uniform answered the door and led him into the front room to wait. He'd never seen a place like this before: Everything was so polished. The tabletop was so shiny it looked like glass, but it was wood. He took a closer look at the crystal bowl on top of the piano. It was full of colored glass fruits: apples, pears, peaches. He picked up one that was supposed to be a plum. It wasn't the right size for any variety he knew of. He was putting it back when someone came in behind him.

"You must be Elmo's brother." He turned. "I'm Mickey's aunt. The boys are upstairs disassembling their telescope; they'll be right down."

"You're Mr. Conlin's sister?"

"No, his sister-in-law. My sister is married to him."

"This plum doesn't even look like one," he said, holding it out.

"It's an imitation," she said.

"I understand that."

"It's a decoration."

"Why not fresh fruit?"

She got hot. "It's my sister's; my mother gave it to her; we have some at home too." She was bristling. She couldn't weigh more than eighty-five pounds, he thought. She dropped her hands from her hips and stepped back. "Would you like a glass of sherry?"

James started laughing. He couldn't help it.

"What's so funny?"

"I've been reading English mysteries lately and they're always drinking sherry. I never thought I'd be offered any, that's all."

She went over to the sideboard and set out glasses that were only as big around as the first knuckle on his thumb. He tried not to laugh again. He had to explain. "It's just that the glasses are so small."

She actually stamped her foot. "What would you like to drink out of, jelly glasses, you clod." She put the decanter down and started walking out of the room.

"I didn't mean to offend you. I'm sorry. I'm just acting silly. What was your name?"

She stopped. "You'll laugh." He shook his head. "Cornelia." She waited. "It's an old family name."

"My name is James," he said. "It's an old family name, too."

"OK, James, I'm pleased to meet you." She was probably younger than he was. But she looked so stern.

"I'm pleased to meet you, Cornelia."

She came closer. "We did an autopsy on a cadaver your size last quarter."

He nodded. It didn't seem to matter what she said: he wanted to laugh. He wanted to touch her. He didn't know what to say next, and she waited. "Do you want a steady job picking plums?" he finally said.

She started laughing. "My brother-in-law has several dinner stories he tells about you people. But I'm sorry, I'm too busy. I'm in my second year of medical school. I'm well-occupied."

He heard himself say, "I'm impressed." He'd never talked like this before.

"I bet you are. Are you impressed enough to accompany me to a gathering of fellow students tonight?" She was looking up at him with a smirk on her face. "Saturday night is our night to howl."

She drove in her car, which, he was surprised to see, needed a lot of body work. The seat was ripped, too. He'd phoned Grandfather and said that Elmo wanted to stay another night. He was wearing his Hawaiian shirt under his FFA jacket: it was the only thing that would fit him. He'd taken the year pins off the front, but there was still the stitched yellow emblem on the blue corduroy. That was funny, too. What difference did it make? What difference did it make why she'd asked him? He was going. He started laughing again, and she joined him.

It was some kind of big hall with only a beer bar. He bought them a pitcher and they sat down at a long table. She knew everyone and tried to introduce him above the noise of the place. All the girls looked alike, clean cut, the same size, thin, perfectly dressed, with fussy hair. The boys were the same, but they were louder, he noticed. Everyone had good teeth.

He hadn't had a drink since that night with Claude. The beer tasted good, but he was going to take it easy. He sipped. Cornelia kept his glass filled. People talked to him. One, about football. Because he was big, he knew. He broke it off and had a long conversation with an older man with glasses who said he taught at the school. James mentioned in passing that he was a podiatrist himself: for years Grandfather had tried to get relief from his corns and only found help when an itinerant podiatrist came through and treated everyone in the district. He came back every year now.

"He's a very good one, too," Cornelia added. "I considered podiatry myself as a profession before I was admitted here." The doctor nodded, holding onto the table to keep his seat on the bench. But he was interested in what James was saying, chiming in with "agreed" every couple of minutes.

"It seems to me," James went on—a phrase Cornelia had used at least nineteen times so far—"that the medical profession has to be relieved of some of the minor parts of the body so it can concentrate on some of the major problems. Polio. Jungle rot. Frost bite."

"Agreed," the doctor said.

"I'm perfectly happy, from both a professional and financial point of view, working just on the foot. It's enough for me. Hammertoes. Ingrown toenails. It's challenge enough. When I operate, it doesn't matter that an MD has to be in attendance. You're doctors."

"Agreed."

"Even if I know as much, if not more, than most people do about the foot."

"Agreed," Cornelia said.

"But why not allow podiatrists to move up, say, to the knee, maybe even up to the hip? That's not so much. You recognize us. Podiatrists are a reliable group."

"Agreed," the doctor said.

"We're not chiropractors. Or optometrists. We've relieved you of dirty feet. Four or five percent of the total human body. And more importantly, if, say, we did move up to the knee, how much business are we taking away from medical doctors? A very small amount. Athletes. Car-wreck victims. And if we went as high as the hip, a few old people who fall. We need to expand, to move up the leg some. And you need to spend more time on the upper half of the body, where the more important parts are located. You've given animals to the veterinarians. Hair-cutting to the barbers. Why not make it foot, knee, and hip for podiatrists?"

"We need a podiatrist on the faculty," Cornelia said. "Let *them* hit the knees of this world with a rubber hammer; we're not carpenters. It's undignified. Let them have the hip too. There's plenty left."

"She's got a point, doctor," James said and started clapping. Everyone around the table joined them. His throat was dry and he took a long drink of beer. He could feel her next to him. She was talking to someone on the other side of him now, and he kissed her on her open mouth. She was startled but gently clamped down on his upper lip with her teeth. People started whistling and he pulled away. She went on talking as if nothing happened. When the bar closed they went with a couple of carloads of other people to a restaurant. And after that, to someone's house up overlooking the bay, where they danced.

They were riding back along the ocean. He was leaning back in the seat. The air coming in the window smelled of drying kelp. He took a deep breath. He didn't feel like himself. Not with her. Like somebody else.

"You show a girl a pretty good time."

"You were surprised that because I'm big I didn't drool on myself?"

"That's not what I meant."

"For a rich girl, you're not bad yourself."

"We're not rich; we have a slowly declining business, as my brother-in-law Michael would say. Which means we're nearly bankrupt."

"Sounds like farming."

"You want to see our family pride?" She didn't wait for

him to answer but turned off toward the city. It didn't make any difference to him where they went.

When she stopped it was in front of an old three-story brick building with dirty and broken-out windows. There was an odor he couldn't place. They went through a side door that she opened with a key. Over the hum of machinery he could hear the sound of metal conveyor belts moving. A few men wearing paper hats were working different kinds of refining machines. It was hot inside. The place was dingy, dirty in the poor light.

"What do you think?"

"Not bad." She was watching him. "Interesting."

"It's our own chocolate factory. Since the turn of the century."

He saw a shadow move; it was a rat the size of his fist. He hoped she didn't offer him any samples. They wandered around. There were so many pipes running overhead he couldn't see the ceiling. They dripped water on them. She didn't seem to notice. "Shirtsleeves to shirtsleeves," she said. When he shook his head because he didn't understand, she explained. "First generation makes the money, and the second loses it. We're even a little slow doing that."

"My family never got out of the first shirtsleeves stage," he said.

She took his arm. "Come on, let's get out of here before I get maudlin."

She phoned him Monday night. They went to China-town to a place where they knew her and then to a foreign movie. It was in subtitles and he could barely follow what was taking place. Some strong man in the circus beat his wife and drank a lot of wine. Nothing was happening. He was amazed to hear Cornelia start to sob. Loud. Blow her nose. She held onto his hand and squeezed it during the worst parts. Other people were crying all around him. He felt embarrassed. When it was finally over and they were outside she asked, "What did you think of that?"

"It was OK," he said.

"You didn't like it." She became indignant. Like with the glass plum. "Hasn't anything sad ever happened to you? That affected you strongly, that changed your way of thinking?"

He got hot; she was looking down her nose at him. "Yeah, there's been a few things. My father blew out his brains with his .38. That kind of took the wind out of me."

"I'm sorry, James," she said.

He calmed down. "He couldn't take it, I guess."

"I can understand that it's just an option."

"I never thought of that, an option. But he had other options. He had me and my brother." He didn't go on. He didn't want to think about it.

The next Saturday she invited him to the beach, and he had to buy a new bathing suit. He was up to two hundred and thirty-one pounds. He hadn't weighed himself in a long time. He was still filling out.

They followed a path down through some brush to a secluded beach. There were rock cliffs going straight up and only a few other people nearby. He hesitated in taking off his shirt and trousers. He felt like a monster beside her. She was putting oil on her shoulders. "Come on, I'll put some oil on you." He took off his clothes. He felt self-conscious. He lay on his stomach. She rubbed the oil into his neck and back. "Did anyone ever tell you you have an immense neck?" He had to laugh. "It's a nice neck, but a very large one."

He sat up. "That's what made the difference."

"What?"

"That I'm big. In grammar school, I was the tallest. I was class president every year. In high school I was the captain of the football team. The prom king. I got the prettiest girls. All because I was big. Because my grandfather was big and my father was big and I'm big. I go in the army and because I'm big they think I'm tough and they make me corporal, sergeant, then staff. Just because of my size." He knew he was working himself up, but he couldn't stop. "I had nothing to do with my twenty-inch neck."

"Was your mother tall?" she asked, still kneading his neck. He didn't answer. "What about your mother?"

"She went off when I was thirteen. With someone that worked for us. She was medium height, I guess: five five, five six." He was glad he couldn't see her face.

"I caught my father in bed with a neighbor," she said. "A friend of my mother's. Walked right in. What do you say to that, Jimmy?"

He didn't know what to say. "Not Jimmy, James," he reminded her.

"That's right. Your grandfather is Jim. Your father was Jimmy. And you're James the Third."

"That's better."

"We'll get by all this," she said. "When we start making our own mistakes. Then the people around us won't seem so important."

"I've got a good start today, after almost four years in the army."

"School doesn't give you that opportunity. I can't seem to break out of my family orbit. I will, I know I will. I bring it on myself. I could keep away. But I can't. I make a point of visiting my father at his office. The last time, the bank had sent an appraiser to go over the books, and he was in the outer office. My father was putting a golf ball into a drinking glass, wearing a silk shirt and smoking a three-dollar cigar. Dignified-looking man. I could introduce you; you'd be impressed. Tailormade suits. Wants to know if I can loan him some money for lunch. I know he's going to take his girlfriend out. He has no imagination: You know who he takes out now?" James waited. "A stripper. I went to see her show. My father thinks he's some kind of rich playboy. I gave him the money, a check on my scholarship account. He folds the paper into his shirt pocket like he's earned the money. Come on," she said, "let's go get wet. Enough of this light banter."

He was never sure what was going to happen next with her. Over the summer vacation she had been working in a pharmaceutical company lab, a place she said was important because she was making valuable contacts. He seemed to be always waiting for her to call back. They saw each other two or three nights a week and some weekends. They were friends, she told him once, good friends. He tried to convince himself there was no sense in worrying about it.

When he didn't hear from her he went home one weekend. The weather had changed, it was cold for October, and he was wearing two sweatshirts and a stocking cap. Some of the early plum trees were losing their leaves to the wind that was coming out of the southeast. He had on his rubber hip boots, too, stuffed with old newspapers and magazines for protection against the rattlesnakes around the place. He had added the insulation when his grandfather had speculated that snake fangs would go right through the rubber boot. He hated snakes: when he worked in the grass it always took twice as long because he was careful and always on the lookout. He was replacing some old wood fence posts with new metal ones up near the house when Elmo came by driving the John Deere, with Mickey, Mr. Conlin's son, sharing the seat. "James," Elmo called. "Mickey's aunt is at the club." He wasn't listening.

"Aunt Cornelia," Mickey said. "She wants to see you."

"Get off the tractor." James shouted to be heard over the engine.

"We're driving," Elmo said.

He lifted Elmo off first, then Mickey, and got up stiff-legged. He didn't have time to change his clothes or get the pickup. He hadn't shaved since Friday morning either. He made the John Deere move. Elmo was yelling after him, "I'm telling."

She was sitting on the front steps of the Quonset hut. She waited until he turned off the ignition before saying, "I've come to see how you rich farmers live."

"Why didn't you phone me first?"

"I just came for the ride. It was an impulse. Michael brought down the contractor who's going to build the new club."

James almost lost his footing getting down from the tractor. He walked over to where she was sitting.

"What's wrong with your legs?"

"Nothing. It's my protection."

"Against what?"

"Snakes."

"You mean your hip boots?"

He sat down beside her on the steps. "I'll show you." She helped him get his right boot off, pulling at the heel, and then she shook it, upside down. Four *Life* magazines and a lot of newspapers fell out.

"What's this for?"

"So the snakes can't bite me."

She started laughing. "You're afraid of snakes?" She was cracking up.

"Those snakes don't care how big you are. They can still kill you."

She was still laughing, slapping her hands together. Then she surprised him by giving him a big hug while he tried to get off his other boot. Almost pinned his arms to his sides. "Are there any around here? Everything's cultivated."

"There were when my grandfather first came." She opened her mouth but she couldn't laugh anymore, no sound came out. He put his big hands around her waist and lifted her up off the ground. "You pip-squeak," he said, and set her up on the tractor seat. He drove the tractor with one boot on right across the lawn to the front steps. "Come on," he said, lifting her down, "it's lunchtime."

Grandfather was at his best at lunch. "We used to use your family's powdered chocolate, Miss Carleson, but they discontinued it. Can't find it in the store anymore."

Chewing and swallowing her mouthful of food before answering, Cornelia said, "More people tell me that." Her back was straight and her chin was up. "I mentioned it to my father, but he said there's no market for it anymore."

"Business, it's business," Grandfather said, and he started in. "We used to have eleven different varieties of plums. A different section ripe every couple of weeks. You never tasted anything like some of them, Yellow Egg, Grand Duke. May until November we had plums. Brokers tell me a plum is a plum. Taste doesn't matter. And don't confuse the issue with different names. We'll buy only the summer plums. Pick them stone-hard and pack them green. People from New York City don't know any better. How many varieties do we have left, James?"

He thought for a minute. "Six, counting the Presidents, and there's only about thirty trees left of that."

"It's a losing battle," Grandfather said.

"How interesting," Cornelia said. "I never realized how complicated merchandising plums could be." She took another spoonful from the glass bowl of home-canned peaches and said, "I bet I know who did these peaches." She was feeling at ease now. "That tall hired girl you told me about, that makes you rhubarb pies."

"She's not here now," James said, avoiding everyone's eyes. "Who wants some of Grandpa's coffee? I'll get it."

She looked out of place sitting in the kitchen. It was like one of the people in his paperback mysteries had come to life and was visiting. He was so excited he couldn't eat. He'd force himself to take a bite and then forget to chew. Even Elmo was taken with her, allowing her to cut his sandwich and pour his milk. He and Mickey were showing off, eating twice as much as they normally would, smacking their lips and rubbing their

stomachs. She helped clean up after lunch and shook Grandfather's hand when they left the house.

He took her on a tour of the place. She insisted they ride
on the tractor instead of taking the truck. He got her back to
the club in time for the ride back to the city. He was too shy
to kiss her good-bye in front of everyone. They shook hands
formally.

"What do you think of her?" he asked his grandfather that
night. He'd waited until Elmo went to bed.

"I'm the last one to ask on that subject. Women haven't
had much luck in this family," he said.

James knew what he was talking about. His grandmother
had died a couple of years after his father was born. During an
operation: They butchered her, his grandfather had told him
once. He'd had a sister he couldn't remember, Veronica, three
years older than Elmo, who'd died of meningitis. And his
mother ran off. He thought of his father. Christ, no one had
any luck in this family.

"You'd have your work cut out for you."

"How's that?"

"She's going to be a doctor. She's used to different things
than this," and he waved his hand around the front room.

"They don't have that much. They just pretend."

"That could be worse," he said. "There's no pretending
with a plum orchard. Your father tried that with your
mother."

James had been slouching on the couch. He sat up. "I
don't want to hear that."

"You asked me."

"What about Conlin; he married her sister," he said,
louder than he meant to. They laughed at him, not only at his
two-tone shoes, big cigars, and deals, but at the way he tried
to impress them. Ready to buy anything, a plum orchard, a
pickup, because they had one. When he came to the club
now he wore the same clothes Grandfather always wore, wool

shirt, khakis, lace-up three-hook boots and a brown fedora,
only his was black, as if the clothes made him like Grandpa.

"He's got money, you don't."

"I can get some; it's not that hard."

Grandfather didn't answer, just sat there in his chair and
recrossed his slippered feet on the hassock.

"We'll see," James said, standing up, then going out

By Thanksgiving he'd taken the high school equivalency
test and passed. Had gone to see a counselor at city college.
He could start the spring semester and major in business, he
decided. He had been taking out a twenty-five-dollar allot-
ment since he enlisted, which came to almost two thousand
dollars with his other savings. He was trying to decide how to
invest it.

Cornelia was back in school. They got together occasion-
ally. When he complained she told him, "James, I'm going to
become a doctor. I hope you understand that." When he
hadn't heard from her in two weeks he parked in front of the
apartment she shared with three other students. But she never
came back that night. He had Elmo phone Mickey to see
where she was, but Mickey didn't know. He wrote. He sent
a telegram: Remember me, James the Third. He invited her to
Thanksgiving. Never heard a word.

He went home for the holiday and sat around watching
TV or reading his paperbacks when he should have been
outside working. The barn was leaking like a sieve because
two pieces of tin had blown off the roof, and the John Deere
was broken down in the middle of the orchard. He felt listless.

Greta phoned Elmo on Thanksgiving Day. Talked to
Grandfather. Wanted to talk to James. "How are you, Greta?
We're enjoying our turkey. I basted it a couple of times, but
Grandpa did most of the work. Two more months and I'm
out. That would be nice, if you could come for Christmas.

You could show us how to make mashed potatoes. I can't get the lumps out." He handed the phone back to Elmo.

He was in the last rank on the parade ground, waiting to be inspected by the captain, when he saw her car pass and park on the street opposite where he stood. He was sure it was Cornelia's car. It had the same dented front right fender. He hadn't heard from her in six weeks. He had to wait as the inspecting officer moved from man to man.

When it was his turn he did it all automatically: brought his rifle up, snapped open the bolt. The captain didn't take the rifle. Just looked him over. "Squared away, Sergeant."

"Thank you, sir." He waited: All the while he wanted to fly to where the car was parked. She had never come on the base before. At Dismissed he ran as fast as he could, holding the rifle at high port. People were staring at him but he didn't care. She rolled down the window of the car when she saw him coming. He slowed down when he got close enough to see her face. It was her; she wasn't going to drive away. She got out of the car when he got to the street. "I don't think I've ever seen you in your uniform before," she said.

"Where have you been? Why didn't you phone me back?" He tried not to sound like he was whining. Or angry.

"I should have told you, James. Three weeks ago I went to Carson City and got married."

All he could think to ask was, "To a doctor?"

"No, you never met him. He owns the place I worked at this summer. I quit school for now." She smiled at him. "I guess I'm my father's daughter after all."

All he could think of was the time when Elmo was three or four and their mother was still at home and she swatted him on the rear. She must have been mad, because she never spanked them. Elmo had been astonished. He'd started crying; then he'd taken a handful of his shirt over his chest and yelled as loud as he could, "Look what you've done: You've broken my heart, you've broken my heart." James felt the pain there but didn't want to reach up. It was real.

"Here." She handed him a glass plum. "You liked the other one, didn't you. I couldn't find one like my mother's. Does it look like a plum?"

He looked down at it in the palm of his hand. It was too small. "It looks like a Santa Rosa," he said.

"Remember me, James, because I'm going to remember you." She got back into the car.

"I'm going to college in the spring," he said.

"I know you'll be a good student," she said, looking at him. And she released the emergency brake and drove down the street. She made a U turn and came back. From the curb he watched as the car came by. She looked straight ahead as she passed.

He didn't tell anyone. Who was there to tell? His grandfather? It wasn't important. He was just a passing fancy to her. She was just using him. That wasn't true. She had seen more to him than his size. He kept the glass plum buttoned up in his shirt pocket. He could feel it as he walked.

He lost his temper with a corporal. Over nothing. He'd asked him to turn down his radio; he couldn't read. The volume went up. He had learned something in the army: to leave everybody alone, to control himself. He broke the corporal's jaw. He must have kicked him, too, because all the corporal's ribs on one side were cracked. The captain got him off. No court martial. He came in late, drunk, one morning. Out of uniform. They restricted him to the base. He didn't bother to go to the mess hall any more. Ate at the snack bar. He was surprised when he weighed himself on the penny scale in front of the PX. He'd lost nineteen pounds. The captain allowed him to go home for Christmas. Told him, "You're getting out in a couple of weeks. Keep your nose clean. You've been in here five times now." James stood in front of his desk, swaying.

Christmas eve he went up the porch steps, late, he knew that, but they were still waiting up for him. "It's Saint Nicholas," he yelled, picking Elmo up out of his chair and dancing with him in front of the tree, kissing Grandpa on top of the head. Greta was there. He went over and hugged her, too. Kissed her on the mouth until she pushed him away. "Merry Christmas. I'm going upstairs for a minute and change out of my uniform. I'll be back. Don't worry." He went up the stairs using the handrail.

He didn't remember anything until Grandfather shook him awake. "James, James," he could hear him say. "I'm too old for this. You've got to go talk to her. Get her to stop."

He didn't understand. "What? What?"

Elmo came in with a glass of water. He thought it was to drink, but Elmo threw it into his face. He sat up in bed. "Elmo," he yelled, "I'm going to break your arm."

"There's a woman down there in the truck who wants a ride back to the city," Elmo said. He heard the horn then. Then again, a longer honk.

"She won't come in. She doesn't want me to take her to town for the bus. She wants you to take her back," Grandfather said.

"The hell with her," James said. He couldn't remember bringing anyone home with him. The horn sounded again.

"You want any more ice water?" Elmo said.

"You throw any more on me and I'll throw you out the window." They all listened again to the sound of the horn. "Just tell her to stop."

"She's got herself locked in the truck and won't listen to anyone," Grandfather said.

"Let her honk, then." He wanted to close his eyes. He looked up at his grandfather. Greta was standing by the doorway. Elmo. There was no use saying he was sorry. "I'll go," he said, "I'll go."

Elmo had some coffee for him by the time he got downstairs. The honking kept up. He took the cup with him out the door. She had the lights on, too. The truck probably won't start, he thought.

"You OK?" Elmo asked.

"Never felt better," he said, handing him the empty cup.

"You want me to go with you?"

"No, it's all right," he said, lightly knocking on the truck-door window. "It's me," he said to the woman inside.

He took her all the way back. He had picked her up at the NCO club. She fell asleep as soon as he turned the pickup around. He enjoyed the ride. There was no traffic. He kept the window open, let the cold winter air blow against his face and keep him awake. But he didn't need it. He knew where he was going.

But when he got back home again he was tired out. He didn't think he could get out of the truck. He just sat there. Elmo came down and opened the door. "We're almost ready to have dinner," he said.

James sat at the table, making himself eat. Raise the fork, chew, then dig in for some more on his plate. "Sure good," he kept saying. They were all watching him. He didn't look up. He had a funny thought. He started to giggle. But he made himself stop. "I feel . . ." He didn't go on. They were staring at him. He was laughing hard but he got it out. "Grandpa, I bet now I can fit into Elmo's shirts without any trouble."

BLOSSOMS
1955

He knew it had to be his feet. They'd poisoned his whole body. It felt like his insides were going around and around. Like they were parts of a whirligig, mixing the pain up enough where it wouldn't drain down toward the holes he'd cut in the sides of his new black shoes to relieve the pressure on his corns.

"Grandpa, we're here. We're at the hospital," Elmo said.

He opened his eyes. "I was thinking," he said, "did we prune the greengage?"

"We got that whole section."

"I don't remember that." Elmo was staring at him, his hands still on the wheel. Elmo knew too much.

He had to get out of the truck. "Well, we might as well go in. They need our money as much as we do." He got the door open and got outside and hobbled over to the glass swinging doors. And finally reached the desk.

"I called," he started out. But it was like he was dreaming again, as if he were watching himself as he slept. The nurse behind the desk, writing things down, was waiting for him to speak. Elmo was standing back, carrying his fedora he'd left in the truck. He tried to explain every-thing.

"This was Sunday and we have no family doctor. We don't get sick very often. I phoned and they told me to come in. To tell you the truth, I feel awful." That was the only thing he heard come out. It was hard to know what anyone else was hearing.

They laid him out on a metal table in the examination room. Gave him a shot of something, but the pain still came. "I'm going to get James," Elmo said.

They hadn't seen James much since he got out of the army. He didn't want to stay here, he'd said. First it was cross-country driving, a moving van. Then he was in the midwest doing something on a gasoline barge. Finally he was supposed to be in Alaska homesteading with Claude Knight, growing cabbages. The only way they ever heard anything was from Claude's folks. Claude wrote now and then. James, never. The hell with plum trees, he'd said before he left the last time. But James would find his place, just like he had.

When he'd finally reached California he knew it was the last stop for him. He was as dependent on the seasons now as the plum trees were. Pruning, picking, spraying, irrigating, smudging against the frost. He couldn't imagine himself not seeing the orchard when the trees were in bloom in the spring-time. It was like strolling across a pink sky after the sun had dropped out of sight.

Elmo was holding his hand. Did he groan out loud? "I'm OK," he said. "Did you tell them we have medical coverage?"

"I gave them the card," Elmo said.

It was the smartest thing he'd ever done. Elmo had in-sisted on going out for football. Because James did, he guessed. But he wasn't James. He didn't weigh a hundred and eighty-five pounds besides being six feet at fourteen. Elmo weighed a hundred and five as a freshman, was two or three inches past five feet. But he never got the insurance until after

Elmo broke his collarbone. It had cost. Better late than never with Elmo.

He never knew what to make of him. James yes, James was like himself. Big. Bull your way through. Elmo was so smart he knew things you were thinking before you could say them. It gave him the advantage, but he never used it. He waited for you. Other times he'd look at you like he didn't understand the language when you talked to him. It made a person uncomfortable.

He was getting his growth now. Skinny. Arms too long. Looked like he might fall when he got up out of a chair. His voice was changing and there was acne all over his forehead like red measles. Spent hours with his telescope on a platform he built out on the roof.

He started fading away again, and felt Elmo grip his hand harder. What a funny feeling.

"What are you doing, Grandpa, taking a vacation on us? I thought we were going to overhaul the John Deere."

James's voice. He felt sleepy, but he wanted to respond. "How much do you get for those cabbages up north, James?" he asked.

"Don't know, never waited until they were big enough to sell." He heard Elmo's laugh too. "Lousy climate, like living in a freezer with a herd of mosquitoes after you." He wanted to make his eyes open but he couldn't. It felt like they had grown together.

"How do you feel?" Elmo asked. He sounded closer.

"I can't feel anything," he said. "Just tired." He slipped back. He and his sister were rowing out to check the trot line. It took a long time to haul up the floats. There was nothing. The seagull guts dangling from the hooks were all untouched. Not even a crab.

There hadn't been anything in the traps he'd set for the

shorebirds. Lorraine sat slumped down in the bow. They let the boat drift. He wondered if they were going to be able to get back against the tide. Their last resort was walking up to the slough where the rushes grew. Pulling up as many as they could to eat the roots. They tasted like raw potatoes if you got all the mud off. Chewing. Swallowing them down. The crunching sound you could hear only in your own head.

He took hold of his oar. "Come on, Lorraine, let's go see if dinner's ready." She lifted her head. Her eyes finally focused on his face. "Dinner," he said.

She caught on. "That beef stew should be ready," she said, crawling over to her place and fitting her oar in its lock.

"Coffee and hot corn bread," he said, slicing his oar down, pulling back against the bay water with all his might.

"You want dinner now, Grandpa?" Elmo asked. "You weren't awake when they came around. But I don't think they have any corn bread."

"I ate before I came into town," he said. He and Elmo had two country sausage patties and eggs for breakfast.

"Grandpa, you've been in the hospital five days," Elmo said. "They operated on you day before yesterday."

"Did they get all my corns?" he asked.

"They took your prostate out," James said.

"What do you know about that. I had rickets once," he added. "Lorraine had them too. Before we went to live with the Clarks."

"That's your sister, Grandpa?" Elmo asked. "Back east?"

He couldn't answer, he had to sit quiet at dinner. The Clarks didn't allow any talking. Just eating, which was all right with him. He could never get enough. He sat there until every bowl and platter was empty.

"I like a boy who's a good eater," Mrs. Clark said.

"Well, we've got us one," Mr. Clark answered, putting his arm around his shoulders.

"We've got to go," James said, "it's past nine. They're

supposed to run you off at eight now." James's big hand squeezed his shoulder. He felt Elmo kiss him on the forehead.

From the kitchen, James heard Elmo on the phone talking to Greta after they got home. "He's going to be all right. You sure you can't come up? You know how much he'd like to see you. James is right here; do you want to speak to him?"

"How are you, Greta; how's the job? You like working inside like that? I couldn't do it myself. I don't care how much they paid me. I'm going to stick around for a while. Take care of things here until Grandpa gets better. Thanks for the invitation, but I'm going to be busy. The roof over the kitchen is leaking so bad the plaster's coming down. I imagine I'll have to reshingle the whole thing.

"What model did you get? You must be doing OK. That comes with power-glide. I'd like to take a ride in that. Good talking to you, here's Elmo."

"Greta, I just want to tell you how much I miss you. Without Grandpa here," Elmo whispered so James couldn't hear. "There's nothing to do. I don't even feel like stopping at the A and W and eating a couple orders of french fries. Well, write me then. I wrote you four times last month and I didn't get any from you. I know you're busy. When am I going to see you if you're working over Easter week?"

Monday, James started in on the roof, tearing the old shingles off the porch first. When Elmo came home from school he went up the ladder to help. The old redwood shingles were worn down and weatherbeaten, so thin and warped they shattered like old leaves when they pried them up with wrecking bars. "What are we going to do if it rains?" James asked, the heels of his boots locked between two roof boards.

"It's not going to. I looked up the forecast in the paper," Elmo said. "And then phoned the meteorologist at the airport. He said there's no chance of rain."

"What does he know," James said.

When the sun was behind the orchard James yelled over to Elmo below him, "Go down and cook up something for supper."

"You go down, James; I'm busy, too."

"Elmo, if you don't get down I'm going to throw you down." He shied a shingle at Elmo and just missed hitting him in the head.

Elmo went down the ladder, yelling back up, "I'm not cooking for you. Just for myself."

When it got dark James came down. There was a skillet on the stove, heaps of fried potatoes and four pork steaks. He was too tired to think about going in to town to the hospital when Elmo came downstairs. "You going?" Elmo asked. "You better change."

"He doesn't even open his eyes. Doesn't even know we're there," James said.

"You're not going, then?"

"You shouldn't either; you don't have a license." Elmo walked right out the front door. James was going to get up to go, but he didn't. He had his boots off and he didn't have the strength to go and get his town shoes upstairs.

Someone had come into the room. "Grandpa, you better? It's me, Elmo."

He opened his eyes. "You know who you resemble? I was thinking about it all day. Lorraine, that's who. You've got her two bumps on your nose and her cleft chin. Same gray eyes, even the same color of hair. James looks like me and your father. Because we got so tall, I guess. It made us look the same."

"What happened to her?"

"She got married, had five or six kids."

"You ever hear from her?"

"Used to. I went back a few times. With your grand-mother and your father. But when Mrs. Clark died we had a falling out. I haven't heard from her since."

Elmo was sitting next to the bed, watching him. Just like Lorraine. He had that untouched look on his face, no matter what happened. He was interested. He wanted to know. He did look like Lorraine. Was she still alive? She was older than he was by four years.

"In those days when I was young, younger than you are now, if you didn't have anybody, people took you in. You used their name if you wanted and you helped out until you could do a day's work. Earn your own way. We were lucky with the Clarks, they treated us like their own. They didn't have any kids, so there was no bickering there."

"What happened with your real parents?"

"My father died with cholera. I don't remember him. I was seven, eight when we went to the Clarks. My mother died too, that's what the Clarks told us. But I found out later she'd married a man who didn't want us. He had a business, lumber mill, I think it was. My mother told Lorraine, who must have been ten, that she was to take care of me." He stopped, his throat was dry, and took a sip of water out of the bent straw in the water glass on the tray.

"She just left you like that with nobody?"

"I had Lorraine. She worked, helping with the wash for the neighbors, making soap. I herded cows. We shucked corn. Anything so somebody would feed us. You have to under-stand it was different then. If you didn't have anything it was your own fault. The county let you starve. The church ran an orphanage, but we didn't want to go there. This was sixty years ago. I just had Lorraine."

"I don't remember you talking about her before. What happened to her?"

"Mr. Clark—we always called them that, Mr. or Mrs., but they were our mother and father, it doesn't matter what you call people you respect—he had a stickpin, garnet, I think it was, even though he said it was a ruby. Mrs. Clark had a carnelian brooch with a gold setting. They told us that when they died we'd each get a piece of jewelry.

"I went back when Mrs. Clark died. I paid for the funeral. Let Lorraine have all the furniture in the place. I think I asked for Mrs. Clark's Chinese sewing basket for your grandmother. Took a dozen decoys I'd carved when I was your age, mostly mallards, I think. We couldn't find either the brooch or the stickpin. Everything was in a mess; Mrs. Clark had lived alone for ten or fifteen years after Mr. Clark died. But Lorraine had looked in on her at least once a day, I know that.

"I wrote Lorraine that I wanted the stickpin when she found it and to send it along. Never came. I more or less forgot about it. We were close. I'd have done anything for my sister. They'd never come out here. I invited them enough times, offered to pay for the tickets, but they wouldn't. So I went back with your father and grandmother. Her husband was wearing the stickpin. He was nothing but a blowhard, was the editor of the weekly paper. He said the stickpin wasn't the same one. Lorraine didn't say anything.

"I said a few things I shouldn't have, I guess. And we left that night. Went to a hotel, then came home. I never heard from Lorraine again."

"You never talked to her because of the stickpin?"

"That's right." Elmo was waiting for more, but he couldn't think of anything else to say. He didn't understand. He couldn't understand. Not at his age. It takes years to do something mindless, and to hold to it. You have to have done it yourself to understand someone else. "How's Greta?" he asked to change the subject.

"She's OK, can't come down for Easter vacation. Penney's wouldn't give her the time off. She sold more than anyone else in her department last month."

"She's a good girl."

"No use me going up there if she's going to be busy. I thought I'd go over and see Mickey. Mrs. Conlin phoned and invited me. She wants to take us to the planetarium. If you think you'll be all right without me," and he giggled.

"I'm on the mend now. How you getting along with James?"

"The same. He's bossy. Thinks I have to do what he says. He's so worried it'll rain before the roof's done, he's going to have us up there with umbrellas to keep the kitchen floor dry."

"Just hold on, I'll be back in a couple more weeks. If there's no complications, the doctor said. He'd be the last one to know. Go see the Conlins. I want you to. James is like me, and your father, too, I guess; likes nothing better than to make himself miserable." They both shook their heads.

"Elmo, we didn't expect you back until tomorrow," Greta said. He'd just thrown open the front door and was astonished to see her there in her green robe. He went in running, yelling "Greta, Greta," holding her as tight as he could, then trying to lift her with the same bear hug.

James came down the stairs, shaking the whole house. "What happened?" he asked.

"Mickey put some poison oak in his mouth at the park. I told him what it was, but he had to show off. Mr. Conlin was coming down to the club, so I got a ride back. Did you see Grandpa?" he asked Greta.

"We went in once when I first came," she said. Elmo had just noticed James had come down wearing only his shorts. "We finished the roof off, Elmo," Greta said, trying to get his attention. "Got the flashing on all around the chimney." James hurried back upstairs. "Got all the rain gutters back up." Elmo stepped away from her, was staring at her. James came hurrying down again with his trousers on, shirt tucked in, but barefoot.

Elmo started backing out of the room, keeping his eyes on Greta. James was standing beside her now. "We were thinking of going into town to see Grandpa and then eating supper out," James said.

"I'm not hungry," Elmo said.

"You can drive my new car, Elmo; it's got power brakes," Greta said.

Elmo ran up the stairs.

"Quit acting like a baby," James yelled up after him.

As he went past James's room he noticed the unmade bed, her slip neatly folded on the chair. The room she usually slept in hadn't been used. There was no bedding on the mattress.

Before they left Greta came upstairs, knocked on his door, but he wouldn't answer. "Elmo, you're making things worse than they have to be." She didn't say anything for a while. "We'll bring you something back; don't cook anything. Maybe some pizza with anchovies. Would you like that?"

He heard her go down, then the sounds of the car. He kept reading, tracing the stars with his finger on the map he'd bought at the planetarium. They were all named after people or animals. He knew more about them than he did about people down here. You could depend on the stars. How could she do that? He kept reading, watching the drops that fell onto the page join and build on the constellations until there were just too many, and he put his head down on the map and closed his eyes.

He took the long way, just in case they were already coming back. With the top down the old Buick cut across the constellations like a shooting star. It was too late for visitors so he parked in the hospital lot and slipped in through the emergency-door entrance. No one saw him. He took the stairs instead of the elevator. His grandfather's door was open, and from the light in the hallway he could see the long shape of his body stretched the length of the bed under the covers.

"Grandpa. Grandpa. Are you awake?"

"I wondered if you were going to come."

He hadn't really been wondering; he knew Elmo would come. He'd been wishing there was some way words would be enough. Elmo sat in the chair next to the bed. He waited. When Elmo didn't say anything, he said, "They were here. They left about an hour ago."

She'd cut her hair. It was as if she was out of focus and needed an adjustment, like on Elmo's telescope. A couple of years before, she'd stopped wearing it in braids. But now the bun, along with the hair, was gone too, and she had short curls. It made her neck seem even longer than it used to be. She didn't remind him of herself at fifteen now. There was too much change. He had to summon the time she'd spent that first summer with them. Tall. Wearing jeans under her faded-out dress. Face sweaty from picking, streaks of sap on the white undersides of her arms. Those braids, one hanging down her chest and the other in back. The pockets of her dress full of handkerchief and wallet. Skinny, narrow-shouldered. Taller than James then. Looking out of her blackberry eyes, making sure she saw everything, to tell Elmo later that night, their bedroom doors open to each other's voice. So he'd heard, "Elmo, you don't have to worry, we're always going to be together. It just takes time, like everything else."

"They were lucky to get that roof back on before the rain came, Elmo. I heard the report on the radio. As soon as you start a project like that the worst always happens. When we poured cement for the foreman's house it got so hot, a hundred and ten at least, that the stuff was setting up in the mixer before we could get it into the forms."

"She was mine, Grandpa." Elmo said it quietly. "Greta belonged to me."

"Things don't work out like that," he said. "You have to understand it's her choice. Not just yours or James's. It's what she wants. And it's not easy for her either. She was crying her eyes out when they were in here. Whatever reason she has, you have to respect that."

"No, Grandpa, from the very first—the seven years between us doesn't make any difference, doesn't mean anything, she said that. She told me she'd wait for me until I got older. She promised me. We had an agreement. She waited until I left, then came down to be with James. I know how it was."

It was too dark to see, but he knew the look that must be on his face now. It was the same look Lorraine had when she tried to explain how important it was they make a good first impression on the Clarks. "You want to eat, don't you? You don't want to starve to death, do you?"

"This is not like we're selling a lug of Red Beauts. It's not a sure thing. There's no plan in these situations that you can depend on. You know as well as I do that Greta's a woman now. And you're still a boy. It would be like grafting a pear on a plum; it's not natural. You have to let things take their course. You have to see things the way they are. Not the way you planned them or want them to be. You know what happened to your father. He never faced up to the fact your mother didn't want to stay. He built his whole life around that she left. The hell with everything else. The place, you two boys, everything. He could have been alive today if he'd let her go. Let it pass. But he decided to kill himself instead. You think about that. What a waste. To spend your life trying to change something you can't do anything about. Can you understand that?"

Elmo didn't answer at first. "How many more days you got left on your holiday here?" he finally asked.

"They're letting me out Saturday. I convinced them I had no more money."

"I'll come in early for you, then. We got behind out there

without you supervising. You're going to have to do twice as much to make up."

"You can depend on me."

"I better get going," Elmo said, standing up.

"Elmo, remember what I told you about my sister Lorraine and what happened between us?" He could see Elmo's head nod. "What she did wasn't right, but what I did, forgot all the good things that went before, wasn't right either. I could buy a thousand of those stickpins if I wanted. But I'm never going to see my sister again."

"It's not the same thing, Grandpa. I need Greta. She's what I want. What am I going to do without her now? Who do I get?"

He wasn't going to say anything, wandering into the front room where Elmo was doing his homework, sipping from his coffee cup, standing there by the lamp. "I should have made up with Lorraine." He had been going over this since they'd last talked about it.

Elmo put down his pen. "It's not too late."

"She's probably dead. I don't have the energy to find out for sure." Then he heard himself going on to his grandson. "I had no one to talk to after your grandmother died. I couldn't help it, the way things turned out with your father." Elmo sat there and listened. Had he told this before?

"Your father thought it was going to be easy. I made the mistake of thinking I wanted something better for my kid, wasn't going to let him go through what I did. Education. Hard work takes the edge off a person's imagination. You dream, but you listen to your stomach too. Your father never knew that. He never did anything he didn't want to do. I sent him to college. I kept him out of the army. Got him a deferment. He picked a woman for his wife that no more belonged on this place than a date tree would."

He wasn't able to stop; Elmo sat there, waiting for the ending.

"I had nothing against the woman. I handed everything to him on a plate. He tried to do the same for her. We would have been bankrupt in a couple of years if I'd let him have his way. Borrow, buy three thousand acres of bottom land. Big-time farming. Mechanize. Buy more equipment. More and more land.

"I said no sir, I wasn't going to lose everything on one roll. Farming is a gamble, but you try and get as good odds as you can." He took a sip of coffee and looked out the window. He saw the lights of James's pickup and cut it short.

"So for ten years he sat there pouting. Until he lost his wife and then himself."

The door slammed. James threw his bag up the stairs before he came into the front room. "They've got a nice little operation up there," he said. He'd come back from visiting Greta, up at the Seidmeyer's motel. "They had the NO VA-CANCY sign up by three P.M. every day. He's got a whole new wing going in. Got three acres to build on. He's going to double the occupant capacity by this time next year."

"He always was a good worker," Grandfather said. Elmo had finished his essay and had picked up a magazine. He was leafing through it, ignoring James.

"I gave him a hand with the bathrooms, got most of the toilets and all the sinks and showers installed."

"People are traveling more every year," Grandpa said.

"I forgot," Elmo interrupted, "when did you buy the marsh, Grandpa? Mr. Conlin was asking."

"Let's see, I bought my first piece of ground with money I saved working on the railroad. Five acres, where this house stands today."

"And you bought two hundred thirty acres where the Red Junes start from the money you made on the commodity market," Elmo said.

"Soybeans," Grandpa added. "Only time I ever played."
James sat listening, reading from a paperback he'd taken
out of his back pocket, nodding his chin along with each
parcel.

"I got a hundred twenty acres from where the foreman's
house is operating a dragline when they put in the levee."

"And the whole marsh from where the duck club is to
where the orchard starts you got when you sold the milk
cows?"

"That's right," Grandpa said, "sixty acres."

Elmo watched him from the table. For the first time since
he was home there was red in his cheeks and he was sitting up
on the edge of the cushion of his chair, gesturing with his long
thin arms as he talked. The top button on his wool shirt was
fastened, and the closed collar made his uncut gray hair stick
out in back like the tuft of feathers on the head of a diving
duck. He'd lost so much weight that his six feet five seemed
stretched out even longer. His bony knees looked like turned
knobs under his creased khakis. In profile he was a third the
width of James. As if there might be two more of him somewhere in the shadows that you couldn't see.

"Your father got that hundred seventy acres of early
plums by the river. The owner wanted to sell, but cash. We
had almost decided to go to the bank, that's how desperate we
were, but at the last minute we talked him into taking twenty
percent down, and waiting until we harvested. They were
ten-year-old trees. At best we could have come up with maybe
another twenty percent. Big frost hit and burned up everyone
else's late plum blossoms. When we sold, we got a price,
enough to pay him off."

"You got the fifty-five acres by the road at auction. How
did it go?"

"I stopped by just to get a cup of free coffee. They had a
big pot always on the boil. I was on my way to buy the John
Deere. James was with me. I remember that because it was

near the Fourth and he had a flag he bought at the five and dime, waving it around in everyone's face.

"They started out low, but no one would say anything. Auctioneer tried working the crowd, but no one would bid. I knew the trees but didn't especially like Nubianas, never had any use for them, don't ship well. But it was like my hand raised by itself and I heard my finger snap against the edge of my hat brim. The auctioneer saw my signal and they were mine.

"It made six hundred forty acres, a whole section. That was enough. I couldn't even dream of having any more. That's all we could handle. Enough for my lifetime, your father's, and you boys too."

"You got the John Deere too, from money you got back from taxes."

"The check was laying in the PO box that day," Grandpa said, sitting back in his chair and crossing his long legs.

"Greta said to say hello to you two," James said. Grandpa looked toward him. "Elmo, I'm talking to you. Greta said to say hello." Elmo was examining the palms of his hands, not answering.

"How is she?" Grandfather asked.

"She's fine. While I was at it, I asked Mr. Seidmeyer if I could marry her."

"Did you," Grandfather said, lifting himself by stages out of the chair. "Congratulations," he said, shaking James's hand. "I know you'll be happy."

"Her stepmother was more excited than Greta was, carrying on. She started in that night making the trousseau. They want a big wedding, maybe have it here if it's all right with you, Grandpa. In the yard."

"That would be fine," he said. "This is a perfect place for a wedding. Inside or out, there's plenty of room," he added, sounding excited.

James stretched his big arms up over his head. "I'm tired; that's a drive." He watched Elmo flipping through the maga-

zine again as if he hadn't heard anything and was sitting alone
in the room.

"You go on and act that way, Elmo. But you're going to
have to face facts sooner or later." And he went out. They
listened to him go up the stairs and into his room. Then he
came back out and shouted down the stairwell, "Besides, she's
too tall for you." And he laughed. They both acted like they
hadn't heard.

"You want some hot chocolate, Grandpa?" Elmo asked.
"I got some of those small marshmallows you like."

"No, I don't believe I will. Thank you all the same. I'm
trying to cut down on my liquids after nine o'clock. So I don't
have to get up at all hours." He stood up, Elmo watching him.
"I can't seem to get my old body to where it was before. You
think they might have cut out some of my liver or something
else where I get my energy from?"

"No, it's because you're not eating enough. You don't eat
enough to keep a bird alive," Elmo said.

Grandpa, over by the french doors, lowered his voice to
say, "He's right, Elmo, facts are facts."

"I don't accept those facts, Grandpa."

"Elmo, she wants to marry James. You have to accept
that."

Elmo looked up at his grandfather, his right leg going up
and down as if some machine inside him were making it move.
"That's beside the point," he said.

He was awake at the regular time but lay there in bed not
wanting to get up. It was Saturday; he heard the sounds of Elmo
going downstairs into the kitchen to put the coffee on, then
James. Never a word between them. Trying to be quiet for him.
James going out, letting the screen door slam. The sound of the
John Deere in the barn starting up. The old two-by-twelve
floorboards snapping down, then springing back under the

weight. James was supposed to disk today. The yellow mustard was waist high in the orchard. Sleeping alone had been the hardest thing to get used to when his wife died.

He'd picked his wife because her name was Renee and she reminded him of his sister Lorraine. He told her both things after they were married a couple of years, to see what she'd say. "That's as good a reason as any. I became really partial to you when you started bringing me my first cup of coffee in bed."

She always made him try for the best in himself. He wanted to give up so many times. They'd lost a crop to hail and he lost heart. "What else would you rather do than own a plum orchard? Sleep all day?"

Or the time he was ready to sell the place. Pay off everyone. "You have to decide if you want to live without taking any chances or it you want to take a few. We have a lot of years to fill in before we kick the bucket. Might as well make them as exciting as we can."

She was wrong there. They were married almost fourteen years and she died. Ruptured appendix. There was no thinking about that.

When he carried on that time over the stickpin. Stomped out of Lorraine's house and into a hotel. She followed, which surprised him. But before she could say anything, he'd yelled, "I don't want to hear it. She's no better than he is. Mr. Clark promised me. I don't want to hear their excuses from you. You can't smooth over this. They're nothing but thieves." She stood there, still in her coat, with that look, and never did say a word on that subject.

Elmo was supposed to go into town to pick up an order of new smudge pots. He'd worried himself into ordering them after he realized it was almost fifteen years to the month since the last big spring frost. There was no screen door slam; Elmo didn't make any noise.

He should get up now. He spent too much time in bed.

But he started thinking about Lorraine. Was she even still alive? He could phone her. Find out. That operation made him remember it all. She was probably dead by now. Better not to know.

He didn't shave, went down, drank a cup of coffee. He had no appetite. For something to do he started in on the dishes. He could tell which was James's plate; he never rinsed them off. Covered with egg yolk. He had been careful not to even glance at the phone on the wall. But now he was staring at it. With soapsuds still on his hands he went over and dialed information. "Can you give me the number of Lorraine Johnston, Meridian, New Hampshire?" That was the last address he had for her. He waited. "Thank you," he said. Maybe she doesn't have a phone, he thought. He went back to doing the dishes. He thought a minute. Elmo. He hadn't heard the truck start up. He called out "Elmo?" Looked out the window. Then went out the door in a hurry, letting the screen door slam.

The pickup was in the garage. He should have gone by now. It wasn't like him not to go in early and get things done. He knew they needed to put the pots out, fill them with fuel. No telling when the temperature would start dropping. He noticed the side door of the barn was hooked open. Even James wouldn't leave it open unless he was inside. Elmo, never. He tried to hurry.

When he got to the door he could barely breathe and had to hold on to the door frame. Elmo was hanging by a rope from the rafter. A cluster of old rusted sash weights dangled below his boots.

He couldn't speak. There was no breath in his lungs to draw on. He closed his eyes and felt like he was going to pass out. He had to get him down.

"I'll go in to town, Grandpa, as soon as I'm done. I've got another four minutes." Was that Elmo's voice?

"Elmo," he tried to say, but there was no sound. The

Elmo came out the second time and he heard himself ask, "What are you doing?"

"I'm stretching myself, Grandpa. I read you can gain up to three or four inches this way. People do it all the time to meet civil service requirements if they're too short for the job."

He noticed his legs were bending by themselves and he was sitting down in the doorway. He tried to yell, "Get the hell down from there" but couldn't.

"See, I made a holder for myself out of the plow harness. Doesn't even leave marks."

He could feel Elmo's hands on his face. His long legs were dangling down the three steps to the ground. "Are you OK? You're all sweaty." He still couldn't talk.

"I rigged up those pulleys so I can get up and down. I'm up to thirty minutes a day. Using about a hundred pounds now. I think I've gained an inch."

"You're going to grow, but you have to be patient." He was surprised his voice sounded so normal. "You haven't got your last growth yet."

"I need to get taller, Grandpa."

"Why?"

Elmo didn't say anything.

"Answer me, Elmo." He waited. "That's not going to make any difference. Not if you were seven feet tall. She wants to marry James, not you." He was shouting. "When I came in here I thought you had hung yourself. Elmo, that's what I thought. You'd done what your father did. It was more than I could stand. I wanted to die too. All three of us would be dead."

"I wouldn't do that, Grandpa."

"That's what I thought." He got control of his legs, forced them under himself, and stood up. "I've had enough. You're going to behave yourself. If you love Greta so much, you act like it. She's marrying James. I want you to promise me." He couldn't look at him. Couldn't wipe away the tears that kept dripping off his nose onto his hands.

"I promise, Grandpa, I promise."

When he opened the door Greta gave him such a big hug he didn't think she was going to let go. "I missed you, Grandpa," she said. Joyce edged around them. She was half the height of Greta: it was like letting a loose ball into the house. With her two-ax-handle-wide rear she went through the rooms in a few quick bounces that made you dizzy to watch, giving off whoops when she saw what Elmo had done. Yelling back at him, "Jim, this place looks brand new." They had come down two days before the wedding to help get things ready.

"I always liked the side yard, with the trumpet vine growing up the wall of the house," Greta said, looking out the window. "Those three plum trees." There was no wind but sprays of pink petals sailed down on their own, covering the ground beneath the trees like a reflection.

"We could have had it at the motel, but it wouldn't be the same," Joyce said. "It looks like a month on a calendar out there," and she pointed to where Greta held the curtain open. "It was her choice. She didn't want it in a church."

"We never go," Greta said. "I couldn't see getting married in one."

"Well, Elmo's been out there working on the yard for a week now. Clipping, weeding; there isn't a dandelion left in the lawn."

"It looks nice," Greta said, looking over at Elmo.

Elmo tried to smile back. When they'd come in he'd shaken hands with Joyce and put his hand out to Greta when she let go of Grandpa, but she stepped around and gave him a big hug, too. He stood there with his arms to his sides, his eyes closed. "My Elmo," she said.

Grandpa went on, pouring himself another cup of coffee, leaning back in his chair at the kitchen table. "Painted the wrought iron fence. Washed the windows; can't remember when that was done last. Painted the porch. Even got the mailbox to stand up straight, out on the road. Painted that too. The outside is ready," he said.

"You can see that," Joyce said.

"Elmo's made a suggestion," Grandpa went on, talking faster, like he did when he was excited. "It's been holding at about fifty degrees, but you can't depend on the weather this time of year. He's been phoning around"—they all looked at Elmo, who turned red—"and it could turn cold on us. He thought, and I agree with him, you might consider having the wedding indoors, in the front room. We'll fill the place with blossoms, be like being outside. He's painted the ceiling where it leaked and we can move some of the furniture out." He stopped for Greta to say something, but she didn't. And he went on. "The minister we made our arrangements with doesn't care; it's all the same to him. But he did say," and Grandpa winked at Joyce, "since the Garden of Eden, inside weddings seem to last longer." They both whooped with laughter.

"I'll have to talk to James," Greta said.

An hour after they arrived Greta was sitting at the sewing machine finishing up the dress she was going to wear after the wedding. Joyce sat at the desk in the living room going over lists, written on a strip of adding machine paper, of things that had to be done. Elmo stood at her shoulder making comments. "You don't have to worry about the chairs for the sit-down dinner; the minister loaned us all his from the church." She crossed that off. "Same with the card tables; he's got twenty he's bringing." She crossed that off. Grandpa went out to look at his old blue suit he'd hung on the side porch to air. He sniffed it. The mothball odor was fading.

James came up the front steps two at a time shaking the

whole house, yelling out, "All those who are coming to town better get their coats on. It's nippy." He went over and kissed Greta on the top of her head, and she leaned down and kissed the back of his hand that rested on the sewing machine. Joyce got up. "An even forty-five," James said to Grandpa. "Not supposed to get any lower."

"Barometer is falling," Elmo said.

"It's broken," James said. "The sun's out. No wind from the south. Come on, I've got to pick up my new suit before the store closes. You need anything, Grandpa?"

"No, I already laid in ten pounds of rice for the festivities." Just he and Joyce laughed.

"Elmo?"

"No, I'm ready."

"You want to do me a favor?" James said. "Put a shine on my good shoes. I'm not going to have time." Elmo nodded. "Let's go," he said, opening the door and waiting for Joyce and Greta to pass through before stepping out.

All that morning people were arriving for the wedding the next day. All the Seidmeyer side came in one bunch: Joyce and Elmo stood at the door, welcoming them. Mr. Seidmeyer. "Call him Eddie," Joyce said to Elmo. Delores and the twins Cynthia and Linda, Greta's half sisters, who were going to be flower girls. Joyce's sister and her four daughters and their husbands. A great-uncle of Eddie's who lived in the county. Two carfuls of neighbors who had businesses near the Seidmeyer motel. Five girls who were going to be the bridesmaids; they either worked with Greta or had graduated with her. Because they lived so far away, they had all been invited to stay at the house, and they came in with arms full of sleeping bags and pillows. Grandfather and Elmo had already moved their bedding into the foreman's house to make room.

"That's not necessary, Jim," Joyce said as they got ready to go there after dinner. "It's your home."

"Easier this way," Grandpa said. "Makes more room, and you'll all be together."

"It's nice," Elmo said. "I had enough paint to do one of the bedrooms for him. The place is like new, never been used. A lot smaller than this old place, but easier to keep warm." He whispered to Joyce, "He needs the rest. He's getting tired out."

Greta started in. "Grandpa, it won't be the same place without you." She lit a Pall Mall. Elmo had never seen her smoke before.

"It's just for one night," Grandpa said.

"It's a good idea," Joyce said. "Elmo can watch his plum trees if it starts to freeze up."

"We'll be back for the festivities tonight," Grandpa said at the door. Claude had wanted to throw James a bachelor party in town but both Joyce and Grandfather had joined in and persuaded him to hold it in the barn the night before the wedding. Joyce had said that she and Eddie would supply all the booze if it was held out in the barn. Claude, who was James's best man, finally agreed.

"You got this place fixed up pretty good," Grandpa said to Elmo, looking around the kitchen of the foreman's house.

"It wasn't in bad shape to begin with. And after I convinced the horned owl to move out of the attic and the mice to leave the pantry, there wasn't a lot of work to it."

"I'm going to lie down a bit. I haven't seen that many people since I went across to the city last."

As Elmo came in with another load from the pickup Grandpa called out from his bedroom, "I'm proud of you, Elmo. You're doing good. You're going to make a slam-bang usher tomorrow."

Elmo stepped into the doorway and then crossed to

the foot of the bed. "I couldn't think of anything else to do," he said.

They made James get up and sit on the seat of the John Deere where everyone could see him. Joyce was the only woman allowed, and she worked as the bartender, standing in her heavy coat behind an old paneled door set on top of two upended field lug boxes. The door was covered with liquor bottles and at each end there was a washtub full of clear chipped ice with brown and green bottle necks, gold and silver caps, sticking out.

Grandpa stood nearby watching, holding a glass of brandy he sipped on. Elmo was on one side opening beer bottles for Joyce, Eddie Seidmeyer on the other, not saying two words, swigging from the same beer bottle until Joyce reached over and took it, "It's all suds, here," and handed him another. There were a couple dozen of James's old friends from high school, Future Farmers, neighbors.

Claude and his father had brought half a pickup load of ice for the beer. Joyce had got the owner of the Rio cocktail lounge in town, who'd known the Clarks for years, to roast two twenty-five pound turkeys and two hams in his restaurant ovens. Everyone had brought something to eat. The old workbench that ran halfway along one side of the barn was covered with food. And everyone was helping themselves, eating from paper plates, standing or sitting at the card tables Joyce and Elmo had set up.

There hadn't been any cows or hay in the barn for thirty years, and Elmo had swept the loft and hosed down the floors, but still fine pieces of straw kept filtering down, and there was the faint odor of manure. He had plugged in three electric heaters a day before the party, but it was still cold inside the barn and everyone was wearing their coats and some their hats.

Claude had brought a phonograph and four Patsy Cline records which were played over and over. Some of the guests were playing darts on Elmo's board nailed to a stud. There was an arm-wrestling contest and two poker games going on. At different times Claude handed up to James a two-quart canning jar full of beer to chugalug. As James raised it to his lips everyone stopped what they were doing and began counting out loud. One. Two. Three.

"I'm glad I'm not young anymore," Grandfather said, watching. Eddie chuckled.

"You never got drunk, Grandpa?" Elmo asked, winking at Joyce, who was listening.

"I have, but I had a right to."

"How was that?" Joyce asked.

"They talked me into taking the pledge when I was ten, in grammar school. Made me sign a paper not to drink or smoke until I was twenty years old. Gave a copy to me, and the principal kept one copy in his log. He used to walk around town after school, his hands behind his back, on the lookout for temptation. He was at every picnic and every outing where there was anything to drink. It took me until I was sixteen before I headed out of there. After I left the state of New Hampshire I felt my oath wasn't legal any more. And I've been making up for lost time ever since."

"What about you, Elmo, are you going to follow in your grandfather's footsteps?" Joyce asked.

"Can't say, but every time I try a sip I start hiccuping. I'm staying with this." He raised his glass of orange crush.

James tried to get down from the tractor but everyone started yelling and rushed over and forced him back up. He sat on the seat of the John Deere, slightly bouncing from side to side. The right flap of his cap hung loose as if that ear had grown in the light of the hundred-watt bulbs that hung from the ceiling. When he emptied a beer bottle someone would pitch another one up to him and he'd open the cap with his big thumb and forefinger. Every once in a while he'd cup his hands around his mouth and yodel, and then the guests would answer.

Elmo came back into the barn. "The temperature's gone down some more, Grandpa."

"We don't have to take it serious until thirty, maybe twenty-nine," he said. "I don't have the temperament for gambling. I'd light up the smudge pots at thirty-two degrees if Elmo here would let me."

"When I was a boy," Eddie said, speaking in his slow shy way, "we used old tires, set them on fire and got them smoking. Covered three acres of sheepnose apples. Got down to eighteen once."

Grandfather was so surprised at Mr. Seidmeyer speaking he couldn't think of anything to say for a minute.

"How many tires to a row?" Elmo asked.

"Don't remember," he said. He always looked away from whoever he spoke to. "We poured coal oil on them to get them going."

"Never heard of that," Grandfather said. "But it has to work. Same as smudging; it'd protect the trees from the cold air. As long as there's no wind. You might as well pray as try and smudge when the wind's blowing."

"Mr. Clark," Claude called out. "Come over and say a few words about your grandson. Just a few words," he added. Elmo and Joyce laughed.

Grandfather moved closer to the tractor and looked up at James, who had a smear of beer foam on his upper lip and was smiling back. "It's true I've known him the longest," he started out, everyone quieting down. "But I never could tell what he was going to do next. Can you imagine any one of us going up to Alaska to grow a crop?" "Not me," someone yelled back. He took a sip from his glass, enjoying himself, waiting for the laughter to die down.

"Well, he surprised me that time, just like he did when he

picked a wife. How did I know he was going to pick one of the best women I ever had the pleasure to meet. And I'm not the only one who thinks that either. He's my grandson, so I know he's not perfect."

"Don't we know that," Claude said. Everyone laughed.

"Marriage is a serious step, but James is ready. Thank you." There was clapping as he walked back.

Claude jumped up on the wheel of the tractor and balanced himself with his arms out. When he was able to stand steady he slapped James on the shoulder. "He's the best friend I ever had," he said, wiping his nose with his sleeve. "They're going to make a nice couple." There was hooting and more clapping.

"Mr. Seidmeyer," Grandfather said.

He took a half step towards James. "I don't know what to say," he started out, looking at James's boots. "I got a new son," he finally said. And Grandfather led the clapping.

"Elmo, you say something," Joyce said, "you're his brother."

Elmo stood where he was and cleared his throat. "I know you and Greta will be happy," he said.

"That's nice," Joyce said, hugging Elmo.

The guests who had the ride back to town started leaving around twelve. Claude and the ushers had brought their wedding clothes and sleeping bags and planned to sleep in the barn. "I'll give you a hand taking this stuff back in," Elmo said to Joyce.

"Leave it. There's not enough food left to say so, and no one's going to bother the drinks. Take your grandfather home. He looks all in."

It was only two miles to the foreman's house and Elmo took it slow, stopping at the bumps and easing the old pickup over the potholes. He passed the house and went the whole length of the orchard to the marsh, then came back. The headlights flashed against the rows of white-blossomed trees and they seemed to move in the light with the truck.

"The temperature is dropping," Elmo said.

"There was no frost warning last I heard," he said back. "You're beginning to sound like me now. I thought I got to provide the bleak side in this family. You got the smudge pots out?"

"All of them. I kept the new ones back to use where we'll need them if it really drops."

When they got back to the foreman's house Elmo read the thermometer on the porch out loud. "It's thirty, Grandpa."

He came over to look. "Let's wait a bit, maybe twenty-nine at least, before we give the alarm. Try and get the local station on the radio. See if they know what's happening."

They sat on the small kitchen chairs, Grandfather with a blanket around him, still wearing his hat and coat. Elmo had turned the heater up to high and had all four gas burners on the stove on. He fiddled with the radio dial. Got up to check the temperature, looking through the window, spotting his flashlight on the numbers.

"It's the same."

"We don't want to lose those blossoms, Elmo."

"Why don't you lie down? I'll let you know."

"I'm already here," he said. "The place is warming up now." He loosened his hold on the blanket and scratched the back of his neck. "You know about me and the plums out there. It was a close thing, us ending up with those trees instead of a bunch of mooing cows." He had to talk.

"I started with the dairy business because like everyone else we had a few milk cows back home. And of course I thought I knew about them. But mainly because I got the lumber cheap to build the barn. Someone had put in a big order and then went under. The wood sat there at the railroad siding for a year before I made an offer."

"I never knew that," Elmo said.

"That's how I went into the dairy business. Built the barn and bought the stock at auction. It's funny how you make decisions in this life. You're going to find that out when you get older."

Elmo nodded.

"I only lasted six months in the dairy business. You don't know about cows from having one or two. They are the dumbest critters a person could think up. And there were ten thousand regulations you had to abide by. Plus the outfits who bought the milk made these fruit brokers seem like honest people. Not able to get good milkers. Never able to leave for a day without some new disaster happening. Diseases. They got a new one every week.

"All around my ten acres were these orchards, self-satisfied, quiet, I can't think of the right word. When the fruit was green I'd think of them as money trees. When it was ripe I'd imagine the plums as jewels. I'd stop, park, walk out under them, the branches so heavy with fruit they were propped up with boards. A simple five-month season if you wanted to go that way. Tranquil, that's the word I was trying to think of. I'd just stand there, peaceful, maybe eat a plum.

"Some of those trees were three feet thick, maybe thirty, forty years old. The limbs had gone to hell but the trees were loaded. I'd stand there and chew up a plum among those trees, it was shady, and I felt a goodness I'd never felt before."

"What kind were they?" Elmo asked.

"California Blues, I think. I didn't know anything more about plum trees than I did about banana trees. But I knew I didn't like cows. That fall I took a chance on the commodity market and bought more land. Planted seventeen hundred whips by myself. Then I sat there five years before they produced a single plum. But not once, no sir, did I ever retract the statement that this was the business for me."

"Grandpa, it's twenty-eight on the porch," Elmo said, looking out the window.

"You better go light the smudge pots, Elmo. Get all the help you can, don't you and James try and do it all by yourselves now. Use the bin trailer, load the extra ones on and put them all over on the river side; it'll be colder there."

Elmo was putting his jacket and gloves back on. Then he was out the door running. Down the steps, then out the gate. He was able to see him because of the white towel he had around his neck like a scarf.

The truck went out of the yard like a rocket. He loosened up on the blanket some more and let it fall back off his shoulders. It was getting warm. He reached over and turned off the four gas burners on the stove.

He should have put a phone in here; it would have made things easier. He ought to go out and give them a hand. The faster the smudge pots were lit, the safer it was going to be for the plums. But he didn't get up as he heard trucks coming down the road.

Four of them. Then Elmo on the John Deere, pulling the bin trailer. He couldn't hear anything once the equipment passed. But he waited, holding his breath, until he saw the lights from the torches. The lights moved at a trot, going up and down the rows. He could imagine the popping sound as they were stuck into the tanks and the fuel ignited.

He saw the early blossoms feeling the first wave of warmth, smiling down at him. His wife, Jimmy his boy, and of course Mr. and Mrs. Clark. Lorraine his sister. All safe now.

PEACOCKS
1956–1959

When he ran he kept his eyes closed as long as he could. The connection between himself and the dirt path that paralleled the orchard was what kept him from running into a tree. The loamy soil was just soft enough to carry his heel print. Enough to keep the connection. On the other side of the path was the levee that kept the water in the slough away from the orchard. Whenever he felt himself veering up the bank he made himself keep his eyes shut until he was sure he was back on the path by the plum trees his grandfather had planted. He knew them as well as anyone could. He'd been up in every single tree. He was well connected with the orchard and his grandfather.

It was easy keeping his eyes closed because he knew where he was going. He could run forever this way: his feet kept sending his imagination the right direction. But the pain was getting worse, his kidneys were burning red hot. It was hard to breathe, but he made himself keep going. He wanted to make it all the way back to the house for the first time. Grandpa would be sitting on the porch waiting, watching his pets. He tried to outrun it, went faster. He must be almost past the last section, Queen Rosas. When the bile started coming up he remembered what Jesse, his coach, said: it doesn't really hurt until after you stop, so keep going. Then he started vomiting and opened his eyes so he wouldn't get any on his shoes. He leaned forward, his arms stiff against his knees, spitting, trying to get it all out. Gasping, feeling his whole body hurt. When he could breathe he stood up and started for the house. He still had another half hour left of his workout.

He could see the roof. The house was just right for the two of them. All on one floor, so his grandfather didn't have to climb steps, like in the main house. Each had his own door off his bedroom into the bathroom. Plenty of privacy for his grandfather, who never came out into the kitchen in the long johns he wore summer and winter. He dressed for his first cup of coffee. The place was small enough to heat easily in the winter and cool with one fan in the summer. He had set up his telescope on a platform outside the attic window. And the porch was perfect for his grandfather, two steps from the ground and his peafowl.

Grandpa was watching him come up. The peafowl were pecking and scratching in the flower bed. The cocks were too young to have any of the big feathers. He got a kick out of how his grandfather treated them. Named the three males after the Three Stooges. The nine females had no names. Had trained Moe to hop up on the porch rail and beg for the cracked corn he kept in his shirt pocket.

He started out first. "Well, how's the stock, are they all fed and watered? Getting ready to roost for the night?" He untied the rope around his waist and started jumping, easy, just lifting the toes of his shoes enough to let the rope pass under.

"Can't say," Grandfather answered. "They're so slow. If they don't hurry up and grow some of those tail feathers I'm ready to give up on them. I won't be responsible. They're just like chickens.

"Now that I'm semi-retired and only a consultant in the plum business, I thought I'd raise these birds. I'd seen them in the catalogue for years, but never felt I was ready to buy." Elmo kept jumping, the sound of his grandfather's voice caught up in the rhythm that the rope and his feet were moving to. They both knew they had heard this before. "I thought they were a sign of prosperity: when a person raised something he wasn't planning on eating or selling, it gave you a certain distinction."

Elmo looked over at his grandfather. He'd changed again. Not just thinner than before, but he seemed like he was shrinking too. He was shorter than the six and a half feet he used to be. He himself still had a foot to go to catch up, but there wasn't the difference there used to be.

When he heard the car, it was too close for him to get away. He kept jumping, faster now, trying not to watch her ease out of the car. Her stomach was so big she had the seat all the way back. She reached inside for the hot dish with a blue towel over the top. Grandfather had stood up, stiff-legged, and he went to meet her. "Well, Greta, you didn't have to go to any trouble, but we appreciate it, of course." She stopped nearly every day with something.

"It's no trouble," she said.

He turned the rope slower, not to miss anything.

Grandpa took the bowl. "I got the others washed up," he said. "I'll get them."

"That would be nice. I forget where they are. I keep looking for them."

"I got a little behind," he said, opening the screen door with his foot, carrying the bowl with both hands.

She turned awkwardly to watch him jump. It looked like she was leaning back so far, to compensate for her stomach, that she would go over backwards. "How have you been, Elmo?" she asked.

"I'm fine."

"We don't see you much any more."

He jumped slow now, barely bringing the slack loop around. "I've been busy," he said. Then he heard the pickup. He didn't turn around, just kept jumping. James stopped right next to him, so he had to bring his arm in to miss tangling the rope on the truck mirror.

"Like old home week," James said. Grandfather came out the screen door carrying a cardboard box rattling with Pyrex bowls and tin pie pans. Elmo kept jumping.

"What I want to know is why don't you two come up and eat with us instead of making her bring the food down to you?"

The rope caught on Elmo's head and he let it hang on his shoulders, breathing hard. "We don't ask her to bring it," he said.

"Well, she can stop, then," James said.

"I don't mind," Greta said. "It's only a couple of miles."

"How did the pruning go?" Grandfather asked James, taking the box over to Greta's car.

"We're half done. Another three weeks, unless we can get the prima donna to help."

Elmo didn't answer; he wasn't going to fall into that trap again. "I do my share" sounded like an admission of guilt when he said it to James. And then James would snicker. The sound made him want to close his eyes.

James got out of the truck, hooked the heel of his boot on the bumper. He had a gut on him now. Almost as big as Greta's. His leather belt cut into the middle of it as if it were separating a couple of sausages. He looked bigger than any two heavyweights he'd ever seen. "What exactly have you been doing?" James asked. "Let's hear it; I'm interested."

Elmo saw the look on Grandfather's face, as if he was going to see something awful. Greta was holding her stomach from underneath with both hands. "Ever since we've come

back from our honeymoon, you act like you're a guest here.
When I can find you. You live down here, that's all right with
me, but you're not doing your share. Those plum trees can't
take care of themselves. Grandpa can't work anymore. Greta
can't either. That leaves you and me."

He didn't have to answer; he could just look at him.
Infuriate him. His face would turn as red as the bulb on the
porch thermometer. James was too easy. "I've been pretty
busy," he said. "Going to school." Saying it out loud he
realized he'd been catching the school bus for almost eleven
years now. It sounded like he needed more, so he added, "I
was elected class president. I have to stay for council meetings. And I have sports."

James snickered. "What sports?" He'd been All League in
his freshman year, playing football. All State in the shotput.

"I'm on the boxing team."

James laughed out loud. Elmo felt himself start to lose the
connection he had with the ground.

"I had to sign a card," Grandfather said. "He's got a
punching bag in the shed. I've got four clippings from the
school paper too, if you want to see them."

"When are you going to fight next?" James asked.

There was no way out. "Next month at the Elks'."

"I've got to see that," James said, getting back in the
truck. "Come on, let's go," he yelled over to Greta.

"That woman can cook," Grandfather said. He'd barely
touched the Swiss steak Greta had brought over. Elmo was
sopping up the last of the gravy with his fifth piece of bread.
"Maybe we ought to go up there for dinner when she invites
us. Say on a Sunday."

"You go ahead," Elmo said.

"He's your brother."

"Remember when we went up there?"

"It takes a lot of compromising when you're first married," Grandfather said. "Two different people."

"Did you ever slap around our grandmother?" Elmo asked. He had to ask; it was worse not to. "I was just wondering," he added.

Grandfather took his time answering. "I was guilty of a lot of things, but not that."

They hadn't seen anything that time. Just heard the yelling, waiting for someone to open the door. Greta had been crying, face pink, eyes floating in tears. They sat down at the table and he started. "I never met anyone so stupid. I tell her to pick up my boots and get the case of shotgun shells I ordered. She forgets both of them. Drives all the way into town for a hot-fudge sundae. Dumb."

"That's not necessary," Grandfather said.

"It is, believe me. She's stupid."

"If anyone is stupid it's you, James," Elmo said. "She graduated from high school; you didn't."

"Well, well," James said, smiling, "look who's speaking up."

"That's enough," Greta said.

"You're not big enough to take seriously," James said to Elmo.

No one said a word the rest of the dinner. He wouldn't go back. He didn't want to be connected with that business.

The next time, he came home from school and Greta was there, her lip cut, her eye swollen almost closed. Grandpa was putting hot cloths on the side of her face. "Do this for me, Elmo; I'm going to talk to James." He had no choice. He squeezed the cloth out, folded it into a rectangle, and put it over her eye. What was the connection between them? Before, she had been like an older sister to him. No. That's what he made up for his grandfather, after she married James. But she should have married him, that's what he thought at the time. At fourteen. With seven years difference between them. She should have waited for him. But now the connection between them was much less. He was almost a spectator. Someone who was watching a movie, then went home when it was over. "Oh, Elmo," she said, taking hold of his wrist. He didn't know what to do, how to act. He didn't understand this. How could anyone do something like that if they loved a person. Would he ever do that?

When Grandfather came home, she went back up to the house. "I told him," Grandpa said, "what kind of a man it took to hit a woman. I made him listen. Made it as plain as I could. I explained I wasn't going to have anyone on my place like that. It's not you boys' yet."

It stopped for a while. Then Greta went to the hospital with her nose broken. She said she fell. James took off, was in town drinking with his friends. Grandpa went after him. Elmo drove, parked in front of the Rio cocktail lounge, and followed him inside. James was sitting with Claude at the bar, swigging beer out of a green bottle. "I hope you're satisfied," Grandpa told him. "She went back to her folks."

"Good," James said. "I was getting tired of her anyway," and he laughed.

Grandfather backhanded him across the face hard. It was like hitting a tree. The place quieted down. "You sober up," Grandfather said. "I want to see you six A.M. out in that orchard. Or don't you come back." Then he walked out. Elmo stood there for a minute, staring at his brother. He didn't want to leave him. Then his grandfather called out at the door, "Come on, Elmo."

He was doing his math at the kitchen table when the phone rang. "What's wrong with him? Elmo, is that you?"

"It's me, Joyce." He didn't want to hear what was coming from Greta's stepmother. It was amazing, all these connections. It reminded him of Tinkertoys; you just kept adding more and more, going up and up. Was it natural, all these connections people had? Greta, his sister-in-law, her real mother dead, had her father Eddie, and of course Joyce, three half sisters, and James, her husband, and she was going to have a baby. They all meant something. Where he had his grandfather. And James. Sometimes. But more, say, than the photos of his mother, who he couldn't remember; she'd left when he was little. Or his father, who he could remember, that he'd found dead. His parents were like someone you didn't know that you read about in the newspaper. Interesting. But nothing to do with him.

"I'm not letting her come back there, Elmo. You can tell him that for me. Not when he mistreats her like this. And I can tell you, Eddie is upset; he's ready to come down there. Somebody better start talking some sense into that boy before it's too late."

He wrote down *James* on the paper. Grandpa's name. Then his own name. Grandfather was fifty years older than he was. James was nine years. Was time important? He needed more information for an equation. For an answer. "Who was that?" Grandpa asked, coming out of his bedroom. Elmo wasn't going to tell him. He was having to go in to the doctor almost every week now. He was skin and bones.

"It was Joyce."

Grandfather shook his head. "What can we do?" He kept a shining new thirty-gallon galvanized can in the entry way full of feed for the peacocks. He lifted the lid and filled the pocket of his wool shirt with cracked corn. Went out. Elmo could hear him tilt his chair back and the sound of the first peacock hopping up on the porch.

He watched from the kitchen window as another peacock jumped up on the railing and displayed its train of feathers for Grandpa. It was like having your own rainbow handy to look at. They made him uneasy, those birds. The way they waited for you to admire them. As if there were more to it than that. They didn't belong here. They didn't have any connection to

this place. He couldn't imagine anything else that came close
to a peacock. He tried, too. Combining different kinds of
ducks from the marsh, a kingfisher and a red-winged blackbird, spring plum blossoms with California poppies. It was no
use. The harder he tried, the less anything would come. He'd
seen something almost close enough once, but never got the
chance to decide. It was a painting by someone with a name he
couldn't pronounce. Two fat naked women in a field drying
themselves after taking a swim in a pond. It wasn't only the
colors or the figures, it was the feeling there was something
else that was there that you couldn't see. But someone had cut
the picture out of the magazine before he could bring it home
from school to compare with the peafowls. One time when his
grandfather went to town he tried to catch one. He was going
to chase it down, get a hold of one, get a closer look. But it
took off, train of feathers and all. It was the first time he'd seen
one leave the ground. It flew better than a pheasant. It was
like seeing a hydrangea bush take off. He kept away from
them after that.

He wasn't nervous; it was just that he wasn't used to so
many people watching. The whole Elks Club was filled, must
be a thousand people. He had heard them from the storage
room where they were dressing. He'd stayed in there after the
bouts started, following the fights by the yelling, which was
off and on like someone was opening and shutting a door.
Then he moved over to the doorway.

He hadn't wanted Grandfather to come. But he'd insisted.
James had to stick his big nose in. "What's wrong, you don't
want him to see you get whipped?" It wasn't that; he was going
to win. But his grandfather had never watched him fight before,
and it was going to make him feel exposed. Immodest. As if all
the efforts they made to be clothed, even when they got up in
the middle of the night to pee, were for nothing.

James brought him. They were sitting down in front, both of them so big the people around them were already trying to shift their folding chairs so they could see. Grandpa was still taller than James. By getting fatter, James seemed shorter at the same height. Elmo knew if he made six feet it would be a miracle.

After they awarded the trophies for the bouts before him and the cheering died down he came down the aisle. This was all familiar. Jesse there with the stool. He didn't look at the other fighter coming into the ring. He wouldn't do that until the bell. There was no connection between them. He wasn't responsible.

They went out to the middle for instructions. The other fighter tried to stare him down. He decided it would be better to fight outside under the stars. The announcer gave their names and the other fighter's tournament win in a trip to Chicago. Not only wouldn't it be so smoky, there'd be the constellations he knew. Jesse was taking his robe off his shoulders, wetting his mouthpiece before putting it in.

He moved to the exact center, watching. The whole trick was not to allow his eyes to go to any part of the other boxer but his nose. He imagined he was a flying railroad spike aimed at the middle of his opponent's head. There was the usual feeling out. It was going to depend on who was just a little quicker and who was in better shape for three two-minute rounds. That's what Jesse always told them.

Jab, he had the reach. His opponent's face began to get red; his eyes seemed to shift around, trying to get out of his head. "Stick em," Jesse kept yelling from the corner. It was almost too easy. The other fighter was getting concerned because he wasn't hitting anything. Getting wild.

He breathed easy, sitting on the stool after the first round. He'd heard James yelling, "Killum, killum." Now he was yelling, "Don't let up on him, don't lose him." There was a certain satisfaction in doing everything right, in order, exactly as he'd planned. He didn't understand why, but he always had the feeling he was the only one in the ring. That would be another good reason to fight outside.

He went out the second time, moving toward the center, knowing what was going to happen. His opponent came out fast, charged, swinging furiously. Then he threw his right hand, the leather connecting, making a satisfactory sound as it struck. His opponent sat on the canvas with a bewildered look on his face, his coach waving a towel, the referee yelling, the spectators in an uproar. He leaned against the ropes, not breathing hard yet, wondering if he should order two or three cheeseburgers after. He hadn't eaten any dinner.

The other fighter got up. He didn't want to look surprised, didn't register anything as he went back out. It was the only time in any of his nine fights that anyone had got up. But the kid's eyes were fixed now, and he went in hitting him with both hands at will.

The referee stepped in and pulled Elmo away, his arms locked around his chest. The crowd went crazy; then there was a new burst of yelling as the referee put Elmo's arm up. This had been the main event. He got the winner's trophy, which was the same as the one they gave the loser. He always thought that was funny. Then the judges selected their fight as the best of the evening and they both got another trophy. More yelling. James and Grandpa were at the ringside when he climbed down.

"You looked good," James yelled above the noise. "I never thought you had it in you." Grandpa patted his shoulder. Jesse came over. "He's a natural," he told them. "He's got fast hands and can hit with either one. You saw that. He's easy to coach, I'll tell you that. He can go all the way to the national finals if he wants." Elmo nodded, decided he'd get all three cheeseburgers.

There was something pleasant about people coming up and congratulating him. People in town. Kids at school. Betty, a girl he'd ridden the school bus with, eight years to grammar school and two and a half so far to high school, came up blushing. "You pack a wallop, my father told me to tell you." He never knew what to say, except thank you. For her he said something different: "That's a kind thought."

Since Greta left, Grandfather had been cooking. Liver. Heart, braised. Spent all day scrubbing tripe on a washboard and soaking it in salted water for stew, red stew with potatoes and carrots. Brain fritters. Kidney pie. It was as if he was trying to find something Elmo wouldn't eat. "This is what I was raised on because it was cheap. Rich people threw this away with the guts," and he'd hold up a piece of liver with his fork. He didn't eat much, but he made Elmo eat. And James, when he stopped in at dinnertime. He'd stopped drinking and going to town after work. He'd been up to see Greta once. But she wouldn't come back.

A couple of weeks after his fight at the Elks Club they were sitting around the table after a dinner of brains and scrambled eggs. "That was tasty," Elmo told his grandfather.

"You're just trying to get on my good side so I'll make them again tomorrow." They both laughed. They were cracking English walnuts for dessert. Elmo put his halves on the oilcloth near his grandfather's plate. They looked like dried flowers there. It was one thing he would eat. Lately when he told his stories he'd been going back, Elmo noticed, to his wife or his sister, never staying in the present very long if he could help it.

"I want you to consider quitting that boxing business," Grandfather said. Surprised, Elmo waited. Cracked another nut. "You took that other boy apart at the Elks Club. Just like you were pruning one of our plum trees." He pointed out the window toward the orchard. "It was too easy for you. You were like an executioner up there."

"I don't pick my opponents," Elmo answered.

"Some people shouldn't do things without knowing the

same thing could happen to them. You're one of them. If it were James, I wouldn't waste my breath. He'd do the opposite. So would I, probably, for that matter. But I'm going to leave it up to you."

"I don't understand what you mean."

He lowered his voice, as if someone could overhear them. "You have to be careful, Elmo. What you do. You're my grandson. In the end it's going to be you that gets hurt."

Elmo slowly shook his head.

"You're too smart, Elmo," he said louder. "And now your hands are too smart." He got up. "I cooked this lovely dinner; you wash up," he said, going for the feed can.

He kept running, working out after school. It was habit, mostly, but he couldn't decide whether to quit or not. He kept going over what his grandfather had said. What difference did it make if hitting someone were easy or not? Betty offered to give him a ride home after a student-council meeting. She had the family Plymouth for the day. Her father had the dealership in town, but they lived on thirty acres of pears down the road from the plum orchard. They stopped at the A and W and kids in other cars came over to say hello. They passed James on the way to town. He honked when he saw Elmo. "Who's that?" Betty asked. "I don't recognize the pickup."

"Don't know," Elmo said.

Grandpa was sitting on the porch. His pet peacock Curly was on the rail, its plumage spread out. He got up out of his chair when Elmo introduced him, a few kernels of cracked corn dropping off his washed-out wool shirt and khaki pants. He took off his fedora to shake hands with Betty. "I know your father," he said. "You'll notice we have nothing but Dodge pickups."

"Best farm truck on the road," Betty said.

"She's slightly biased, Grandpa." Elmo went to get some

cracked corn for her to feed to the peafowl. They ate right out of her hand from the first try.

"They must like you," Grandpa said. "They won't do that for everyone. Won't do that for Elmo."

"Because I run them off the porch with a broom. You don't hear them at four A.M. screeching."

After Betty had driven off, Grandpa said, "Nice girl."

"You're just saying that because your peacocks liked her," Elmo said.

"You don't see a flaming redhaired girl with two million freckles every day."

Teasing, Elmo asked, "You notice things like that still?"

"I'm not dead yet," Grandpa said, whacking him on the shoulder with his fedora.

There was a boxing tournament in the city over the weekend. Elmo mentioned to Jesse that he wanted to move up a class to welterweight. "You're giving away your edge; they're bigger kids. They'll outweigh you." Elmo waited until he was through. Jesse was a gardener at the high school who had boxed in the navy. His team was the only one at school that was winning this year. Jesse almost strutted when he went into the teachers' lounge for coffee. "Don't worry, I know what I'm doing," Elmo said.

He won five matches and the division title. He was on local TV with Jesse, who was shorter than he, picking him up in a bear hug around the waist after the last fight. He was interviewed in the dressing room by a sportswriter who covered high school athletics for the city paper. When he got home, people he didn't know phoned to congratulate him. Grandpa didn't say anything, handed him the phone.

Betty phoned him. "I saw you on TV," she said.

"I guess I'm just a celebrity."

"My father said you could be in the Olympics."

"Me and Joe Palooka. I don't know if I want to go that far. It's kind of like astronomy. I used to think that people

were almost like constellations. You can only know so much
about them, as much as you can see, and then you have to rely
on your imagination. I was wrong; because people are so
much closer, it makes it harder to understand them."

"You're losing me, Elmo. But go on."

"I'm losing myself," he said. "Hitting someone in the
ring is like making contact with a constellation. Draco, say.
You get to know more. You see what I mean? There is a
connection. But not as much as, say, between your sisters
and you."

"Keep going."

"Maybe boxing is getting down to the basics. Between
yourself and who you think you are."

"I'm changing the subject," she said. "Did you get the
assignment in math?"

He laughed. "You know better; I finished that on the
bus."

"That was a silly question. A scholar like you. I have to
go now. You phone me next. My mother thinks it's undignified."

"I promise," Elmo said.

Grandfather went into town for an appointment and the
doctor put him in the hospital. "They want to run a few
tests," he told Elmo when he came into his room. "They must
know I had some more money left." Elmo sat next to the bed
to be able to hear him whisper, "Take care of my pets for me."

"I will, Grandpa."

"Don't be stingy with the feed."

"I won't." There was nothing to be worried about, Elmo
kept telling himself.

The necessary three parking places were empty and he
maneuvered the truck just right, ten feet from his grandfather's window, then hurried inside. "I got a surprise for you,"

he said. His grandfather lay on his side, looking in the wrong direction. He started to turn toward him. Elmo knocked on the window with his knuckles for the bird. He had tethered the peacock up on top of the case he'd brought him in. He didn't think the stupid bird was going to cooperate. Just then he raised his train and the plumage spread out like a fan catching the summer light. The iridescent blues and greens moved like water.

"That's old Moe," Grandfather said, sitting up. He was looking better after this operation than he had after the first. He might be gaining weight. But he was still white as a sheet. He'd been in here the whole summer. The peacock collapsed its feathers. "Greta's just left; brought the baby in. He's going to be big like me and James," he said. "On the other hand, Greta's tall too, of course. Said she's pregnant again. That's rushing it, I'd say." Elmo stood still at the window, waiting for the peacock to answer his knocking again. "How's the picking going?"

"Right on time. We're in the California Blues."

"You'll be going back to school next week."

"If James gives me permission." Elmo laughed. "He's got Claude helping in the plums; he'll get by. Greta comes when she can."

"How are they getting along now? I didn't want to ask her."

"All right, I guess." He didn't want to tell him about the latest episode. How could they do that: call each other names, throw things, hit each other. Was he missing some connection between them?

"They wanted to name the baby after me," Grandfather said. "I said don't. Three Jameses are enough. Gary is a good name." Elmo looked down at his grandfather. Listening to him, he could feel his eyes tear up, his eyelids blinking them away. He bent down and hugged him. When he let go, he saw his grandfather was embarrassed.

Greta had left him a pan of meat loaf and potatoes. He sat at the kitchen table eating, not bothering to get a plate. Between going in to the hospital and working in the plums he hadn't been doing much else. He was so tired when he came in he sometimes fell asleep eating. He decided to phone Betty. He had meant to a dozen times. He hadn't seen her since school let out in June. He knew she'd got a job in town as a lifeguard at the pool.

She answered the phone on the first ring.

"May I speak to Betty Jean Briscoe, please?"

"This is she."

"This is Elmo Clark. Would you be interested in attending a movie classic, *Creature of the Lost Lagoon*, this next Friday evening?"

"Is this a date we're discussing here, Mr. Clark?" She started to giggle. He could hear her whisper to someone in the background, I have a date, I have a date.

"I think it would come under that category."

"Then I accept."

She could have said no. But then on the other hand he could be underestimating his own resources. He was looking at himself in the mirror over the sink. The pimples were gone except on his forehead and his hair hid them. Five o'clock shadow; he needed to shave once a week now. If he fought again he'd be a middleweight; he'd gained. But he was through with that. He looked closer, from a different angle, at his reflection. If he did look like his grandpa's sister Lorraine, she must have been a knockout.

Someone honked their horn out front. It could only be Mickey Conlin. He went out, the peacocks bobbing out of his way. "You want to go hunting tomorrow morning?" Mickey called out before he got near. He was sitting in a new red sportscar convertible Elmo didn't know the name of until he got close. Mickey's father had leased the marsh from his grandfather for his duck club five years ago. He brought clients over from the city to shoot. Mickey was convinced he and Elmo were the same. Because they were both sixteen. He had been in the auditorium when he'd boxed in the city. He had his nephew Cameron with him.

"Some of us have to work for a living," he said, resting his hands on the door. It was what his grandfather would have said.

"Come on, Elmo, the place is loaded with doves."

It gave him some pleasure to refuse, probably, he thought, because Mickey wanted him to come so much. "Can't. If I don't help James, my name's mud. You've got Cameron, he's lucky. You going to hunt tomorrow?" he asked him. "You got your four ten with you?"

He finally nodded, then spoke. "Yes. I remember how you showed me, Elmo. Keep the butt tight against the small of my shoulder." At nine he was already a better shot than Mickey.

"Don't shoot in the trees where there's still plums."

"I won't," he said.

"Next time," he said, backing away from the car.

Elmo brought his grandfather home Friday morning. Helped him out of the car. "I can walk," he said, holding onto Elmo's shoulder. All the peafowl came across the yard in mincing steps, the males expanding their feathers. "They're happy to see me," he said, hauling himself up the steps by the railing. He sat down in his porch chair and Elmo went back to the truck for his things. The peafowl came up on the porch, wanting to be fed. Without him asking, Elmo got the juice can of cracked corn and handed it to him.

"No matter what happens, I'm not going back to the hospital," he said as if he were ending a long conversation on the subject. "I'm staying right here."

"The doctor says you're fine," Elmo said.

"That's right," Grandfather said. "He said that the last time, too."

* * *

It was almost time for him to leave to pick up Betty. "You're sure you don't want to go along?" he asked his grandfather. They both laughed.

"You don't need a chaperone and that movie you told me about would keep me up nights."

"You're going to be all right?"

"If I'm lonely I'll phone Greta. If I get hungry I'll cook me up one of my peacock friends out there. Did I tell you I met someone in physical therapy that told me he actually had one of those critters for dinner? I was telling him about mine and he told me the story. I didn't tell you this yet?"

"No you didn't," Elmo said, not looking at the clock.

"Thought it would taste like pheasant. Cooked two. With orange slices, stuffed them with carrots and onions, like we do with ducks. Low heat. Basted them with their own drippings and white wine. Put it out on the table in front of his guests. Had his carving knife all ready, sharpened it with the steel." Grandpa made motions of sharpening. "Tried to take a slice off. Wouldn't cut. Kept trying. Everybody waiting. Put it back on the cutting board and got a heavier knife; didn't do the trick. Tried a cleaver next, brought it down, never dented it. He had to take the guest out to a restaurant." The last time he told it, Elmo remembered, the peacock had been put on a chopping block and hit with an axe.

Mr. Briscoe opened the door, looked past him. "How many miles you got on that pickup?" he asked.

Elmo was ready; he remembered coming to birthday parties here: Mr. Briscoe had once wrapped up a colt for Betty in tissue paper and led it into the dining room. "One hundred and seventy-two thousand and six tenths of a mile, give or take a few feet."

"You Clarks, you're running it into the ground; I can't make any money off you. I can't even remember when I sold that truck." He sounded indignant. He led him into the front room and pointed to the couch for him to sit down. Elmo perched on the edge. He never had a chance to be nervous; Betty came right out and he stood back up. Being out in the sun must have made her freckles multiply, he decided. There were at least a million more, the color of red ants.

"Did he sell you a new pickup yet?" she asked him.

"Not yet." He wished he could seem as at ease as she was.

"How come I haven't seen your name in the paper lately? Give up boxing?" Mr. Briscoe asked.

He was going to say, "No time. I've had to work." But for some reason he heard himself going into a longer explanation. "I liked it at first because a person has to concentrate so much, with the conditioning and the training. The actual fighting was secondary." Mr. Briscoe was looking puzzled. "Then I got so I liked getting ready more than the actual boxing, so I've decided not to do it any more. I just work out now."

Betty's mother came out of another room. She'd put on lipstick, he noticed. She had the same red hair and freckles as Betty had. "How's your grandfather? I heard he was in the hospital."

"He's home now, feeling much better."

Betty took him by the arm and led him toward the front door and opened it. "Say hello for me," Mrs. Briscoe said at the door.

Mr. Briscoe followed them down the walk. "Tell him I can get him a good deal on this year's model."

"You promised," Betty said as she got into the pickup. Elmo shut the door for her and went around.

"I know," Mr. Briscoe said, "but it's not every day I see you hold your breath when I start to say something. I couldn't pass it up." He started laughing, took his glasses off to wipe his eyes.

Elmo drove down their road wondering how long it took an individual family like the Briscoes to develop the connections between each other and how long with an outsider. Would an outsider not having the same past ever be connected well enough? Greta wasn't a good example. Maybe the connection between a person and object was more important. His grandfather's peacocks. Or a person and what he thought. Just what he could think up inside his own head. The connection between himself and himself.

"What are you thinking?" Betty asked.

"Just, when was the last time I changed the oil in this old wreck. What were you thinking?"

"If I hid my shampoo so my sister wouldn't use it."

They took back seats, right under the wall where the beam of light came out of the projectionist's booth. He must have sat next to her at least a hundred times on the school bus, in classes. But he felt uncomfortable, as if he had no control over his body. His stomach might gurgle, he might pass gas, drool, snort. He shifted himself again.

"You can hold my hand, Elmo," she said, "I'm done with the popcorn." He picked it up. It was warm and he could feel the echo her pulse made from the flat of her thumb. After the cartoon was over and the movie started she whispered, "You can kiss me if you like, but only with a modicum of passion."

"Do you think I need all this direction?" he said. She closed her eyes, he noticed as he leaned toward her. He kissed her once and said, "You're going to have to wipe your mouth of the popcorn butter, Miss Briscoe, if I'm going to be able to gain purchase on your lips."

Walking back to the pickup, they passed the Rio. James must have seen them, because he and Claude came outside. James was yelling after them, "Lookee here, what do I see?" slurring his words. Elmo had to stop; there were people passing. James was so drunk his fly was half open and he had to brace himself with one hand against the blue tiled front of the bar to stand. Claude, weaving slightly, stood alongside him. "Aren't you going to introduce me?" James asked.

He wasn't embarrassed, Elmo told himself. This was nothing. "This is my brother James," he told Betty, "and his friend Claude. Betty Briscoe." He had been holding her hand but now let it go.

"Pleased to make your acquaintance, Betty," James said. "Out on the town, huh. Why don't you come in and I'll buy you a drink." He tried to straighten up, and took a few steps toward them. Took Betty by the arm. "Come on, I know your old man." He tried to take a step backward and almost fell, pulling Betty with him.

"That's enough," Elmo said, getting between them and pushing James away.

"Who do you think you're pushing?" James said, and he tried to shove Elmo back, lost his balance, and fell over onto the sidewalk.

Claude punched Elmo from the side and knocked him down on all fours. "Son of a bitch," he said as he kicked him in the stomach. Elmo noticed Betty had her hands over her face. He would have liked to reassure her. This was just funny. If he could get his breath to laugh, he would. There was no connection between her and what was happening. She shouldn't be bothered by this.

"Wait a minute," James was saying. "Just wait a minute." He got back up. "That's my little brother." Elmo got back up too, holding his stomach. His head was ringing like a bell, as if his tongue was the claque. Claude had stepped back, both hands clenched and down low like an old-time boxer, ready for him. He wasn't as drunk as James. He blinked his eyes. Elmo aligned himself with the North Star and moved in.

Claude swung too soon and he stepped in and under, bringing his fist around. The skin over Claude's cheekbone split and he felt his knuckle pop against the bone. Then noting he was still aligned, he brought his right hand around. Claude crumpled like a piece of wastepaper.

James came toward him, weaving back and forth, his hands to his sides. Elmo hit him in the face. It was like hitting a sponge. "How do you like that?" Elmo told him, saying it every time he struck, until some customers came out from the bar and stopped it.

He remembered Betty then. She wasn't there. He walked as fast as he could to where the truck was parked but she wasn't there either. He just started walking, not knowing where to look next. He looked in the couple of stores still open as he passed, going all the way back to the movie. He was worried now. She couldn't walk home; it was too far.

He phoned her house. Her mother answered. "Mrs. Briscoe, Betty and I seem to have got separated somehow."

"Her father went to pick her up. She phoned here. She was upset."

"Thank you, Mrs. Briscoe," he said, not knowing what else to say.

James's face looked like a plum that had been stepped on. He wouldn't come into the house so Grandpa could see him. Talked to Elmo from inside the cab of his pickup. "Whatever happened," James said, "it was probably my fault. I don't even remember what I did," he said. Elmo didn't believe him. "You don't know how bad I feel about this. I'm married and have a kid and another one on the way. I have to decide what comes first." Elmo was embarrassed. James was serious. "I was thinking this morning, what if I lost Greta. I'm going to straighten up." He started the pickup. "Claude said you got lucky last night. I told him we were lucky you didn't kill us both. If it makes any difference, I'm sorry. I'm sorry about the girl. I remember that much. I'm sorry, Elmo."

He was going to phone Betty but he put it off. Decided

to wait until school started. They both had U.S. history first period. She sat at the front. After class he caught up with her outside in the hallway. He didn't know how to start out. He just walked along beside her while she ignored him. She finally stopped and sat down on a wooden bench. He sat beside her. "I don't know what you want me to say," he started out.

"We don't act like that in my family," she said. "We don't go in for excess. You were as much to blame as they were." She had placed her books on her knees. This was not important, he decided, starting to enjoy the situation. There was no connection between them. "You Clarks are always doing something. You're famous in the county for it. When I was little, I heard about you. I used to watch you on the bus and think I might catch you changing into something else."

She's being dramatic, he thought, and he started to laugh. She jumped up and walked away, surprising him. He yelled after her, "You have too many freckles anyway. I can't see you without trying to count them." She kept going, never turned around. "It's a nuisance," he called after her.

"I feel like I've been pregnant all my life," Greta said, sitting in the kitchen with Elmo. He didn't answer; he was thinking of Betty, who he'd taken to the drive-in movie last night. Greta had to repeat herself. Elmo managed to nod and grin. They heard Grandpa's feet hit the linoleum floor. Elmo got up fast. "I'm getting the hell out of here," his grandfather said. "You and me are going to take off, Elmo. I'm not staying here any more." Elmo took him by the shoulders and eased him back in bed. "Are my clothes handy, Elmo?"

"They're handy, Grandpa," he said, putting the covers up around his grandfather's chin. "You rest some more; then we'll make some plans. These trips take some time." He went back out into the kitchen.

"His mind wanders," Greta said. "What did the doctor say yesterday?"

"He wants to put him in the hospital. Again. He thinks he's had another stroke. He'll come back, get better; he's not that way all the time, you know that."

"Do you want me to come tomorrow morning?"

"If you would. I got them to let me go just eight to twelve. You don't mind?"

"No, it's no trouble. Gary sleeps all morning. I'm too round to do much but sit." All the peafowl were waiting by the screen door to see if anyone would feed them. They scattered as they went out to the car.

When Elmo came back inside his grandfather was sitting up again. There were veins that stayed out on his forehead now, surrounded by brown spots the size of quarters. His eyes stared out of his head, fixed at what he saw. He was looking around the room, lost. "Where were you, Elmo? I was looking all over for you."

"I was out shucking some early corn, for a surprise."

"Lorraine and I used to shuck corn. I was better than she was. I did twenty bushels in one day. Don't deny your family, Elmo."

"I won't, Grandpa."

"She was a good sister to me. Couple of years ago I tried to phone her, planning on making up."

"I didn't know that."

"She had no number." He lay back down and closed his eyes. "I was too late."

James came in while he was boiling the water for the corn. It was staying light longer now; it was almost seven thirty. "How is he?" James whispered. "Maybe we should take him into town, like the doctor said."

"He wants to stay here. I can take care of him," Elmo said.

"Greta said you can't stay cooped up here all the time."

"I don't mind. She's going to come in the morning so I can go back to school. They got after me."

"Claude's got the packing shed ready to go. I'm going to give it a week before we start picking the Red Julys. I could come in the afternoon until then."

"No, half a day of school is enough," Elmo said.

James got up. "Call us, Elmo; I can get here in a minute."

When the corn was done he took a knife and cut the kernels off a cob into a bowl and added butter and salt and pepper. He sat by his grandfather's bed. "Open up, Grandpa, I've got some corn for you. Open up." He put a few mashed kernels in between his lips and saw them slide back out when he tried to swallow. His grandfather began to ramble on with his eyes closed, how he'd caught three porcupines eating up his young trees. Put them in a gunnysack and hauled them out by boat to a small island. Couldn't knock them in the head, he said.

When he drifted off Elmo went back to the kitchen and ate an ear of corn. It was sweet. The peacocks were roosting; he heard them shifting their tail feathers. He ate the rest of the corn, then sopped up the butter with a piece of bread. "Elmo," his grandfather called out, "are you there?"

"I'm here, Grandpa. I'm here." He did his homework. Then tried to remember the time difference between east and west. It would be eleven o'clock there. He picked up the phone anyway. He got the operator and told her what he was after. She said she'd phone back. He did the dishes, waiting.

The phone rang. "I found a Vivian, but no Lorraine."

"Would you try her?" He listened to the rings. They made him think he was going back into the past. Carrying all his grandpa's stories.

"Hello," someone said.

"Are you any relation to Lorraine Johnston?"

"May I ask who's inquiring?"

"My name is Elmo Clark. I live in California."

"My mother was named Lorraine. She died four years ago."

"Did she ever mention a brother? My grandfather's name is Jim Clark."

"I remember Uncle Jim. He came out here to see us. I'm her daughter. I must have been nine or ten when I saw him last."

"It's complicated," Elmo started out. "My grandpa is sick and he's been mentioning your mother. His sister. I thought I might get them together, but I guess it's too late."

"I don't know what to tell you."

"There was a disagreement," Elmo went on, wanting to finish it. "Over a stickpin that belonged to your grandfather and was supposed to go to my grandfather."

"I don't remember anything like that."

"I'm sorry to bother you like this; it's just that he's sick. I wanted to see if I could tie up some loose ends, I guess."

"I've been to California. I have a niece in San Diego."

"Well, if you come out again, be sure and stop," Elmo said. "We'd be happy to see you."

Elmo was giving his grandfather a sponge bath the next morning, before Greta came. "I must be in sorry shape if I can't even wash my own neck," he said in his old voice, as if he hadn't had a stroke.

"You're just lazy," Elmo said. "You remember me shaving you last time?"

"You almost cut my nose off." He laughed. "You got coffee out there, or you going to keep it for yourself."

"You finish and I'll get you a cup." He kept talking, wanting it to last. "Greta's coming over in a little while."

"What for? They having trouble?"

"No, no, she gets tired staying up there at the house by herself. She'll bring the baby and you can keep her company while I go straighten out that teacher on a few calculus problems."

"I like Greta," he said. Elmo came back with a cupful of hot coffee. He took a big gulp. "Now that's what I call coffee." He took a deep breath. "I never thought I'd get over your grandmother dying. We had been married less than fifteen years. But I had to, because of your father. When he killed himself, I had you and James to keep me getting up out of bed. You see what I'm getting at, Elmo."

"I see," Elmo said, "but you're not going anywhere."

He hadn't been in school in almost three weeks. But Betty took notes and got his assignments, then gave them to the bus driver, who put them in the Clark letter box and picked up the homework. She sat next to him in math. "Truant," she said, when walked into the classroom and saw him back. "I'm so far ahead of you now in the race for vale-dictorian you won't even be close enough to hear me give the speech."

"I'm the one that taught you how to invert in dividing fractions. In the fourth grade, remember that? How soon they forget their betters."

She reached across the aisle and gripped his wrist. "I missed you, Elmo." It surprised him for a minute; he didn't think she was going to let go. The teacher had come in and was writing on the chalkboard.

He wouldn't let himself think about her. He wasn't in control when he did. She wasn't in the fantasy that made him have to pull out his shirt in front to get up out of his seat, or jam both fists in his front pockets to hide the bulge. She made him forget things. Big things like why he had to go home after school. Or little things like how many trees did they have of Abundance. She made him forget. He didn't know if he had his eyes open or closed sometimes. If late at night, unable to sleep, he was seeing the peacocks in his grandpa's bedroom or if he was imagining it.

There was no math problem he couldn't find the answer for. He had to remember that. It was important. All he had to do was make himself think. Put his mind to work. Let his imagination pick up the answer and bring it back to him. He had even gone to church with the Briscoe family. When Betty had asked him he'd said yes. He hadn't been in church since he was eight or nine. And then because one of the town churches sent a bus out for the kids. He waited every Sunday out by the mailbox because of the cookies. Each woman in church brought a different kind. There were peanut butter, date, oatmeal, brownies, lemon, raisin, and some with frosting and multicolored sprinkles. The bus had broken down after about a year and they never fixed it. He never went after that. He sat next to Betty, feeling her leg against his, the rest of the Briscoes lined up on either side. When they sang Betty held the book open and he could hear the sound of her voice next to his ear. He closed his eyes and imagined the springtime orchard, him running. The singing was like what he saw then. The shape of the wind as it blew the spray of petals against him. The petals falling on his head and shoulders until he opened his eyes. His grandfather laughing at him when he came back to the house. "Your Easter hat," he said.

After class they walked together. "How's your grandfather?"

"He's getting better. I was talking to his niece last night in New Hampshire. I think we might go there for a visit. See that end of the family. As soon as he gets a little stronger."

"It's warmed up early this year. Time for our first swim." She waited; when he didn't comment, she went on. "I can hardly wait to dive off the barge. I could meet you up there today."

"I'll see," he said.

"I'm going to go anyway," she said.

When he got home everyone was asleep, Greta on the chair, the baby on the couch, and Grandpa in his bed. The oven was on and he could smell cake. She must have been baking all morning. He cut himself a slice of Greta's homemade bread, spread it with butter, then sprinkled a spoonful of sugar over the top. Went back out, taking big bites out of the bread. The peacocks all followed him, but he ignored them.

He started working on the twelve-foot wooden ladders for the coming season. The pickers busted hell out of them. He couldn't blame them, heavy as they were. He started replacing the broken steps. Taking his time. Examining each ladder, sorting out the ones that needed work.

James came by, stopped. "It's hot for May," he said. "It's going to hit eighty."

"They're all asleep," Elmo said.

"We're going to eat with you tonight, if that's all right. She's got enough grub cooked to feed a picking crew."

"I'll be back by then," Elmo said. "I'm going to take a ride soon as I finish these."

She was already there. He saw her father's car parked up on the levee. Then, coming down the bank, he saw her, already changed and sitting on the barge. He hurried. The wooden barge had drifted in here years before. It was tilted up so one edge was almost in the water. He'd been coming here since he was in the sixth grade; James had brought him. He would never have found it by himself. The tules closed in around it on three sides like tall grass. A raft of yellowed tules and driftwood that looked solid enough to walk on floated at the far end of the slough.

He could hear the lap of the water as he changed into his swimming suit in the cabin. He noticed her clothes halfway stuffed into a brown bag. Someone had put a quilt over the old mattress that had always been there. He folded his trousers on their crease and put his shirt over the back of one of the chairs. He made himself go back up the stairs and out into the sunshine.

He lowered himself next to her on the edge of the barge, put his feet in the water too. "It's too cold to go in," he said.

"You can't let your senses overcome your mind," she said back. He laughed; he had told her that once. "Have you ever seen a naked woman, Elmo?"

"Mamie Eisenhower," he said, and added when she started giggling, "in my religious dreams."

She started talking in an Okie drawl, too. "Have you ever known a woman? In the Biblical sense?" she asked.

"I think you're going beyond the bounds of good taste," he said, splashing her with his foot.

"Have you?" she asked in her normal voice.

"A gentleman never reveals a lady's name or past." He looked over and saw her face was flushed. She really wants to know, he thought. Not looking at her, he said, "Claude took me over to the city."

"How was it?"

He thought. "I don't know," he said. "On one level, interesting to do what I'd been hearing about since I was five and thinking about since I was eleven. On the other hand, I would say under those circumstances it was a little overrated, but I'm just starting out."

"What was her name?"

"I don't think she ever told me. But she was a Christian, which gave me some comfort—she was wearing a cross."

Embarrassed, Betty laughed. "I was wondering if we might try it one of these days," she said.

He could barely talk: the words wouldn't come out right. His mind felt like it was shutting down. "You sure you're ready for the big step into adulthood? This is the final pubic right of passage." He didn't correct the word; he couldn't think of the right one.

She hadn't noticed. "I'm ready," she said. "Some days I feel like I'm ready to bust."

"Any particular day?" he asked. Neither was looking at the other.

"Maybe today," she said, getting up and walking back

across the barge. He heard her go down the steps into the cabin. He sat there awhile before saying in a loud voice, "Well, I can't think of anything better to do on a sunny day like this."

"Where in the hell have you been?" James yelled, coming out of the house when Elmo drove up. "He's in there crying because he thinks you're not coming back." Elmo ran, scattering the peafowl. Greta was by the bed holding his hand, with the baby in her lap. Both the baby and his grandfather were sobbing as if their hearts would break. "I was out checking on the railroad fares," he said loud as he could, to be heard. "I think we can get tickets straight through, changing at Chicago. We can each take two suitcases," he said all in one breath.

His grandfather looked at him, stopped crying. James had taken the baby into the other room. "They still have sleepers?" he asked, his face all wet. Elmo nodded. "It's going to have to be the train," Grandpa said with a big sob; "you're not going to get me on an airplane."

He stayed home the next day, phoned Greta to say she didn't have to come. He did their wash in the old wringer washer. It was another warm day and he hung the clothes outside to dry. When the sun was directly overhead he brought out the rocker and set it on the porch. Then he picked his grandfather up, wrapped him in two blankets, and took him outside. He didn't seem to weigh anything.

"Well sir, take a look at those peacocks of yours. They are nearly the perfect pet; all they do is eat and sleep. They must need all that rest and nourishment just to show off their feathers once or twice a month." He looked over at his grandfather, who was staring into space, eyes open, unblinking. The words made no connection. He remembered them verbatim from when his grandfather had spoken them.

He went in the house and changed the sheets on his grandfather's bed and then took him back inside. Tried to get him to eat something. "All right for you, Grandpa, you're going to have to eat twice as much for dinner." He went back in the kitchen with the bowl.

Betty phoned at three thirty. After he said hello she said, "Well, I'm glad you didn't die for love." He was able to laugh. "I've got your assignments; do you want me to bring them out? I didn't get to the bus on time."

"Put them on the bus tomorrow," he said. "I need a rest from all that brain work."

"I'd like to see you," she said in a lower voice. "Just stop and visit." He didn't answer. Nothing would come out. "How's your grandfather?" she finally asked.

"He's fine. I took him out today and he had a good time, sitting on the porch. I better get the wash in off the line," he said before she could say anything else, and he hung up.

He had all the clothes in the basket when Greta drove in and got out of her car carrying a Pyrex bowl and something wrapped in a towel. "I made some carrot cake, Elmo," she called out.

"He's going to like that," he said, following her inside. She put the things down and went into Grandpa's room. Elmo put the basket of clothes down, opened the towel, then the wax paper. It had white frosting.

"Elmo," Greta said. He licked his fingers, went toward the doorway.

"Grandpa," Greta said, leaning over him. She took a face mirror out of her purse and held it up to his nose.

"What are you doing, Greta?"

She felt around his wrist and put her ear to his chest, then shook him by the shoulders. The old head rolled. "Call the doctor, Elmo," she said. "Grandpa's not breathing."

"No, Greta, he's fine, he's just asleep." Elmo went over and straightened the blankets. He could hear her call the doctor, then James. Elmo brought a kitchen chair in and sat beside the bed, holding Grandpa's hand. "You're not going to guess what we're going to have for dessert," he said. "Your favorite, carrot cake. She put white icing on, a thick layer. It's going to be so rich we're going to need a lot of hot coffee."

James came into the house, slamming the door shut. He was breathing hard and the sound filled the bedroom. He put his big fingers on Grandpa's neck. Left them a long time. "He's dead, Elmo."

He knew he was being calm and reasonable. "He's not dead, James. I'm talking to him."

"I know dead, Elmo. He's dead."

"He wouldn't leave me here, James, I know that. Not alone. He's not dead." James went out.

"I was thinking, Grandpa, about our trip out east. To the eastern seaboard, as you say. I think the fall is better. I'd like to see those leaves you're always talking about. We should go out there before it gets too cold. I don't want to run into any of those storms. I'm too partial to this California sunshine."

The doctor, who was also the county coroner, came in, felt around with his stethoscope, then carefully took the folded-down sheet as Elmo watched and put it up over Grandfather's head. "He's gone," he said, "he's gone."

Elmo took the sheet down. "He's all right," he said, laying his head on his grandfather's chest.

"Your grandfather had some arrangements with one of the funeral homes in town. I'm going to send for them now, take him back with us."

"He's staying right here," Elmo shouted, sitting up. "He's going to get well. No one's going to take him anywhere." He jumped up, knocking over the chair, and put up his fists. The doctor backed out the door into the kitchen.

Greta tried to come in. "Elmo."

"No, Greta, he's staying right here."

He heard them talking and they all went out. He locked

the front door and turned off the lights. "It's early," he said aloud, "but we both need our rest. We've got a big day ahead of us tomorrow." He sat down at the kitchen table to wait.

He'd been up and around when the knocking started. Had got the water just right and was shaving his grandfather. "Elmo, it's me, Joyce, I want to come in."

"Hold on," he called back. "I'm almost finished here." He wiped his grandpa's face off with a towel and went to the door.

Joyce stepped in as soon as he opened it, with James and Greta right behind her. Eddie and Claude stayed on the porch. The kitchen was crowded. James and Joyce went into his grandfather's bedroom. "I was getting him ready," Elmo said, following.

"I can give you a hand," Joyce said.

"He was awful shy," Elmo said.

"I know what you mean."

"Maybe you could brush his blue suit. It's hanging in his closet." Elmo went back and took the basin of shaving water and dumped it into the bathtub, washed out the pan, filled it with warm water.

When the suit was brushed he put it on his grandfather. Joyce knotted the tie and Elmo put it around his neck, buttoned the top button of his shirt. He couldn't think of anything else.

Eddie and Claude had gone back to the main house. James was sitting at the table with Greta. Joyce was folding the wash. When no one was looking, Elmo slipped a piece of carrot cake wrapped in wax paper into his grandfather's pocket. Then he walked out and sat on the porch, his feet up on the rail, throwing single pieces of cracked corn to the peafowl.

When the sun was over the edge of the orchard two men

came in the hearse and wheeled a gurney into the house and then came back out. Elmo didn't look. Didn't move. Kept throwing feed, making the peafowl run for it.

"Let's go up to the house, Elmo," Joyce said. "We could all use some breakfast."

"I have a few things I have to do first," he said. "I'll be up later."

"You promise," Greta said, putting her hand on his shoulder.

"I promise," he said.

He sat there a long time. His head was emptied out. There was no connection between what he could see and what was going on inside. He closed his eyes for a minute. There was no relief there. When he opened them there was the same thing. The yard, the peacocks, the road, and then the orchard. He thought, if only I could imagine the hardest math problem and then come up with the right answer, I could do anything. But there was nothing but his grandfather in his head. Inside. Like the chick inside an egg when you hold it up to the light. That was never going to come out. There was no more room to imagine an answer. He threw the last of the feed, got up and went into the house.

He found his twelve gauge in the pantry. He took his time, loaded, filled his jacket pockets full of shells. By the time he got back to the porch there were only five or six in sight. They must know, he thought, aiming. He got those and two more behind the house.

He dragged the dead ones, as he killed them, to a big pile of tree trimmings, higher than his head, that hadn't been burned yet. He swung them up by their legs to the top. The others couldn't get away; he took his time. Where could they go? What could they become? A tree?

When James came driving up in the pickup, he was surprised. Then he realized they must have heard the shots from the main house. One took off from behind the rhododendron bush and he blasted it. Slowly James opened the truck door. "Just stay right there, James," he yelled. "I'm attending to my own business here." James sat still, his legs hanging out the open door, his elbow on the window frame, watching.

He nailed the last ones by the clothesline. They seemed like they were waiting for him there. He emptied the rest of the five gallons of diesel around the base of the pile and capped the can. He snapped the kitchen match alight with his thumbnail. Then threw it in. There was a whoosh and the still-green plum trimmings sizzled and foamed as heat from the flames climbed up the pile. He looked for the peacock feathers, but there wasn't any sign of them that he could see.

BUCKAROO PLUMS
1967–1970

What's wrong with Elmo? she wrote on the bottom of the third page of the report. He's selfish. Inconsiderate. He will not face his responsibilities. [me]. She retraced the brackets around *me*. Her mother had told her that the weekend before last, when she was finally allowed to go home. They were in her old bedroom, she was trying to find a navy blue lambswool sweater she'd left, and she was complaining to her mother.

"You knew what you were getting into. You've lived within five miles of the Clarks your whole life."

"Mother, I didn't mean it that way."

"You're not going to change him, Betty. Did you really expect to? Look at his brother. That whole family. I recall the time James cut the telephone pole in two with his truck, drunk as a skunk. We were passing on the highway. Took every deputy in the sheriff's department to take him in. The boys are the same way. I don't know how many times they've been kicked off the school bus."

"Here it is, I knew I hadn't taken it." She held the sweater under her chin and looked in the mirror. It wasn't

going to work. Did she mean her and Elmo? Or the sweater
with her too-dark gray skirt? Why was she always looking for
clues? Examining everything to death. It was like trying to
learn ten foreign languages at once, loving someone. You had
to know how to understand instantly as they switched back
and forth from one to another. Plus interpret tone, emphasis,
pitch. Volume.

Do I try too hard? she wrote on the next page margin.
Yes. Do I want too much? No. Do I love him enough? I don't
know. She underlined I don't know. This is foolishness, she
wrote in capital letters, and picked up the booklet again. She
started looking over the diagrams. No, she wrote. They had
tried that before and were cited. In the margin she wrote, See
page 19.

This job was unbelievable. My office, she thought. My
own bathroom. My own secretary. A month ago she'd given
a talk at a conference in front of almost two hundred people.
Who listened respectfully, and clapped after she finished. In
three years she'd come this far. She was making almost as
much money as her father. Two hundred times more than
Elmo. He didn't care. He still spent money as if it were water.
One of her father's terms, speaking of the Clarks. She went
back to reading the report, stopped to glance down at her
watch. Another hour. Friday.

The traffic wasn't bad: she got halfway home before the
cars started backing up on the freeway. She commuted to the
capital so Elmo would be closer to school, the experimental
station, and most important, his plum trees.

What had happened in three years? The three years
they'd been married. When did it start to get complicated?
They had been lovers before. The word made her think of
them naked. There weren't any complications then. It had
been like finding someone more perfect with each discovery.
"The scandal of it all," her mother had said, and they had
laughed, when she and Elmo spent the summer working in the

orchard, living in the foreman's house. Her oldest sister'd had a baby before she got married. It was their beginning.

Could she love him more than she had that summer? On a hot August night they sat in the bathtub in cold water, eating their dinner. Elmo had put a board upright against the faucet end to rest his back against. She sat facing him, her feet braced against the sides to keep her from sliding down the sloping end. Whatever she'd cooked they ate off the old plates with the bouquet-of-flowers design. Liver and onions, which he tolerated and she could eat every night. A heaping plate, dipped in flour and fried with bacon and onions till it was almost charcoal. Eating with their fingers, picking up the slices whole and snapping bites out of the sides, the plates resting on their knees as they chewed. Her breasts floating like two feeding bottom fish, he'd told her once. "You like your food on the done side," he said.

"You have to love me," she said, holding up a slice and spying through the moonshaped bite on the edge, "no matter how much I eat."

"Don't concern yourself with that," he said. "But please stop dropping the onions in the bath water. I'm not sure what they might do to our reproductive systems."

She had painted the bathroom walls international orange and the ceiling white. The sides of the old claw-foot bathtub green. It was like being in the castle at the bottom of an aquarium. Then he had painted their bedroom in twelve-inch stripes, white, green, and yellow. Up and down the walls and across the ceiling. After they lay down, holding hands, their heads on the same pillow, she watched the full moon come through the open window. In the third grade, wearing their George and Martha Washington paper hats, they'd held hands marching to the auditorium for assembly. Sometimes getting on the bus they'd hold hands. She could remember every time. Her father had kidded her: "Elmo's your squeeze." She never knew what he was talking about. He was always saying things like that. Until they were in the eighth grade and both of them were at the same Halloween party. He had tried to lift her off the top of a stool, his arms locked around her waist. She couldn't think what game they were playing.

Then September, and it was time to go back to school. But Elmo wanted to stay in the foreman's house. Live there, work in the orchard. It was like arguing with one of the plum trees. "Elmo, one, there's not enough here for both you and James. Picking, packing: in the busy season we can help. But what about the rest of the year? Two, he's got Greta and the boys. Three, six hundred forty acres: is that going to be your life?" He wasn't going to listen to reason. "Are we going to sit here in the winter, in this old house with our sweaters on, after pruning, and wait for the trees to bud? Go into debt in town and hope for a good crop to pay them off? Plums aren't getting any price for the farmers. There's just too many." It was the first time she'd realized how hardheaded he was. It wasn't just that she knew better. He was obstinate for its own sake.

They went back. She graduated. Elmo took his time. Took half a load to be able to come back and help James. But he went along and took the civil service tests with her, just like he was looking for work like everyone else. Agronomist, he put down on his application forms. He had started out in horticulture, but he moved around a lot. He once took a course in medieval stringed instruments and built one out of wood. Played it for her. That had been so funny, Elmo singing. But then a couple of months ago she'd seen Meat Science on his schedule for this quarter. "Meat Science, what's that?" Her tone had been querulous.

"Production methods. James has got an idea to raise pheasants commercially. Have hunters come out and shoot them. I thought I better get prepared."

"There's an opening as an inspector at the agency. Just drive around checking out complaints. You could still go to class." He didn't answer. She didn't pursue it either. Words like that came out on their own. She couldn't blame them on her mother. She didn't have any control over them. She had walked into the air pollution agency just as it was taking off and become an expert unaware. Elmo was going to stay where he was. Going to school, helping James, working at the agricultural station. But she always had the feeling they were waiting for something. Some signal, like when the bell rang for recess in grammar school, for their lives to start. She turned off at her exit. Five minutes to home.

Elmo always got up, if he was sitting, when she came into the room. Waited for her, with that look. He had cut himself shaving in that same spot on his jaw. It was still startling seeing him, knowing he was just a few feet away, that she didn't have to open any more doors to be with him. She loved his nose. Big long nose made his whole face look like his grandfather's. But there was no other family resemblance. James was tall and heavy. Elmo was just a little taller than she was and weighed fifty pounds more. There had always been that joke in the county: Elmo looked like the Raleigh spice man. His mother running off later. Gray eyes that turned colors while you watched, chin cleft so deep it looked like a scar. Stood straight like his grandfather used to and talked like him, too. He was a Clark, no one would ever have mistaken that after he spoke.

"Welcome home," he said and kissed her fervently, as if he hadn't seen her for months. Hugged her. He meant that to be ironic, she was sure. She backed up and almost stumbled on a box of books. He still hadn't unpacked them in three years. That was the trouble: this wasn't his home. She paid the rent. She bought the food. He stayed here when the orchard didn't need him. "Did you get those polluters to listen to reason?" he asked.

"No, but they will; we're going to close them down. Do you want something before we go?"

"I'll wait, Greta will surely try and outdo herself." She had forgotten they were to have dinner with his brother. They always went to the place on weekends but they didn't always eat at James's. The Clark family with just the two brothers left was more complicated than any other family of twenty-five. They lived to be different.

She got some cream cheese out and spread it on half a piece of bread and ate it over the sink. "How did the project go?" she asked, chewing. He made a twenty-hour-a-week part-time job his life.

"Not bad; it's too early to tell. If we can graft on the other varieties that will make the tree self-pollinating and raise the yield and at the same time, and this is the critical part, come up with a tougher plum with a longer shipping and shelf life, then we've got something. I'd take a chance on them myself." He came further into the kitchen. His voice sounded so determined, as if he were grappling with each tree, when he talked about his orchard. Whole-souled, her father would call him.

"Our trees won't last forever: those forty acres of Santa Rosas should have been pulled up two years ago. But we have to put in something better, competitive, or we're just spinning our wheels." He was following her around the apartment, talking, as she put things in her bag for the weekend. He had made the bed, done the breakfast dishes. His gym bag was at the door. The pickup would be gassed and aimed in the direction of the place. He'd been ready since coming back from class at eleven that morning. Waiting. If she didn't go he'd go alone.

"Two hours and eleven minutes," he said. She had dozed off. It was dark and they were in front of the main house. He was waiting for her to get out; then he'd go on to the foreman's house and turn the heater on. She never suggested that they stay at her parents' house. On their thirty acres of pears for a tax write-off. It would be too impractical to get up there at four thirty and go chase the plum trees. He would stay if she asked; he got along with her parents and two sisters. He got along with everyone. No one could dislike an Elmo. Her father had given them a new '64 Dodge pickup for a wedding present, a demo from his Chrysler dealership in town. He had known what Elmo wanted. She'd bought her car at cost, to commute to work. Everyone was so solicitous of Elmo.

"Betty?" Greta came down the steps two at a time. She was as tall as James and walked like a man. Had her hair pulled back in a bun. Wore dresses she made herself for occasions. Greta has to be color blind, she thought, looking at her latest dress. Greta hugged hard, almost squashing the air out of her. Picked up her bag with one hand and kept the other around her waist. Elmo drove away, honking his horn as he went.

The boys came down the stairs like little semis to get kissed and hugged, as if she hadn't just seen them last weekend. At nine and eleven they looked too much like James. He had been sitting in his chair watching the news. He got up too when she came in. The Clarks were polite. Always. James was shy, she'd finally realized. Always tried to shake hands with her. She'd peck him a kiss on the cheek just to give him a start. "It's not going to rain," he said. He just stood there, not saying anything more, until Greta took her into the kitchen. The boys pushed each other to take her coat to hang up.

Greta liked to bake. That old gas range oven popped out cakes and pies as if it were a bakery. "I like your dress," Greta said, stepping back for a better look. She used old dish towels for aprons, knotted tight around her narrow waist. "I can never get patterns for clothes like that." She could remember when Greta married James in the front yard of the house. She'd come with her parents. They'd commented how no one had ever said anything about it, the daughter of an Okie fruit picker marrying into the Clark family.

She set the table, the task Greta left to her to give her a feeling of helping. Sometimes she felt she might start laughing, but it would be the wrong response. Greta wasn't funny. She was just so earnest in her feeling for James and the boys. For Elmo. For her, Betty, too. The family. It was like being respected because you have money. It always struck her as funny.

When Elmo came into the high-ceilinged kitchen it was like five more lights were turned on. She could stop trying to talk. He sneaked up to kiss Greta on top of the head. She was inches taller than he was. They maneuvered like wrestlers to get holds for the best hug. He grabbed the boys and sat them up on top of the old refrigerator and they shrieked and kicked their heels and left black marks on the white. James came in and Elmo got him into an argument over how many tons of prunes they'd sold last year.

James and the boys ate like three machines on the same belt, grinding away until all the food was gone. Elmo ate but talked more. Greta could cook. She always ate too much here. Greta kept getting up for more food; she didn't seem to mind. "Espalier, and you not only raise the yield, you can plant the trees five feet apart instead of twenty. Do you know what that would mean?" Elmo said.

"Grandfather would never go for it," James said.

Greta had three kinds of pie. Lemon, because it was James's and the boys' favorite. Coconut cream for Elmo. Cherry pie because she had once mentioned in passing that she liked it. But if she had her preference, and she didn't really like dessert, it would have been jelly doughnuts.

They stayed until after the weather report and the eleven o'clock news, sitting in the front room, half freezing because the fire in the fireplace was the only heat, Elmo with his arm around her shoulders as they sat on the couch, James with his big stocking feet up on the hassock so they had to look around them. Greta half dozing, her head nodding. The boys upstairs in bed. "How can they say they're going to bomb those people back to the stone age? They're already in the stone age," James said.

"Maybe they meant the ice age," she said.

"They just want to spend, use up all our money on this business instead of putting it where it belongs." James put his feet down on the floor and leaned toward her. "The government must think the food gets to the supermarkets by magic or grows there in the parking lots at night for the consumer to buy in the morning. The supermarket chain gets the money, the middleman gets the rest of the money, the consumer gets the bargains, and the farmer gets the government loans for next year's crop, if he's lucky. Go into debt. We have no farm policy in this country." It was the most she'd ever heard James say.

They slept close together, clinging to each other, to keep warm under four blankets. The second week in December and it was so cold and it wasn't winter yet. Elmo got up to make the coffee and bring her a first cup. He climbed back into bed to keep warm. He turned off the heater at night. She had asked him why once. "Because we always did," he'd said. They'd woken up earlier than usual because of the traffic to the duck club. The hunters coming over from the city. They were going to prune, but it was still dark out. She drank her coffee and slid back under the covers, waiting for it to get warmer in the house. Sooner or later she'd have to leap up, put her feet on the cold linoleum floor, and dress as fast as she could. This cold was supposed to be good for the trees: it took a thousand hours of winterchill, Elmo had told her, before the trees could wake up from dormancy and put out leaf and fruit buds. He knew more about plum trees than he did about her.

If it was possible, it was colder outside, standing on the ladder, pruning the plum trees by the levee. They each had rows. It wasn't just that they were faster than she was—there was no comparison—but they went after the trees like they were trying to get away. Buckaroo plums, she thought. Snap snap. They'd slide down the ladder; they didn't use the steps. Move the ladder, all the time keeping their eyes on their runaways so they wouldn't pull up their roots and be off. Sizing up their adversaries for the next cut. Up the ladder again. Snap. Snap. Snap. Next tree. They would have left her in the distance if it hadn't been for Elmo, who did every other one in her row, besides his own. Greta was faster than James or Elmo. She moved around a tree as if she were giving it a haircut, sometimes not even getting down to move the ladder, holding on to a limb and swinging it over with her feet. The boys took turns driving the John Deere and loading the trimmings on the flatbed. When they got a load they hauled it out of the orchard to a pile to be burned later.

Elmo managed to do five things at once besides the pruning. Teased the boys by dropping his cut branches almost on top of them or leaping up on the tractor and straddling the hood so they couldn't see to drive. Threw pieces of pitch at James's back. "Knock it off, Elmo, I know it's you," he'd yell. Kept telling Greta to slow down: "It isn't how much you do, it's how long you're here that they pay you for." Greta never answered if she heard. The woman was possessed. Once he grabbed her pruners when she was moving her ladder and she chased him like a girl, long legs gaining on him with every step.

She'd worked herself in a packing shed, wrapping pears for shipping. Helped pick their orchard one year when her father hadn't hired the work out. Her mother's father, who died when she was little, had owned a cannery. She knew the life. But this was different here: not just more trees, six hundred forty acres worth, a whole section. This orchard stole the life out of you. The trees nurtured on the Clarks like a parasite. Dependent for everything. Irrigation. Spraying. Pruning. And then the picking. And there was no profit. They weren't even making money. It was their sport.

Even when she had worked herself up to a lather, wearing all the clothes that would fit, she was still cold. Gloves, hat, scarf, Elmo's wool shirt, jacket, wool ski pants, boots. Look at her now. Up and coming executive in a wide-open field. Was she making puns to herself now? She liked her job. She sometimes got to use the chemistry she'd majored in at college. Her managerial skills were innate, from her mother, who'd been president of every club in the county at one time or another.

Elmo was creeping up her ladder. He bit her on the calf of the leg. She ignored him until he started wobbling the ladder a little and she had to grab a branch for balance. "Stop it," she yelled at him. He climbed the tree she was pruning. "Wipe your nose; I've never kissed a woman with blue lips before," he said. She used her Kleenex and when he leaned toward her, eyes closed, she bit him on the ear.

They ate lunch standing around the John Deere, hot soup out of thermoses; they kept their mugs warm on the manifold of the tractor. They swayed from foot to foot, blowing cones of steam and eating their sandwiches with their gloves on. It was overcast and it smelled like rain. They'd stay even if it started coming down.

It got dark early but they worked right up until they couldn't see enough to find a limb to cut. Then they went in, she and Elmo to the foreman's house to clean up before they went back up to the main house for dinner. They took their boots off sitting on chairs right next to the heater.

"Well, how did you like your day off?" Elmo asked, picking up her hand and kissing each finger in turn.

"I couldn't think of a nicer way to spend a Saturday. It's that wonderful feeling of being outside that's so invigorating," she said.

"And did you ever think of the opportunity you're getting up on that ladder? You could spot some poor air polluter, some farmer burning without a permit or one of those factories across the river giving off too much smoke."

"I never thought of that," she said, pulling off her other boot.

"That's why I try and give you the tallest ladders," he said.

He let her take the first bath and the room filled with steam until the mirror over the sink looked like a block of ice. She got in and stretched out. The heat made her body malleable, loose, like a tangle of yarn. She let some water out and put more hot in, working the knobs with her toes. He looked through the doorway wearing his shorts. "Come and join me," she said.

"I thought you'd never ask," he said. She pulled back her knees and watched him get in one leg at a time, dip, soap himself until he was coated with white suds. Soap always lathered better for him: it was the hair on his chest, she thought. He submerged suddenly, raising the water into her nose. She had to sit up. "Are we going to have time to see my parents tomorrow?" She said it.

"If you like. We can work up until noon."

"I'll phone, then." She could feel her own awkwardness, then anger and outrage. What was he feeling?

"They have to do what we did today every single day until the last part of February, if they're lucky and there's no storms."

"I know, Elmo." Did she sound contrite? "I don't mind helping."

"I have no choice," he said. "And I'm going to do what I can. You don't want to understand that."

"I do, Elmo."

"Why are you being so docile? You usually put up a better fight," he said.

"I'm too cold," she said. "I'm at my best with central heating."

"You go over, take the truck in the morning, and visit. I'll stay; it will give us more time. Come back when you're ready."

She wouldn't answer. Let the warm water put her to sleep.

Now the cars from the club were passing the house again, going back to the city after the shoot. They both listened as one slowed and pulled off onto the gravel apron in front. Elmo started to get out. "Don't answer," she said as he dried himself off. They heard someone on the porch before the knock.

"I left the kitchen light on," he said, putting on clean shorts and then his trousers. He would freeze without a shirt. She wasn't his mother. She could hear him open the door to talk.

"Clark, what the hell, why don't you come down to the club and see us?"

"Busy, Mickey, have to work for a living."

"Here, I brought you some ducks; they're gutted but that's all. You can do your own plucking."

"I'd invite you in, Mickey, but we're about ready to go up to see James."

"Don't have time anyway. Come down one of these times. It's a good year; never saw so many birds in my life."

"Elmo," somebody called out from the car.

"It's Virginia," Mickey said.

"Hello, Virginia," Elmo called back. "You do any good?"

"Three limits, nine more than Mickey."

"Hi, Elmo," another voice called out. "Mickey's told me all about you."

"That's Cindy," Mickey said, and Elmo called back hello to Cindy. "We're going together. It's getting serious. I might ask her the big question one of these days. They accepted me in officers candidate program. After that, maybe. You must be freezing. I'll see you, Elmo. Don't be such a stranger."

"Thanks for the ducks," Elmo said, shutting the door.

He came back into the bathroom. "Mickey Conlin."

"I heard. He's engaged?"

"Almost, apparently."

She started giggling. "You remember that time—we must have been fourteen, freshman—and you brought him to one of our school dances?"

He thought a minute, shook his head. "I used to go stay the weekend at his house in the city."

"He danced with someone, I forget who, and asked, 'Do you do it?' in her ear. She didn't know what he was talking about, thought it was a kind of dance, until she got back to the lavatory and told us. For years later we all used to go into hysterics when someone would say do you do it."

"You don't forget anything."

"Come to think of it, I don't."

She got out of the tub and he handed her a dry towel and dried her back with another. "James says the Conlins offered him a good price for the marsh. The old man did."

"What do you think?" she said. She couldn't see his face because he was behind her. She didn't dare turn. She wanted him to come to the conclusion all the other farmers in the county had come to. She waited, forgetting to breathe.

"It would break up the section. My grandfather got that parcel with money he earned from operating a dragline. We need the money to pay property taxes. They're eating us up. But it would just be the start. We're not going to have the money next year either. I don't have all the answers," he said, throwing the towel into the corner.

She had come home from work early with a headache behind her right eye. She hadn't taken aspirin when it started, let it go until it felt like the whole side of her head was numb, and the eye was tearing, dribbling a stream of warm liquid down her cheek. This must be what it's like to have a stroke, she thought, looking at herself in the mirror. Her cheeks

looked puffy, her freckles stood out like acne scars. She had
tried counting them once and stopped in the sixteen hundreds.
She'd powdered over them, wore turtlenecks and long-sleeved
sweaters until she was almost through high school. Elmo
thought they were wonderful. That she was striking, with her
red hair and every inch of her skin dotted with spots. He had
divided her body into fourteen sections and tried to kiss each
freckle within two weeks. That was the first summer at the
foreman's house, and she had never been so happy. That
wasn't the right word, too mundane. Ecstatic wasn't even
enough. It was like all the good things you could imagine in
your whole life occurring to you all at once, repeated every
second for three months. He took a purple colored pencil and
linked several of her freckles together. She watched him,
tired, sated, hardly able to keep her eyes open at first. "That's
Draco," he said on his knees, wearing just his undershirt.

"How interesting. I hope that comes off, Elmo; I have to
get my Pap smear Wednesday to renew my prescription."

"This constellation is Cassiopeia."

"I'm glad they're good for something," she said. "I used
to hate them."

"Here, this one. Guess."

"The Big Dipper."

"See, you're going to amaze the scientific world. With
your very own planetarium to give demonstrations."

They moved that fall to their first apartment. That was
after they were married. For some reason she'd thought he'd
rejected the whole idea of marriage. One part of her knew it
wasn't necessary: she had convinced herself of that, although
she was willing to marry him. But it wasn't her that pressed
him. She'd heard James say to Elmo, while she was in the
kitchen drying for Greta, "If you have any respect for Betty,
you'll marry her. Living with a woman is too easy." She
hadn't heard what Elmo'd answered.

They went to Reno on Valentine's Day. Just started

driving, and she hadn't any idea until he pulled out a ring in front of one of those chapels. She'd just thought he'd found a good parking space near where they usually ate. "I phoned this place," he said. "You're going to need this." It looked like a washer, but later he said it was a prize ring from a gumball machine. She could only get it on her little finger. She wasn't speechless, but she couldn't think of anything to say. "I have a ring from my grandmother, but they couldn't get it ready for you; sent away for parts or something. Unless you have an objection." It was rare that he was ever disconcerted. Nervous. Not in control of his emotions. He was that now. Not looking at her, holding onto the steering wheel as if they were looking for a street and he were about to make an abrupt turn.

"You're sure?" she asked. "Let's not be hasty here. We could just play the nickel machines, eat, and go home." He was going to say something, opened his mouth. But stopped. "I don't mind being your love slave. It's respectable. My parents don't mind. You don't have to pay me for my work in the orchard now that the picking's done. We don't have to celebrate this way. You can owe me. Your credit is good."

"You're more scared than I am," he said.

He opened his door and came around. She watched him. Opened her door, helped her out. Held her there on the sidewalk, his hands resting on her hips. "If it just takes faith, desire, devotion, responsibility, endless sex, and liver and onions three times a week, I think we have a chance," he said, taking her hand. How long ago was that?

She heard the front door close and came out of the bathroom. "I'm home," she said. He had some books and a brown paper bag. He stopped in front of her. "I have a headache."

"Did you take aspirin?"

"I just did." He didn't move, looking at her. It was as if the room were still crowded with their argument and there was no space to get away. They'd had the worst one yet this morning, last night. On the phone at work, where she'd hung up on him. They were always about the same subject, and so frequent now that there was a shape to them, a form. She thought of it sometimes like one of those purple flowered thistles that grow in patches, sharp leaves and thorns around a hairy purple center. They'd take over a whole orchard if you didn't do something. They were in the apartment, trying to skewer the two of them against the walls.

"I stopped and picked up some liver. If you want to take a chance, I'll cook tonight. You lay down."

"I'm all right," she said. She was wearing her good silk blouse so she got out her apron first. She didn't feel like liver. She wasn't hungry. Turned the heat on and put the frying pan on the burner. She reached up to the shelf for the five-pound-bag of flour. It slipped away from her fingers and she watched in amazement as it came down by itself, landed in the middle of the stove, and burst. "Damn it," she yelled, "I don't want to eat anyway."

He came to the doorway again. "I'll clean," he said, "I'll take care of it; go watch the news."

"You'll take care of everything, won't you, Elmo." She had to say her lines: she had been working on them since this morning. To be able to breathe right, the words had to come out. "Why did you marry me, Elmo, did you think it was going to be easy? Answer me," she yelled.

He waited. He wouldn't argue back yet.

"Why don't you graduate, Elmo?" She paused, gave him the room, but didn't expect him to speak. She knew how to achieve that. "What do you want, Elmo? You can't go back to the plums. There's not enough for both you and James. You can't live there, you know that. What has that orchard ever done for anybody." She stopped to catch her breath, lowered her voice. "You're not your grandfather, Elmo." She waited, almost able to see the effect.

"You mean I'm my father. That's what you're saying. I know. Don't think I don't."

"Elmo, I didn't say that." She was losing control.

"But you meant that, didn't you." He was standing in the doorway, face flushed, trembling, his body distorted, as if he were being pressed against the wall. "Don't you mention either of them."

"I just wanted to get to essentials, to get everything out in the open."

He had stopped listening to her. "There's no connection between any of us. None," he shouted. "We're all different."

She had to go on; she couldn't stop till the end. The thistle growing, the spikes punching holes in her stomach, in her head. "You have to decide, Elmo, what you want. You're sitting here and going to let them take you. Because you're going to show me, aren't you. You're going to show me by letting them draft you. Isn't that right? Why don't you answer, Elmo? Talk to me," she yelled. "You're just waiting for the mail. So you can go. You'll have a reason then. Because you can't face up . . . "

He ran, moved so fast he was a blur, and she heard the front door close. She never had a chance to say what she'd thought up driving home. "You better think about having a baby, or you'll end up killing one in that mess over there."

He didn't come back that night or the next day when she came home from work. He'd never stayed away overnight before. She said aloud, "It's not going to hurt me to phone Greta." But she hated to. Let them know they were having trouble. They knew anyway. They must know. But the Clarks never argued in public, in front of anyone. Never swore. She dropped a bowl of fresh peas once and said shit out loud. They all looked shocked. It was as if one of the peas had spoken the word.

"I was just wondering," she said, trying to get off the phone. "I'm glad." Greta would talk her ear off. The more

indifferent she was toward her, the more kind and friendly
Greta became. "Maybe I'll drive over," she said. "Don't mention I phoned; I'll surprise him."

She could phone in sick tomorrow at the office, she reminded herself backing out the car. There wasn't much traffic.
Everyone was eating. She was chasing him again. But Elmo
never kept score. There was no taking turns or noticing who
was ahead in the argument for him. They'd been together
almost four years now. That wasn't such a long time.

It was after nine when she reached the foreman's house.
There were no lights. Their truck was parked out in front. He
had to be in there if he'd got up at five that morning. She got
out of the car and tried not to make any noise as she went
across the porch and opened the door. She could see where
she was in the dark from the stove pilot light. Guided herself
through the kitchen and into the bedroom.

She listened for his breathing but could only hear her
own as she undressed. Let her skirt drop to her ankles, stepped
one leg free and kicked loose with the other when it tangled,
hitting her chin against the wrought-iron bedstead. Controlled
herself, got everything off and got into bed. Edged over until
she felt the solid warm expanse of Elmo's back. Pressed herself
as close as she could.

"We finished picking the Red Beauts today," he said.
"And they made me think of you."

"You say the nicest things."

"You're a better shade of red, of course." She squeezed
him tighter. "I was thinking."

"And about time," she said, but he didn't laugh.

"I was thinking," he repeated. "Once my grandfather
told me he got my father deferred, kept him out of the army.
He had been in the coast artillery himself, I think, in the first
one. He said it was the wrong thing to do. And James went,
of course. He volunteered to go over."

She waited.

"I don't want to go into the army, you have to know that. Even if I get my degree, and I admit I should, and get into graduate school, they still might take me. It's no guarantee. But I'll try. I do want to stay with you."

"It's not a patriotic war, Elmo, if there is such a thing."

"I know that; I agree."

"We could have a baby." She could feel his back move as he inhaled, then let the air out. Once. Twice. Three times.

"I don't know," he said. "Would it be fair to have one just to avoid the draft? To the baby? There should be a better reason. I like the idea, the more I think about it, of having speckled-faced children. But not that way."

"They'll take you, Elmo, I know they will."

"I have to take my chances," he said.

He graduated: He had the units; it was only a matter of waiting until the next semester. They accepted him into the graduate program, gave him an extra stipend for his work at the experimental station. He signed the whole check over to James. She didn't say anything. He had his priorities. What was there to say? He'd evened the odds he wouldn't have to go.

He was willing to move closer to her job and the station. Further away from the orchard. Three hours and thirteen minutes now. She surprised herself, brought up her chance for a transfer. "I could be head of the whole unit down in the Los Angeles basin. Believe it or not. It would give me new opportunities," she said, quoting the director.

"I went down there once with my grandfather; did I ever tell you?"

"No, you never did." They were sitting in their apartment on a Friday night, not going to the orchard until morning. He had worked late on something at the station. It was so unusual to be sitting on their own furniture. She was reading the paper and he had a book in his lap.

"I forget why, exactly. They had some equipment or something he wanted to see. For almost a week we drove all over down there. I really liked the place. Couldn't understand why everyone knocked it so much. It was like a series of islands crisscrossed by bridges you had to get off of to get on land. Had everything a person could imagine. You just had to find the right stores. I think we were looking for generators. Found a warehouse full. Perfect weather. The ocean like a lake. And when we drove out to see the desert, where they were irrigating an orchard, Grandfather didn't want to leave. He told me, 'I should have planted here. Do you think they get hail? Fifty-mile-an-hour wind? Curculio? Even frost's not allowed. Perfect weather for plums.' "

"And they have the best smog and air polluters in the whole world," she said. "Would you be willing to move down there?" She was laughing when she asked.

"I don't see why not, after I'm finished up here. They have orange trees down there, I understand."

They were at the main house having dinner. Elmo hadn't changed out of his khakis with his new stripe on the sleeve. She'd picked him up at the airport; he'd just flown down from Washington after basic training. "Grandfather would be proud of you: private first class. That high up already," James said. They'd both had a couple of glasses of wine, which was unusual.

"It's general next," Elmo said. "I'm not going to be in long enough for anything else." Greta laughed.

"You won't think it's so funny," she said, "if Elmo doesn't come back." No one looked at anyone. She hadn't meant to offend, least of all Greta.

"Greta's brother Lyman was killed outside of Germany," Elmo said. She didn't know what to add to change what she'd said.

"Who wants pie?" Greta said, getting up. "It's in the past," she said, putting her hand lightly on Betty's arm. "Two orders of lemon for the boys, first."

They drove back to the foreman's house for the night. "You shouldn't open your big mouth all the time," he told her.

"I'm your wife, Elmo; I want to be with you."

"Join the army; then we can be together."

"You're taking the easy way out, Elmo. Don't you see. Why did you marry me?"

"I'll be back in twelve months. Just think, all that time you'll get to use the PX." He laughed. "It'll seem like a long weekend."

She sat back. She heard the words but wasn't sure which one of them was saying them. "If I'm still waiting."

She didn't take any time off during his thirty-day leave. She wasn't angry or upset. This could have been avoided. Elmo went to the orchard, worked with James, or spent his days at the experimental station. He had dinner ready for her when she came home, or took her out. He treated her as if she were the one who was going away.

He talked her into going to the experimental station. She was tired. "Come on, Betty, I want to show you something."

"Do I have to change, or can I wear these?" She wasn't going to climb any trees if she could help it.

"You look wonderful. Put your shoes on." He got down and slipped her heels on her feet. She must have been falling asleep.

He took her hand when they walked down the steps to the truck. He never understood that she got tired: getting up at six-thirty, leaving at seven forty-five to be there before nine. Back at six-thirty at night. Shop. Cook. Clean. He helped too, but she felt he expected her to do everything. She was tired.

He got out to unlock the gate and she noticed in the headlights how young he looked with his army haircut. She had stopped thinking about him leaving. It seemed remote.

Not really a possibility. He never mentioned anything about it or the army either.

They walked past the offices, labs, and hothouses. She had been here a couple of times to pick him up but had never realized how big the place was. It was just light enough to see the rows upon rows of trees that went on for miles. No wonder he liked the place so much.

"Almonds," he said, pausing at some trees they were passing. "They're trying to make the meats flatter so they won't stick out of candy bars. We accommodate anyone here."

He held onto her hand. She was coming more awake by the instant. It was warm for April, already in the eighties. She could smell blossoms on trees somewhere. It was quiet enough to hear your own heart beat. The stars were spread out thick overhead.

"Here," he said, "something I'm trying in this row. See, I'm experimenting with espalier. Two-dimensional trees. Easier to pick; you can plant them closer together. They do this in Europe a lot. Possibly a better yield, if we get the right varieties."

"They look like grapevines instead of trees."

"There's a resemblance. I never thought of that." She couldn't see that well. But they really looked like her mother's pyracanthas trained up on a trellis.

"Here, sit on my jacket right on this spot. Perfect. Close your eyes now."

"Elmo, I've got my good skirt on."

"Close. Now open your eyes." He had put a bottle in her hands. It was tied to a branch of a tree. "See the blossoms inside? Is it too dark? The plums will develop on that branch inside the bottle. As long as it's attached to the tree. When the plums ripen, you cut the branch off at the neck. Then fill the bottle with brandy. Use a funnel. You'll have live Red Beaut plums in brandy. It's your birthday present. Happy Birthday."

All she could think of was he'd given the stipend to
James. It wasn't the money. This is what he was giving her,
she thought. "How nice."

"You don't like it?"

"Oh yes."

"I read about this and thought I'd try it. It has to stay
here anyway," he said, "until the plums are ready. I just
wanted you to see it. Someone will phone you when they're
ripe."

She didn't want to say anything. All she could think of
was that she was going to be twenty-four two weeks from
then. He'd slid his hand between the buttons of her blouse;
she could feel the pads on his fingers. She closed her eyes and
took a deep breath. He was pushing her back against the warm
grass. She took another breath, letting go of the bottle in her
hands. He wasn't going to be here for her birthday, it dawned
on her. Nor the next. He had her bottom lip between his
teeth. She shook her head and pushed him away.

Tuesday he left.

She'd never appreciated her job enough before. She went
to work, came home, and then went back the next day. It took
up the time now. She made it last, made it as interesting as she
could. It was like playing a game that went on and on, kick the
can in the summer evenings when she was a girl, until the
can was flattened, wouldn't stand up to be kicked, or no
one would come out from hiding, but they kept on playing anyway.

Weekends she went to see James and Greta. She stayed at
the main house with them, something she had never done
before, even with Elmo. It must have surprised them as much
as it did her, staying there, but she was more comfortable
there now than at her parents' house. She couldn't help it if
they didn't feel like real relatives. She was always made to feel

welcome. But she never got to know them any better. Never felt at ease with them. It wasn't just because Elmo was gone, either. They seemed so distant. So reserved. Self-contained.

She helped at picking time. Took her three-week vacation then. Time went faster when she was in the orchard. Elmo would have liked her thinking that. But it was true. She'd be climbing a ladder at dawn and then it was lunchtime and then she and Greta would be hanging onto the seat of the John Deere while one of the boys drove home at dark. Greta must have mentioned her working, because when she got his next letter Elmo wrote in his P.S.: I didn't think it was possible to miss someone this much. So please stay off the ladders. I'll worry if I know you're picking. You can barely stay upright handling the pruners. What will happen with forty pounds of plums in a chest bag around your neck? Be careful. Your loving spouse, Elmo.

Once she took the boys back to the apartment and kept them a weekend. Took them to the zoo in the city and then to the planetarium. They called her auntie and took her hands, as big as they were, when they crossed a street, looking anxiously at the cars behind the crosswalk as it they couldn't trust them to wait through the WALK sign.

She never thought April would come around again. The early plums were going to be ready to pick in another month. Elmo was coming home. The closer the date got, the more she went to the place. She'd read parts of his letters sometimes after dinner, or later, in the living room. They all enjoyed that: Elmo could be funny. So that Friday she hurried from work, just grabbing her mail and getting back into the car to make the drive without opening his letter, to be on time for dinner. They were having coffee when she remembered and reached into her purse. There had been photos before: Elmo in front of his tank, the Climax. She hadn't known it was a plum until James mentioned it. Pictures of the crew, bare-chested, tanned, smiling for the camera. There was a photo in this letter of Elmo in a bathing suit. Somewhere. Skinny legs, she thought, and passed it to Greta.

She read the first words and thought she was going to be sick, right where she was sitting. Elmo had extended for two months. They had made a pact, the whole crew, that they'd go home together. Two of them had more time to do on their original twelve months. That was like Elmo, was all she could think. Now it would be June. They'd be halfway through the picking. What about her? "Here." She handed the letter to Greta, who took a long time to read it.

"He shouldn't have done that, Betty," she said, handing the letter back. James was watching them, waiting. "He told Betty he's staying over there two more months," Greta said.

She knew what she'd do if she were alone in her own kitchen. Put two fingers in her mouth and whistle, loud; that's what she wanted to do now, until her face was beet red and she had no more wind. What about me, she thought. What about me?

When she got the telegram her first thought was it was what she deserved for what she had been thinking. She phoned Greta, then left work for the place. James read it over and over. All it said was that Elmo was missing, and it was dated the day before yesterday. She couldn't think. James started phoning. She could hear him from the kitchen. He came back to ask Greta, "What was Al's last name I played football with? He's in the Assembly now. You went to school with his sister."

James got hold of him and he phoned someone in the Defense Department. They waited with her. Neither James nor Greta would leave the house. She knew they should be out in the orchard while the pickers were working. They sat there the whole day, waiting, not knowing what else to do. Not wanting to use the phone because someone might phone them. Not wanting to leave the room and let it out of their sight. She slept in her clothes downstairs on the couch. They waited half the next morning until almost eleven.

When the phone rang it felt like the bell was in her heart. She couldn't help it; she started crying before James picked it up. "It's somebody from Washington, Betty," he said. "They have some information."

"You talk, James. No, I don't want to." Greta sat still, her big hands quiet on top of the desk.

"It's an aide for our congressman; I can't think of his name."

She could hear the voice. She had to know, and she went to where James was standing and put her ear next to the receiver too. Elmo Clark, E5, serial number 1468735. Wounded. Critically, the voice said, reading from something. Broken pelvis. Damage to vertebrae. Fractured skull. His tank apparently was blown off the road into a ditch. It was not discovered until the operation was completed. "He's alive, Greta," she said. Greta nodded her head. The boys were playing Monopoly on the floor near the fireplace. They had stayed too. Gary had just rolled the dice and moved his marker past the Go to Jail corner to the first green property. Must be Pacific, she thought. She left James and the phone and sat down where she had been sitting originally.

"They're estimating it was about three days after the attack that Elmo was rescued from the tank," James relayed. "That's why they sent the telegram." James was speaking at nearly the same time the words were coming out of the phone. "Because of the damage the tank had to be cut open and that took more time. But Elmo was conscious and talking."

She couldn't imagine any of this. It didn't have anything to do with her and Elmo. He was coming back in June.

"All the other occupants were killed outright. This part is from Elmo's battalion commander: He was there when the tank was opened. 'They all think the world of Elmo,' he said."

For the first time James didn't speak, just listened. Said thank you at four different intervals and hung up the phone. He went over and stood next to Greta. "Good prognosis. All things equal, he should be as good as new. Walk again. They're flying him back as soon as possible. After he recovers sufficiently from the operation to remove the bone fragments in his head."

At first it was as if she were unable to say the right thing to him. Do the right things. And he was depending on her. To help him. To get him out of the hospital. Out of this whole predicament. She tried. But it was impossible to know any more what he wanted. She didn't know where to start. The doctors said patience. Time. She had both at first. She went straight to the hospital after work. She took days off to sit by his bed, to hold his hand. Vacation time. Leaves of absence. They understood at work. Made cookies. Sent books. Her director made a lap table for Elmo to write on in bed. She brought him sprigs of blossoms and baskets of plums, when they got ripe. Everybody came to see him. The family, people from town, from work, neighbors. She had such plans, how it would be when he was able to come home to the apartment. After he was out of the casts, the doctors said he could be released for a weekend visit. He wouldn't leave the hospital. After a while, four or five months, the people she worked with didn't ask How's Elmo so often. A secretary's nephew had been killed. At least he's alive, she thought. Going to see him that weekend, she couldn't wait for the elevator, took the stairs instead. When she got to his room he lay semiconscious from new medication they were trying and didn't recognize her. The same thing happened when Greta drove over to San Francisco one Saturday to visit him. They'd met in the parking lot. He'd been to his physical therapy session and was in such pain his eyes weren't focused and he lay there and couldn't even talk to Greta.

After visiting hours ended Greta wanted to drive straight back, but she insisted they eat something first. It was worse in the restaurant: Greta looked like she was going to cry. She'd never come alone before, always with James. She hadn't known what it was like to sit for hours beside someone who didn't care if you were there or not. She had taken Greta's hand, held it during most of the visit. It didn't make any difference to Elmo. Greta sipped from her coffee cup, put it down. "It can't last forever this way," she said. She couldn't think of anything to answer.

She brought picnics to have out on the grounds when he was well enough to go outside in his wheelchair. After the second time he didn't want to leave his bed. Refused to try to walk. Stopped the physical therapy. The wheelchair was as far as he would go. Someone would have to push him. He wouldn't put his hands down to move the wheels. He wouldn't help himself.

"Elmo, I'm not going to be able to take this much longer. I don't know what you want. I can't figure it out. You won't say. You lie there feeling sorry for yourself. And then take it out on me. I didn't do anything to you. You're going to ruin us both, don't you see?" He just watched her from the pillow. The bed looked too big for him. "You can't change what happened. Not with your mother, father, grandfather, or your dead friends." She paused, but there was no reaction. "You don't have to carry all the tragedies. Overload yourself." It wasn't doing any good, she thought, and started to sniffle, but went on, "Until you're smothered. I don't care any more," she said, and ran out.

That evening she came back. "My neighbor," Elmo said, "there in the next bed, who's feigning he's asleep, says we are the best romantic arguers he's heard in the last eighteen months." He never looked at her when he talked, which was rare enough. He listened to anything. But when he talked, he closed his eyes or looked past her. It was worse when he tried to be funny like he used to. He had no humor left.

"I think he used to be a family counselor, because he gives me a lot of advice about these matters." She looked over at the other patient in the room. He had never come out from under the covers, as many times as she'd been there. "He told me he thinks we should never get married. But a long engagement would be acceptable."

"Elmo, what if we move back to the foreman's house? I could get a job in town. My father needs a secretary. We could get those plum trees to dance to a different tune, given a chance."

"I've been thinking seriously of just getting in my truck and driving around the state. Just drive away. Get the feeling for the country again. Maybe take a year off . . . "

His eyes were staring without seeing her. He didn't look like the same person any more. Thin. Chalk white. A scar that went down the middle of his forehead and disappeared in his eyebrow. He wasn't the same person. Or maybe he was the same and she was different.

"Alone, Elmo?"

"That's what I was thinking," he said.

"Good, because I'll be busy myself." They had done this before. They were repeating themselves.

After six months she asked to see a psychiatrist at the hospital. Got Elmo an appointment. He wouldn't talk to him. Wouldn't talk to her for a week. "It's *my* head," he yelled at her finally. "It's mine."

She had to talk and talk before he'd consent to leave the hospital the first time. He didn't want to go. Not even to see the plum trees. She had to get Greta to go with her to the hospital before he'd come back to the place. Then the woman wanted to bring her mother, too. To talk to Elmo. Greta's mother. "I think your coming will be sufficient," she'd said. "He wants to see you. If you don't mind, you could drive over and stay the night, and we'll all go back together. He'll like that."

At the last minute she had to agree twenty times that she'd take him right back to the hospital if he asked. "The fruit's already the size of the first knuckle on your thumb, Elmo. The trees are loaded. You're not going to believe it."

They got to the main house by ten thirty. She didn't look, but she knew he had his eyes closed the whole trip. James carried Elmo up the front stairs in the wheelchair. "Can I just sit here for a minute," he asked. She went over and put her hand on his shoulder, kneading the flesh. "Alone, just by myself?" They all went inside and sat in the kitchen.

"He's going to be all right," James said, "It's just the adjustment."

"It's been fifteen months. They want to put him in a rest home," she said. "The doctors had a staff meeting. They say he's not making any effort. They can't do anything else for him there." Greta kept pouring coffee; James was examining his spoon. She knew what her parents thought. They didn't say it, but she knew. They had gone to see Elmo, how many times, and he lay there, wouldn't speak to anybody. There was nothing she could do anymore.

"They want me to decide," she announced.

"He's not going to a rest home," Greta said. It was such a surprise to hear her speak up that no one said anything.

The boys came running in the back door. "Mom, Mom." They were both trying to speak at the same time. "Uncle Elmo is up the tree in the yard," Gary finally got out. They all went to the window. They couldn't see him with the tree leafed out. Greta made a move toward the door.

"No," she yelled, "he's mine, he's my husband. I'll take care of him." She went outside and walked casually toward the tree. She had no idea what kind of plums they were. She could only tell by the ripened fruit. He had somehow jammed himself up between two branches near the top. One shoe was on a branch; the other dangled free. He was holding on with both hands as tight as he could. The knees of his new trousers she'd bought him were stained by the grass where he'd crawled. His eyes were open and his whole body was straining to stay where he was.

She climbed up to the crook, balancing below him. "I guess we could build a room up here," she said. "It would be hard to make any babies, otherwise." He closed his eyes. The lids were fluttering uncontrollably. She stroked his kneecap until he stopped shaking and opened his eyes again.

"Come on down, Elmo. Greta made pie. The boys are hungry for lunch." He relaxed and loosened his grip. She helped him out of the tree. He tried walking, her arm around his waist, his arm over her shoulder.

"It looks like a good crop to me up there," she said. She had noticed he had two hard green plums and some leaves tight in one fist. He was starting to say something, and she stopped talking and turned her head toward him.

"I can't," he got out. "I can't. Take me back. I can't."

CALIFORNIA BLUE
1988–1989

It wasn't my birthday. So when I got to my apartment and turned on my answering machine and heard, "Gerald, this is Joyce. I'm going to phone back at seven P.M. Be sure to be there. And thank you." I knew what she was going to tell me, Greta's mother, who was living with them now. But I didn't make a move. Didn't phone for reservations. Didn't pack. Nothing. I sat there by the phone waiting, listening to the sleet hit my windows. A New England winter. A snow plow? It sounded as if a glacier was moving against the building.

The twenty-second of January was when I should have got the call from California. Another nine days. Since I'd come here to law school they hadn't missed. Both Greta and James would be on the line, would talk for an hour, James on the extension, interrupting: "You didn't tell him about Elmo. You should have been here, Gerald." They talked about the place. Where they were going next. The boys. It was always me who said I better let you go; this is going to cost you a fortune, Greta. What the hell, James would say. "If you're not my real parents," I told them once, "you're a reasonably good facsimile." I have to write that to Elmo, James had said.

I had to let it ring three, then four times before I could pick it up. "It's me, Joyce, Gerald. James died this morning." I couldn't think of anything to say. "It's clear today, no fog. You can see the coast range." She was phoning me from the front room, looking out the window.

"I'm on my way," I said. "I'm coming back."

"We'll be expecting you," she said.

I was lucky and got a through-flight on a half-empty plane, then caught an airport bus. When I got to town, it was too early to rent a car and I didn't want to phone for a ride, but I was just in time to get a lift with the mail lady. She didn't say much. Recognized me. "I heard about Mr. Clark," she said. "He was a nice old guy." I realized I never knew how old James was. I never thought of him as old or middle-aged. Just James. He always managed to stay the same.

She stopped off the road at everyone's box, snapped open the door and shot in the mail. It was like being on the school bus again. She didn't have any mail for the Briscoes' box, the place before the Clarks'. That's where the orchards ended; a last neat lineup of Bartlett pears and then hundreds of acres of wheat. I didn't know who those fields belonged to anymore.

Ahead I could see the old house, two-story, screened porch, the wintertime trumpet vine like a lattice of ropes holding down one side of the roof. The three old plum trees on the north side. The barn. The wrought-iron fence went around the front lawn in a spoked rectangle. There were cars parked out in front by the gate. The mail lady handed me a bundle of letters. "Give them my condolences," she said.

I stood at the gate a minute until she turned the car around and went back down the road. There was no getting ready for what was waiting for me inside. I couldn't devise a plan if I wanted to. All I could think of as I opened the gate was that the plum trees needed pruning.

I knocked on the front door. Greta took me inside with a hug. "Gerald," she kept saying. Gary came into the hall, pumping my free hand after Greta let go. I felt someone come up behind me and touch me on the elbows and I stiffened them against my sides, then was lifted two feet up off the floor by Tommy. When he let me down he started shaking my hand. I hadn't seen the boys in ten years. "When are you two going to stop growing?" I managed to say. They were bigger than I remembered. When I used to watch them on TV before they retired from football they always reminded me of runaway boxcars from a train.

"I got my settlement," Gary said. "It took five years, but I won." I had read there was a contract dispute that had gone into arbitration and he was awarded three million dollars.

"You just couldn't take it," Tommy said. He lowered his voice. "It's not the game that gets the old guys, it's the high life. I went to bed at ten o'clock every night of my playing days. That's why I'm still in the business and you're a cowboy in Montana."

"You play a child's game, you stay a child, Coach," Gary said.

"All right you two, let me at him," Joyce said. She gave me a squeeze. Greta's mother. She was the only one who had changed. Lost weight, looked more her age, which must be close to seventy now. Still dyed her hair platinum. I hadn't seen her since before her husband Eddie's funeral. I had limited myself to a two-week visit a year after I left for Boston.

The boys' wives came out of the front room and were introduced. Wanda and Connie. They didn't look like Greta. I don't know why I expected them to. They were tall enough. They had to be. Wanda met Tommy in the hospital where she was a physical therapist, after his knee operation. Connie had been the rodeo queen when Gary was the grand marshall, up in Helena. Joyce told me that, standing next to me, and added in a whisper, "They could have done worse." We both laughed. It was good to be home.

Greta took my suitcase and put it by the stairs. "Come

on," she said, leading me by the arm into the kitchen. "We're not going to be sad. He knew and we knew it was coming. His heart just gave out. We talked about it. He wanted it this way, just a family get-together." She must have told that to everyone that came.

"No wailing or carrying on," Joyce added.

"He wrote something, and a will too. Elmo's going to read that," Greta said.

Now that James wasn't here, I'd have to face Elmo. I should be able to do that with equanimity now. I didn't have any rancor toward Elmo. But I still got flashes of him killing my herd of ducks I'd saved from the sports. Taking my money and my custom shotgun. I knew he was back, of course, out of the hospital, but I'd never seen him. Not because I didn't want to. The last time had been when I was in high school. The old feeling of apprehension when I heard his name didn't come this time. I was just curious, that's all. I was ready.

There were five kids sitting around the table having a snack. Two were in highchairs, chins covered with jam. The others were already big enough to sit in chairs. Joyce got a damp cloth and started wiping their faces. Greta picked up the food on the table. Three were Tommy and Wanda's and the two younger ones were Gary and Connie's.

There was food on the counter all the way to the sink: bowls, plates, trays. Pots on top of the stove. Foil-wrapped chrysanthemums were lined up on all the windowsills with the white cards still stuck on their holders. "You hungry?" Greta asked. "We had a late breakfast."

"They fed me on the plane."

"People have been bringing things all morning." She gestured at the food.

"The boys will take care of it," Joyce said.

"Elmo's supposed to be here this afternoon." Greta said. "We couldn't get hold of him until late last night."

"When's the funeral?"

"Not going to be any," Greta said. "James was cremated early this morning. He wanted it that way."

"He left more instructions than there is in a cookbook," Joyce said.

"I could hear him laughing in there in the front room when he was writing it all down," Greta said. I thought she was going to start crying then: we all looked at each other. But she grabbed a sponge and started cleaning off the table top.

"How're Delores and the twins?" I asked Joyce.

"Delores is at the embassy in Uruguay now."

"Paraguay, Mother," Greta corrected her.

"What difference does it make. She's down there working. Never tells us what she's up to. You knew the twins joined the navy. After they graduated from Annapolis they had to go to flight school. Now they're in Hawaii. I sold the motel year before last. Too much for me. Thought I'd come down here and brighten up Greta and James's life. See what happens." We all laughed.

The phone kept ringing; people came to the door with more food. The kids were running in and out of the kitchen. Connie was telling me about her and Gary's new house they'd built on their ranch. I wasn't used to all this commotion. I kept thinking I could hear James scraping his boots on the back porch before he came in, ready to yell, "Damn, Gerald, it's good to see you," big hand stretched out to me.

"You want to come?" Gary asked me.

"They're going in to town to shop at the new mall," Joyce explained.

"No, I think I'll stick around here and help the women," I said.

We sat in the kitchen drinking coffee. No one speaking. Leaning back in our chairs. "I'll sweep," Joyce said, but she didn't get up. Greta, across the table, was going through a small brown box of recipes written on three-by-five cards. "I broke a plate over his head in that chair you're sitting in," she said without looking up. "When we were first married. I left him for two months after he knocked me down and broke my nose."

I couldn't imagine Greta battling James. People in town thought she wore the pants in the family. I never heard her even argue with him. She'd yell at the boys or me when we were younger, but never James.

She was still straight and slim, her hair in tight curls close to her head. The skin parallel to her eyes had creased but she was always the same. She looked up at me. "But loving James was the biggest adventure I ever went on. There isn't a step of it that I wouldn't take this minute."

Joyce got up and took my cup and hers over to the sink. "I hope James can't hear you," she said; "you'd embarrass him if he could."

I washed and Joyce dried the breakfast dishes while Greta vacuumed the front room where the kids had a tent, a blanket over three chairs, and had scattered cracker crumbs all over the rug. Joyce hummed as she picked up the wet dishes. I could see out the window over the sink just to the garage and a section of the road.

The first time I went off to college I came back every chance I got. On weekends, holidays, sometimes just for overnight. To help, I thought, but I couldn't stay away. A couple of hours' drive and I walked into this kitchen and I was home. Worries or no worries, whatever was going on at school, it all passed out of my head when I got to the road. We worked if the weather was good or just sat in the kitchen. Since I'd been in high school we'd talked about getting an old Buick convertible running that they had under a tarp in the garage. We started ordering parts from catalogues; took out the transmission and rebuilt it. James surprised me, had it running and had put on a new top when I came back one time. I made the original old green paint come back to life with three coats of polish.

"Why don't you drive the Buick back to Palo Alto?" Greta asked me. I didn't know what to say.

"Go on, Gerald," James said. "It's a classic."

"If you really want me to," I said.

The green '46 Buick changed things, changed me for a while. Everyone wanted a ride in that Buick. Like grammar school and high school, I was going through college at a sprint; the good grades came like they always did. I took at least two more courses a semester than anyone else I knew, to get through faster. Now, with the Buick, I was traveling in style.

I brought Karen back for a long weekend. She was from out of state, didn't have anywhere to go for Thanksgiving. James almost dropped his fork when he found out her father was a U.S. senator. I hadn't known that either. "In Washington D.C.?" James asked.

"We reside in West Virginia, but yes, he works there." I liked the way she had of looking alongside her nose, slightly askew, when she spoke to you, as if your head were a little to the left of where it should be. There was a gap between her two front teeth and she was just my height. She wore her hair like Prince Valiant and it was never out of place, no matter what we did. She sometimes forgot to put both sides of her makeup on: one eyelid would be blue and the other would be plain. I always checked it, but I never told her. I couldn't resist her.

"A lawmaker," James said. "I've never seen one. I'm glad to know they're real, have children and all that." She laughed. He whispered to me later, "Do you want Greta to make up the double bed upstairs, or do you want to put Karen in one of the boys' rooms?" I didn't catch on. "Doesn't matter," I said.

At dinner James asked, "Your father doesn't happen to be on the Ag Committee, does he? I could make a lot of suggestions."

"No, I'm sorry, Foreign Relations and Finance."

"Too bad," James said.

On the way back to school she said, "Well, besides the fact that he's a farmer, a veteran, a taxpayer, and a second-generation Californian, I don't think I've ever met anyone like him before."

"You should meet his brother," I said.

With the Buick things changed. But I had to keep reminding myself: Enjoy yourself; try to enjoy yourself. I took probably the best-looking girl in any of my classes home for a weekend. James wasn't impressed. Polite. But he found a lot of things to do outside.

Karen came back with me a couple more times that year. I think it was as much to see Greta and James as anything. I'd say, "Let's take a ride" and she'd know where I was going. James always asked about her. "Don't let her get away, Gerald. You're not going to find any better." I was too busy getting through school in three years, but she talked me into going back east with her to meet her parents. She spent her junior year in Florence.

The Buick burned up. James had told me the carburetor was leaking gas onto the manifold. But I never got to it. I had rented a garage. That burned down too. I couldn't tell him. I phoned Greta when I knew he wasn't there. "Don't worry about that old car," she told me. I couldn't go back, not until James came for me one Friday, met me at my room. "Damn, Gerald, those Christmas trees are growing faster than I can handle. Plums, you do the same thing, prune, pick and water, year after year to the same tree. It's unnatural, cutting trees down all the time so people can use them for two weeks. Then plant more. There's no sense to it."

"Gerald, change the water. Gerald. The dishes are coming out greasy," Joyce said. I drained the sink and squirted in more soap and ran the hot water.

* * *

With the Christmas tree money James starting buying back some of the land he and Elmo had sold. There was a rumor that the power company was going to flood half the county for a nuclear reactor they planned on building. Eminent domain; get everything cheap. People were selling. I knew James was up against it. I wouldn't take anymore of the money he wanted to pay me. I had a good scholarship and worked three nights a week at a gas station. And I had my savings, which I tried to give him for the battle with the power company. That wasn't necessary, he told me. We don't have a chance, he said, but I have to try.

He went to the meetings. Spoke up. I went with him a couple of times. When they asked, "Does anyone have any questions?" James got to his feet. He had a lot of questions. He went up to Sacramento. Phoned his congressman so many times they knew him by his first name when they called back. "Is James there?" they asked. Greta went around with a petition. They formed a committee, Save the Farmland. Then the state discovered a fault under the proposed site and the power company's permit was revoked. The fault worried Greta more than the reactor. Better to get a little rattling than get fried, James would tell her.

After I graduated I stayed on for my MBA. It seemed like the best thing to do. I had majored in business, passed the CPA exam. I couldn't stop myself. I just kept going to school. But I came back to help. One Saturday morning we had an auger rigged up behind the John Deere and were drilling holes to plant more Christmas trees. We both had mud up to our elbows and another two acres to do. "That's enough," James said. "We're not going to plant any more of these sons of bitches."

I thought he was kidding. "The money's good," I said, laughing.

"Money's not everything." He whistled after he said that, slapping his leg with his hat. "Did you ever think I'd say that, Gerald?" I didn't answer. "Anyway, everyone and his brother's going into this business. I did four percent less last year. We don't have to kill ourselves anymore." By then they'd made him lose a lot of weight, but he still had chest pains. He was trim now, still over six feet when he stood up straight. He'd begun wearing plaid wool shirts with the sleeves rolled up and a brown felt hat, widebrimmed, like the gangsters wore in the thirties.

"I'm going to start enjoying myself," he said. "This goddamn land has been in my family for three generations. Did you know that?" He didn't give me a chance to answer. "And no one ever got rich from it, and I don't want to be the first. Hoist the auger back up," he said, scraping his rubber boot off on the tire rim. "We'll let the place rest for a while. We'll grow stumps. The folks around here will know the Clarks have gone completely around the bend."

He was serious. We were going to stop. Then he said, "You too, Gerald. You've spent enough time in these fields. You take five too. Think of something better to do with yourself." I got the auger up and threw the shovels on. "Get on," he said, looking at his watch. "It's ten to ten, middle of the morning, and we're quitting."

Karen moved in with me. She hadn't found a place she liked when she came back from Florence. She was an art-history major, going to be a museum curator. "What's this?" She'd picked up the decoy Elmo had carved for me when I graduated from high school.

"A friend made that when he was in the veterans hospital. James's brother."

"Such a simple form. But he's managed a certain tension."

"He was good at that," I said.

She looked down the side of her nose at me. "You lived with the Clarks. They adopted you."

"No, I had my parents. My father left first. And then my mother. She died my sophomore year in high school, in a car accident. I just stayed there. At first because I had nowhere else to go."

"And later?"

It was too hard to explain about later. "I just stayed," I said.

James took Greta to Hawaii that winter. They sent me a card. "These banana trees don't look like a good prospect for us." They went to England next, for a month that next summer. I stayed at the place, painted the house, kept an eye on things. If they wrote me one they wrote me twenty cards. "Better than I expected," James wrote. "Went to Claridges and had tea. Just like I read about. Cost me thirty-three dollars with the tip."

"Not much for orchards here, but you should see the gardens. Flowers."

"Took Greta to Oxford and looked around. Punted on the Thames. Me, James Clark."

The doorbell rang. Greta answered. We could hear her talking. Joyce stepped back so she could see who it was. I had started thinking it might be Elmo. "It's Mrs. Briscoe," Joyce said. I nodded; I had gone to school with a Briscoe. "Her daughter was married to Elmo once."

"I didn't know that."

"They were young, going to college up at Davis. Then they drafted him before he finished. It was too much for him. He came back changed."

Greta came into the kitchen carrying a pot. "Stew. Mrs. Briscoe," she said. "Asked me when the funeral was; hadn't been able to find anything in the paper. I told her there wasn't going to be any. She gave me that there-go-the-Clarks-again look. I mentioned she could donate to the Heart Association in his name. I couldn't think of what to say."

"You don't have to say anything; it's not their business what you do," Joyce said.

I was listening to them and suddenly I felt my eyes well up; tears started coming down my face and I couldn't stop them. I must have made a noise, still standing at the sink, because they noticed. Joyce came over and put her arm around my waist. "It's not James," I tried to say, "not just for James." I couldn't say anymore.

I was sitting in the front room alone. The boys and their families were scattered all over the house. I could hear Greta and Joyce doing something in the kitchen. It was almost dark outside but I didn't turn on any of the floor lamps. The high-ceilinged room looked better in the thin light from the winter sun going down through the lace curtains. Old rug over the hardwood floor, design almost faded away. Two dusty-smelling couches facing each other on either side of the fireplace. James's chair, leather; the boys had bought it for his birthday when they turned pro. The seat was sprung by his weight, as if someone were sitting in it now. The desk, Greta's chair where she always sewed while we watched TV. French doors leading into the hall.

I didn't hear anyone cross the porch or the hinges squeak on the screen door. But the front door opened. He saw me and came right into the room. I must have been thinking of something else because I knew who it had to be but still didn't recognize him. He stopped in the middle of the room. I stood up. His hair was gray now, but his face was tanned, almost ruddy from the sun or the cold. He wore a coat and tie, baggy unpressed trousers and hiking boots. There was no expression on his face: just his eyes moved a little, as if I were hovering.

Greta came in then. "Elmo," she yelled, moving toward him, embracing, kissing him. Then Joyce came in. He was still watching me. Holding onto them, he stepped closer and he put his free hand out. I grabbed it. I didn't know what I expected. Elmo's back. But I didn't feel anything. It was like shaking hands with a salesman.

We ate in two shifts, the kids first and then the adults. Everyone was talking at once, passing the platters around, eating cramped, even with all four of the extra leaves in the table. Before our dinner, when the kids were still eating, Connie had jumped up. "Come on, folks, it's five to five; first call for drinks. Greta, white wine? Grandma?"

"Same," Joyce said.

"Elmo?"

"I'll pass this time," he said. Greta caught my eye. I didn't realize it but I'd been holding my breath.

It was a feast, food from all over the county. There were a dozen ducks, teal, I think, by the size. Only Greta, Elmo, and I ate them, shared them even. "Long time for me," Greta said, holding one up with both hands to take a bite. "James stopped hunting."

"No more ponds. Tules closed them up. The marsh is just for mosquitoes now," I said.

"Whatever happened to the Conlins?" Tommy asked.

"The old man died. Mickey's still around," Greta said. "When your father started buying back some of the old place, Mickey sold all he had. But then when he found out the power company wasn't going to take it, they had a little falling out." Elmo, Greta, and I laughed.

"He has something to do with the mall now," Joyce said. "I see him strutting around there when I go into town."

"You sure no one wants any?" Elmo said, taking the last teal out of the pan with a wooden-handled fork.

"I never did like them," Tommy said. "Neither did Dad."

"That's right, he didn't," Gary said. "There was never enough meat on them for me."

"Tasted like fish to me," Tommy said.

"That's what your father used to say."

"I never even knew people ate them," Connie said. "You never see them in the supermarket."

"I had some in a Chinese place once," Wanda said. "It was awful. Like eating pork fat."

"No one's forcing you to eat them," Joyce said.

"Who wants dessert?" Tommy asked, getting up. "There must be twenty kinds," he said at the counter. "I haven't seen bread pudding in years. There's even custard. Gerald, there's two kinds of chocolate cake, your favorite."

"That's good news," I said. "I'll have a piece of each."

I could have imagined it but I kept feeling Elmo was watching me. I wondered what he saw. I'd never got that tall. It had taken me a year to grow a mustache to look older. My face was the same as it was ten years ago when I was sixteen. I was always asked for ID when I went into bars. Karen thought that was hilarious. It seemed like time wasn't going to have anything to do with me; I was always going to remain the way I was.

I knew about him being a photographer, but it made me uncomfortable when he'd get up from the table and take a picture of us. Sit back down, then get up again a couple of minutes later. Everyone got used to it, stopped posing and smiling, just went on eating. I couldn't help it; I'd stiffen up, waiting for the flash, the click. It made me nervous. I tried to keep my eyes off the section of table where he was sitting. I came here for James's funeral. Nothing else.

When Greta asked me to build a fire in the front room I got up fast and stayed there until everyone came in. The boys filled one couch, with a couple of the kids perched on Tommy's knees. I went and got two kitchen chairs for Joyce and me. Elmo was setting up his camera on a tripod. Then he sat down.

"Uncle Elmo," Tommy said, "we've got to get back to-morrow; I work for a living, unlike this plutocrat here." He elbowed Gary.

"What are you talking about: I never worked so hard in my life, worrying about my money. And since when is coaching working, anyhow."

"James wanted you to read the will, Elmo," Greta said, and she got up and went over to the drop-lid desk she did the bills at and got out a sheaf of typed papers and a couple of torn-open envelopes with a rubber band around them. She handed them to Elmo, who started to laugh, shaking his head, as he looked the papers over.

"Maybe this should be just for the family," Connie said. She was looking at me, but I wasn't paying attention until Joyce said, "What about me? Do you want me to join Gerald in the kitchen, too? I have four daughters: I only carried three for nine months, but Greta's still my daughter."

"I didn't know that," Connie said.

"There's a lot of things you don't know," Joyce said.

I started to get up; I didn't know what else to do. "Sit down," Gary said. "Tommy and me already know more or less what's in the will anyway. He told us when we came down when he was in the hospital. You have to stay."

Elmo was standing patiently in front of the fireplace as if he hadn't heard anything. I sat back down. Joyce patted me on the knee. "He wanted me to stand up here," Elmo started out, "in front of the fireplace, when I read this to you." He straightened up and put his hand in his trouser pocket and started in. "This is the last time I'm going to get everyone's attention, so I'm taking advantage of it," James had written. "I'm dead now and Greta has my ashes up on the top of our bureau. I want Elmo as my executor to scatter them around the property when it's not so muddy. I thought I might last till summer but I didn't make it."

"About the property, I know it looks kind of stark now but it has potential. I left it like it is to give it a rest and us, too. My grandfather when he died gave Elmo and me six hundred forty acres, a whole section of plum orchard. It took some doing but that's what we have now. Four hundred leased and two hundred and forty in stumps. We don't owe anyone either. Not the bank or the IRS. My grandfather, who was a clever man, would be proud of me. The place is free and clear. What you decide to do with it is your business now.

"I wrote my will on the envelopes Elmo's holding, waiting in my pickup for the freight train to go by at the tracks this side of town. It must have taken a good twenty minutes. So I thought I better take advantage of the wait. I wasn't feeling too good and I was on my way to the doctor.

"I just want to say that I don't have any regrets. I was lucky to have you as a family. I lived with Greta for thirty years. And my brother Elmo, of course, he's always provided a little shade when I made things too hot for myself. The boys know I'm proud of them. Both have nice families. And even my mother-in-law, as mean as she is sometimes." Everyone laughed. Elmo waited, then continued. "And of course Gerald, who was born and raised on the place. And my grandfather, I have to mention him. There's nothing else I could have wanted. Goodbye now. Think of me sometimes when you're sitting around the kitchen drinking coffee."

Elmo paused to take the rubber band off the envelopes. "He had awful handwriting," he said. "He had this part numbered. One, my two shotguns go to the boys. There's masking tape with their name on the stocks. Two, that quilt that my grandpa's mother made that Joyce wanted is hers. Three, the medals that I got from the army and the forty-five go to Tommy, who asked for them. Four, my half of the Clark property goes to Gerald. Greta will fill you in on the details. I don't have much more room on these envelopes. Five, the John Deere tractor goes to my brother Elmo."

No one said anything for a minute, just looked around. It was like James was in the room with us.

"What were the details, Mom?" Tommy asked.

"I'm not going to stand by the fire," Greta said.

"It's the warmest place in the room," Elmo said.

"Well, Mother and I get to live in the house as long as we want to, if we need a place. But we have other plans."

"What are they, Greta?" Wanda asked.

"We've got our eye on a house in town."

"You spend all your time driving back and forth, living out here," Joyce said.

"James, as you know, was always closemouthed about money." Everyone laughed. "But when my father died he left me a little, too. We put some of that money into lots in town. When they built the mall they got a little more valuable. We had a building put up, which we leased. To make a long story short, one of the stores is vacant now. We thought we might open a fabric shop. I worked in yardage at Penney's before I was married. That's really all the details I can think of now," she said.

"If that's all," Tommy said, pausing a minute to see if anyone had anything else to say, "who wants to get another chance at that dessert? I never got any tapioca or walnut pie."

"It wasn't for not trying," Gary said.

The wind made the house creak when I came back inside after seeing Greta and Joyce off to town. They had some business to do. The boys and their families had been gone a day but I still hadn't got used to the quiet. Elmo wasn't down yet but I'd heard the shower water running. It wasn't seven yet.

I watched the three plum trees through the kitchen window, the last ones left on the place. Since I was in grammar school I'd pruned those trees: James always left them for me. I thought this was as good a time as any, and went back outside.

I got the ladder out of the shed and a pair of pruners and set up under the Elephant Heart. James hardly ever used the front door if he could help it after we started in the Christmas tree business. I always thought it was because there was nothing to see but the solid green wall out front. But he'd sit on the front steps in spring, though, when I started to get in shape to run, to time me. It was an exact mile from the front gate to where the old packing shed was. He'd always sit on the third step, his long legs stretched down to the walk, holding the stop watch. I started running the mile after James said it might be a good idea, that first year I went into town to school. I made the team. Greta and James came to all the meets. He made comments: "When you hear another runner trying to challenge, speed up. It'll break him. You look like you're running alone, dreaming your way around the track."

"That's what I do to get around there, James, in the first place, daydream." I was surprised he didn't understand that.

"Try concentrating," he told me, trying not to shout. I knew he wanted me to be good at something besides the books, in sports, like him and the boys. "Be well-rounded," he told me once. I did better after he told me about Elmo. "Did Elmo play anything?" I'd asked him, knowing James had.

"In fact he did, he boxed."

I had been surprised. When I last saw Elmo he'd been drunk for about two months and could barely walk steady, much less look like he was ever a boxer. "Was he any good?"

"Elmo was good at everything. Take a closer look at my nose; that's how good he was."

I didn't think about him very often then, but once in a while something would remind me of before, when Elmo was there. Ducks flying, migrating overhead, would do it. I'd stop what I was doing and follow them with my eyes, listening to them call, until they were out of sight. He'd shown me how to drive the John Deere when I was ten. "Get up there, it's a machine." I was worried after he put me on the seat. It made a lot of noise. There was an older boy at school who only had one leg from having a tractor tip on him. "It can't do anything. It's not thinking. You're the one that's going to drive that thing away." He jumped off and the tractor started going. He was right. He couldn't get me off until supper time.

I got the first two trees done and was looking over the last one, standing on the ground deciding how I was going to prune, when Elmo came out. He still wore his coat, clean shirt and tie. Had his camera and tripod. He looked at the tree, standing beside me. "I'll do this one," he said, and went up the ladder. He went right at each limb, as if they were marked. You have to have a feeling for pruning; not everyone can do it. Take too much and you don't get a good yield. Leave too much and the fruit is too small and hard to pick.

"What have you been up to, Gerald?" he asked me, reaching cautiously out over the top of the ladder with the pruners, as if the limb might move.

"I've gone back to school again."

"I understand that from Greta." He waited for me to say something.

"I got sort of bogged down with the details," I said. "Nothing seemed to go like I thought it should, or expected. I kept changing my mind about things."

"That happens," he said.

It had been happening a long time, I thought. One of the games we'd play at 4-H, they'd spin you around with your eyes closed until you could barely stand, and then let you go and run. I'd stop, open my eyes, not even sure where I was. Which direction to go. I felt like that now. I felt like it was always the wrong way. I started picking up his limb trimmings to stop myself from going on. But before I knew it I was telling him about the last fifteen years. How fast I went through school. I was twelve again. I was trying to impress him with something I knew was valueless.

"Then what?" Elmo asked, coming down the ladder to move it to the other side.

"I finally got a job, recruited like a free agent with a good knuckle ball." He laughed. "I worked in the city a couple of years, in securities. But it wasn't exactly what I wanted. So now I'm going to school again." He came down the ladder, finished. The trees all looked identical. Bare-limbed. I always thought when I was a kid that they were ready for their blossom dresses now.

I kept talking. "I never got close to what I wanted." I'd never thought this before, much less said it. "The more plans I made, the further away I got. It was as if the process became the goal."

"You sound like one of those psychiatrists up at the hospital," he said.

That made me laugh for some reason. That he could say that. That I could tell him what I had. "That's what I should have been," I said, "a doctor."

"Not too late," he said.

I had to set the ladder down, I was laughing so hard. He was grinning. Before Greta had driven off she'd said, "Gerald, now don't forget to show him the John Deere." I remembered that when Elmo opened the side door in the barn for me to pass through with the ladder. "I forgot how heavy these are," I said, breathing out puffs of steam. "They have aluminum ones now, weigh as much as a pocket comb." I turned on the light. Elmo had come back after he got out of the hospital, but not very often, and never for overnight. He'd told Greta it was too hard on him. And they never pressed him. So he didn't know what we'd done. I went over and pulled off the tarp.

The old John Deere was better than new now. Elmo just looked. New tires, rebuilt engine, four coats of paint. After a lot of phoning we'd got the old gold letters. He climbed up on the seat, rocked up and down. "I saw in a magazine where they have these things all computerized, air-conditioning, TV. You just sit there," he said. He looked out of place up there in his shirt and jacket and tie.

"I took your custom shotgun, Gerald, you remember

that?" he said, looking down at me. I remembered. Some sport threw it in the pond after missing a sprig I had called down. I dove till I found it.

"I traded it for a tank of gas and a bag of potato chips, up north of Redding. Said I'd be back for it. It took me five years before I got back there. Same old guy was in the store, sitting in the same place. 'I knew you'd come,' he told me, 'but a couple years ago I let my nephew use your shotgun to go pheasant hunting. He was supposed to bring it back. I'll have to phone. Leave me your address.' I had sent him the money. After a couple of months, soon as I got any. Virginia had wanted the potato chips." He caught himself and stopped.

I didn't know what to say. Elmo taking my shotgun had been the last straw between us. He had been drinking then and had taken off. With Virginia.

"I'm sorry I took your shotgun," Elmo said. "I'm sorry I did a lot of things." I didn't know where to look. "Let's take a ride on this thing around the place," he said, starting it up. "Open the barn doors, Gerald, so we can go look over our property."

He drove the John Deere out and slowed down for me to hop on. "Hold it," I yelled, going over and getting his camera off the tripod. Elmo had showed me how to use it. "Doesn't have all the newest devices. Doesn't even have a light meter. Just get everything in the rectangle and press the plunger." I lined him up sitting on the tractor. He looked different through the lens, as if he were already in a photograph.

He waited. Distant. Mechanical. I had asked Greta if he was on any kind of medication. But she said no, he wouldn't even take aspirin when he had a headache. "You're good for him, Gerald; he never stayed over, not even for James and me. You never knew him before," and she stopped. "I don't know him now," I said. I took his picture and hopped up on the tractor.

It wasn't like old times. I was a grown man, twenty-seven;

Elmo must be in his forties. Going down the road in winter. Gray. No sky. Cold. My nose running. Stumps on both sides, as far as you could see. We went fast, as if we were chasing something. This was the place we owned, Elmo and me. I still couldn't believe that James had got back the whole section. I never imagined that. And for owning half, I wasn't expecting that, not in a thousand years. But with the Clarks you never knew. What was I going to do with my three hundred and twenty acres? Without James here. Greta.

We stopped at the foreman's house where Elmo lived when I was growing up. James had tried to keep it up, but it needed paint. The hand's house just behind was ruined. Windows broken, the roof sagged, door open to the weather. Moss on the roof shingles.

Elmo didn't get down, so I didn't. He got us back on the road. Then the marsh: It was a relief, almost, after seeing the houses. I made a point of never coming down here if I could help it, all the times I came back. The tules were eight feet high, thick; they moved like the earth was moving with the winter wind. Filled with blackbirds; I couldn't see any but I could hear them inside. We stopped in front of the duck club. It looked the same. There were two punts, bottom up, on blocks by the steps. Place looked intact, no broken windows. A big padlock on the front door. He surprised me, got down. I stayed where I was.

"If you can't go home again," he said, "you can sure think about it a lot."

For something to say, I said, "Greta told me James bought this from the Conlins because he didn't want to give Mickey a reason to drive back and forth in front of the house to get here." He nodded.

"Whatever happened to Virginia?" It just came out. He was too satisfied with himself. I wasn't twelve anymore. When Elmo had taken off with my shotgun and Virginia, the Conlins would have killed him if they could have found him. He didn't answer. He was busy with his camera. Taking a picture of the club, me sitting up on the John Deere, the marsh.

I sat there. Starting to boil. Losing control after all these years. I never forgot anything. I kept it all in order. All the questions I ever had. All the answers. It gave me a kind of momentum, power over myself. I could quicken my pace, outlast anyone. At school. "I was the top of my class, Elmo. The very best in any of the schools I ever went to." It came out louder than I meant it to. "I never had anything but what you Clarks gave me. Now I've got half the place. I don't need it, Elmo. It has no meaning for me." He was fiddling with the camera. It was like finding my own father; James had got hold of him, heard where he was, somehow. He arranged that I could go see him if I wanted to. I thought about it, but I decided it wasn't any use. He never came to see me. I had all I could handle in high school. I didn't need any more interests. "It was you Clarks that were my family. But I don't want the place. It doesn't matter to me anymore."

"It matters to me," Elmo said, "we're partners now. We have to decide what the best approach is here." I hadn't said it right. He didn't understand.

He climbed back up on the tractor. "Come on, let's go get some coffee. It's too damn cold out here."

We were still sitting in the kitchen after dinner, Elmo, Greta, and I. She was sewing something. Joyce had gone to bed. I was in no rush to go upstairs. As long as Elmo wanted to talk, I was willing to listen.

He looked directly at you when he spoke, concentrating, it seemed, on making sure you were listening. It was disconcerting. He never fidgeted like he used to. He sat there calm as if what he was saying didn't have anything to do with where it was coming from. He looked like one of those TV commentators, there in the kitchen light, who knew everything you or anyone else needed to know, even though he was just reading something printed out by a computer.

"I just fell into it," he said when I asked about the photography. "I was up at the hospital, mostly killing time. But I was almost myself. Feeling pretty good, sometimes. James had come up and seen me. Brought all the local news. And about twenty-five pounds of Greta's cookies." She stopped sewing and looked up at me and smiled. "Peanut butter," she said.

"One day I went to the craft room. There was a whole cabinet full of photographic supplies no one ever used. I started fooling around. It'd been there so long I didn't think the film was any good. I used it anyhow, tried to develop it on my own.

"There was a woman who worked in the office, Mrs. Taylor, whose husband Glen was on the local paper as a photographer. I'd ask him questions through her. One Saturday she got tired of it, I guess, and took me home to meet him."

He sat there and talked as if he hadn't spent eight years in a nuthouse. Mental hospital. He was just learning a trade. It was occupational training.

"He showed me some things and I kind of went from there. I'd get passes and stay out a week with them. Go on his assignments. One time he asked me to cover a lodge meeting or planning-commission meeting alone, I can't remember which. I went.

"I don't know if I can explain this, but the camera gave me the ability to see things for only that instant. For that time only. It cut me loose from the past. By the time the prints were developed, I was free." He was staring at me, hoping I understood. I shook my head, enjoying his discomfort.

"Once, up there, I got to the point where if I went outside my room I had to have my eyes closed. It sounds funny, but it was the only way I could concentrate enough to

even move. To think. But I couldn't go around blind like that
forever. I got better, where I could get around a little
open-eyed. That's when I went down to the craft room. I
imagined that the camera took the place of my eyelids. Just
imagining, like you do when you're a kid. So I could keep my
eyes open. And when I took a picture, then I didn't have to
remember the subject; it'd been recorded.

"Do you understand, Greta?" he asked.

"No, but it doesn't matter, does it? It's nice to have you
back."

He looked at me. I wasn't going to give him the edge.
"I'm in the same boat as Greta," I said. "But now you take
pictures."

"I do clubs, school pictures, sports, photos of the biggest
pumpkin in the county, or the twenty-three-pound German
brown someone caught last summer. That's my job, keeping
the record of things."

Greta had told me some publisher up on the coast had
collected a lot of Elmo's photographs and planned to bring out
a book. I said, kidding him, "You're an artist."

He took it seriously. "No. I'm not being modest, either.
That camera is a machine: An X-ray technician isn't an artist.
We're both using a machine to take a picture. That's all. I'm
a camera operator. Like a tractor operator. If anyone is an
artist in the business, it's the people I take pictures of."

"So photography cured you?" I asked.

"I don't know," he said, getting up and stretching. "I'm
ready for bed. I think in the end a person has to cure himself.
It's the only way it can last."

Elmo was outside. I could see him through the kitchen
window, taking pictures. He was waiting for something, probably a gust of wind to move the limp clothes on the line. I
wondered if there was any film in the camera. I had an awful

feeling there wasn't. He was just pushing the plunger. Getting people to pose, screwing up their faces for him, shoulders stiff, putting their arms around each other. The Clark family portrait. A breeze stirred the bottom of the towel and he took the picture.

He'd spent the morning taking pictures of Greta making cinnamon buns, Joyce and me doing the dishes. "You're doing that so you won't have to help," Joyce said. "That's absolutely right," Elmo answered. He'd set the old camera up, then stand there, not even looking through the lens after the first time, watching the subject as if it were his eyes taking the picture.

"What do you think?" Greta asked, kneading a big lump of dough. I knew what she was talking about. There was something wrong. His manner, maybe. His answers never really lined up parallel with the questions. He was just a little out of time.

"It's not the same Elmo as before," I said, "but it's the same person." Why did I say that: it didn't even make sense to me. "He seems to know what he's doing," I added.

"It was him that insisted you get James's share of the property," Greta said. "James was just going to leave it to Elmo; then let him give it to you."

That surprised me.

"You better go outside, Gerald," Joyce called out from the front room. "Mickey Conlin just stopped out front." I jumped up and ran out the kitchen door across the side yard. Mickey had stopped his car between where Elmo had his camera and the house, and was getting out. I slowed down. Followed him. We hadn't seen each other for a long time. Mickey turned when he heard me but went on to where Elmo was waiting. I looked to see the scar on his forehead where I'd hit him with a decoy once. They didn't need me. Nothing was going to happen here. Elmo was going to nod and smile. Mickey was going to pretend the past didn't exist, had passed from thought.

"Long time no see," Mickey said to Elmo. Elmo nodded. Neither put out his hand. "Sorry to hear about James. I gave a contribution to the Heart Association like it said in the obituary." Mickey had changed. He'd lost his sleek paunchy look and was fit, as if he jogged or played racquetball. His clothes were just right, the open shirt, tweed sport coat, but no chains, ostentatious pinky rings, or wristwatches like before. He could pass for anything until he opened his mouth.

"We thank you," Elmo said.

"We might be able to talk some business now that you own the whole place. I don't know if you've kept current, but I've moved most of my operation from the city over here to this county now. Own a piece of the mall and the other places my father had on this side . . . "

"I still own only half; there's my partner," Elmo interrupted, nodding over at me.

Mickey didn't look in my direction, started grinning, shaking his head. "The Clarks," he said. "They broke the mold after they made you."

Elmo went on, "Gerald and I were going over old times and we were wondering what ever happened to your sister Virginia."

I don't know who was more surprised at the question, Mickey or me. He stopped smiling. I took a step forward to get in between them. Elmo had the intent look of someone who really wanted to know the answer to his question. That innocent look. The bastard thought he was safe now.

"I haven't forgotten, Elmo; you did that to get back at me," Mickey said. "Because I had it made and you were a wine drunk who blamed it on the war. Spent your whole life feeling sorry for yourself, whining about how bad you had it. I was over there too." He wasn't yelling but the words came out of his mouth in segments, like a chain, as if you could see them in the cold air. "I didn't sweet-talk a nineteen-year-old to take off with her, who didn't know any better."

I got closer. I thought Mickey was getting ready to grab Elmo, who was standing there as if he were hearing a radio weather report, wondering whether he should disk before it started to rain.

"She was my sister, you son of a bitch. When we were kids you always thought you were better. Smarter, everything. I used to come all the way over here to see you and you had no time for me, you were too busy. The Clarks, kings of the county. Better than everyone else. The best farmers. Best everything. You looked down on us. I used to beg my father to bring you back to the city when he came over, so you could stay the weekend."

He must have waited a long time to say this because he had it all down, organized, chronological, perfect.

"When I was confirmed I took the name of Elmo, did you know that? Michael Thomas Elmo Conlin. Did you know that? I went to every one of your boxing matches. It was my father who phoned the city papers. And I made you an usher at my wedding." He stopped. Because he couldn't think of anymore, or there wasn't any?

"Virginia's married, has a couple of kids. Her husband is in city planning. She's an architect."

"It can't make any difference now," Elmo said, "but I'm sorry. For everything." He picked up his camera and tripod and stepped back. And while we were watching, he started taking our pictures. When Mickey realized what he was doing, he turned and started walking back to his car. He called back over his shoulder, "With you two clowns' names on the deed I'll have the place back faster than my father got it the first time from James."

We watched him go. Then I said, "Come on, clown, Joyce made us some potato soup for dinner," and I picked up his tripod and camera.

*   *   *

I stayed a week. Then I went back east to finish my last semester. It was still snowing when we landed. I never minded the east coast weather in general. I was here temporarily. This wasn't California. I liked to wear my overcoat and gloves and hat in the winter. Even my galoshes. Putting them on, taking them off. It was like the weather had nothing to do with anyone's life; you just tried to avoid it here. Insulate yourself.

Joyce wrote. Greta. Let me know how things were. The fabric shop was doing well. "You'd think I'd know about the public," Joyce wrote me, "after being a waitress for fifteen years and running a motel for twenty-five. But they drive you up the wall. Years of shopping has made them crazy. They're like snarling dogs. They know what they want and you better give it to them." Greta made me a wool shirt, like James used to wear. "Elmo's been out to the place. I made him and the boys one too," she wrote me.

Elmo sent me a six-by-ten photo he'd taken of the family with a timer. We were all there. The boys and their families in the middle. Greta and Joyce on one end, Elmo and I on the other. All standing in front of the old house. It already looked like a picture taken ten years ago. He'd written the date on the back. Then, in a note: "I did what James wanted, took his ashes out and spread them around where the orchard used to be. Walked around the whole place from the slough to the road to Briscoes', back to the house." And he sent a picture of me sitting at the table, eating my dessert. I decided I didn't look like that. I actually looked happy, eating a forkful of chocolate cake in the kitchen. Part of Joyce's shoulder showed. Karen hadn't understood.

We'd lived together off and on until she finished graduate school. We had a few arguments. She left for two months once and four months another time. A year for an internship in Seattle. We made some plans. Travel. Jobs that would take us all over. Her father had connections. Karen could have a State Department assignment as a cultural attaché, evaluating programs in the embassies. He offered me a job as an embassy auditor. It would take two years to travel around to practically every country in the world, checking embassy arithmetic. We would be together.

I backed out. She started to yell. "You don't want to leave here because of the Clarks. You can't let them out of your sight. You lived there your whole life. James and Greta will manage. They'll survive without you there. Whose life are you living?"

I didn't want to hear that from her. I didn't let her get to me, but I wanted to yell back What the hell do you want? Instead I said, "I changed my mind. You're right, I want to stay. I can't go now."

She grabbed my upper arm. "When do you say you love me?" She was going to say something else. Closed her mouth. "You have to start deciding things," she finally said. She walked out. She didn't come back.

Greta forwarded my California mail. A local realtor had written he had a buyer for my part of the land. A firm offer, he said, at twenty-five hundred an acre. It was a thought. Sell out. Did the Clarks owe me eight hundred thousand dollars? I still wasn't sure why James left the land to me.

Elmo kept sending photos. A portrait of the John Deere, which I hung over my desk. Another photo of the marsh. I looked at it a long time. It looked like someone had cleared out one of the smaller ponds. Cut the tules. It was hard to tell.

I graduated again and came back to California with a sense of relief. It's as if you leave your shadow when you go and pick it back up when you arrive at the airport. I still had the state bar exam, but I wasn't worried about that. And I had enough money to get by on. I had always been a good saver. And when I'd worked I had invested, not only in stocks but in all the things I felt I had to have. The accoutrements that I'd thought about since grammar school. Several sports cars, for a start. A condominium overlooking the bay. Italian furniture. Suits. Racing bike. Stereo. Buying. Buying. Karen used to laugh, opening the boxes I brought home. "Where am I going to wear this gown? And where are you going to wear that tuxedo?"

"I'll think of something," I told her, and went out and bought some opera glasses along with the season tickets. Neither of us liked opera, it turned out. We wore the clothes to company Halloween parties.

When I went back east to school I sold everything. I took one suitcase with me. I got a good price, double what I paid for the condo four years before. I'd got tired of the things I'd accumulated. I'd wanted them so badly at one time. I was disappointed in myself. For the wasted motion. For not understanding sooner.

I'd decided on school again because I was good at it. Law school mostly because it was a three-year program. I thought I needed the time so I could devise a new direction, a good plan this time. Now James had died. And given me half the property. I had to work around that somehow to where I was before. I had to start all over again.

I rented a car at the airport and drove across the bay bridge. It was a clear day. I could see the moon in the morning sky. When I got off the highway and drove along between the orchards I could almost feel the old place.

I had been going through this town as long as I could remember. Buying my school clothes. Going to the movies. Eating at the A and W. Driving back and forth. I parked the car in a downtown lot and thought I'd walk to Greta's house. The town had grown, doubled since I left high school. I knew I could locate the house if I stayed in the old part of town. I turned my head away when I passed the Rio cocktail lounge. They'd caught me buying drinks for my friends with a false ID when I was in high school. Called the cops when I acted up. Couldn't keep my mouth shut. They locked me up. James came and got me out. "Don't make a habit of this," he told me. "It's not good for either of us." I topped that for stupidity by stealing a souvenir hat when I went to the state track meet. The night before, a bunch of us went out and I shoplifted the hat. $3.79. I didn't need another hat; I had four or five. I had thirty-two dollars on me. I started doing these nonsensical things. Acting on impulses. No plan. They didn't let me run. I'd contaminate the team, the coach said. James and Greta had driven all the way to watch and were up in the stands waiting. Just before my race I went up and told them what I did. Later, on the drive home, no one spoke. I started to cry. "Everyone does their share of stupid things," James told me, getting out of the car once we got home. "This isn't the worst thing that's going to happen to you."

I missed the house but found the fabric shop. I walked between the rows, hundreds of bolts of colored cloth, until I saw Joyce behind the cash register. Two other women were measuring cloth for customers, making initial cuts with scissors, then tearing off lengths from the bolt with a big rip. Joyce was ringing up. There were customers everywhere, looking at pattern books, files, holding up the loose ends of cloth from the bolts under their chins.

I watched until Joyce saw me. "That's my grandson," she said. "Take over," she told one of the clerks, and she grabbed my arm and we went out. "I'm supposed to be retired." she said. "I'm working more hours here than I did when I picked fruit for the Clarks." She walked fast for an old lady, talked all the way. They had torn down the old high school; it was a park now. No wonder I couldn't find anything.

"Greta's home," she said. "She gets lunch from eleven to twelve and I get off an hour when she gets back." Their house was brick, one story, two bedrooms, a small porch, with a big magnolia tree out in front. Greta was sitting on the couch drinking coffee and watching TV. "This is so sad," she told

me, her eyes red, pointing at the actors. She got up and put
her arms around me, kissed me on the cheek. Joyce turned off
the set. "Have you been out to the place?" Greta asked.

"I just thought I'd visit you two first," I said.

"We haven't been out there in a month," Joyce said.
"There's no time. Elmo stops, but not for long. Takes a few
pictures and goes out there. Stays a while."

We had lunch, sitting on stools at a counter. It was the
first time I think I'd ever been with them that we weren't
sitting in the kitchen. It made me uncomfortable. Even the
food didn't taste right. We visited, then I walked them back to
the store at one o'clock. They gave me a key to their house so
I could let myself in when I came back.

I walked to where the car was parked. Greta, like always,
like James used to, had asked, "Have you heard from Karen?"
I had written her about James. And she sent me a note back:
"I might be needing to see you soon, when I get back." She
was doing some oral-history project in Madagascar. "I'm running out of authentic subjects." She's fine, I just got a letter
from her, I'd told Greta. When she comes back, I'll bring her.
I promise.

When I turned off the highway the place looked the
same. But then I saw the first piles of Christmas tree stumps.
And cleared land, not much, maybe twenty acres near the
house. Out a couple hundred yards in the field was the John
Deere. That had to be Elmo. From the car I watched him get
off the tractor, set the cable loop around a stump, get back on,
then heard him gun the motor forward and pull the stump out
by the roots with a shower of dirt and a puff of black smoke.

He saw me and waved. I got out and waved back and
started walking out. Taking my time, trying not to get my
shoes full of dirt. "I wondered when you might come by," he
said. "Joyce said you'd written you were coming back." He
wasn't wearing a tie now. One of Greta's wool shirts. But not
the felt hat, like James had worn. Not yet.

"What are you up to?" I asked.

"I thought I'd pull some of these stumps out. I didn't like the idea that James was out here where nothing was growing."

All at once I was indignant. I knew what he was doing. "I'm not helping, Elmo. This place is an anachronism. It's got no business being here anymore. I'm going to sell my half."

He acted like he never heard me, waiting for me to finish. "I got some whips ordered for the winter, the older varieties, mostly. There's a market for good plums. I figure to put in thirty. acres. It's slow work. But I have all fall, if it doesn't get too wet."

For some reason I thought, if this is what my first thirty years of life are like, how are the next thirty going to be? I had to ask. "Did you clear in the marsh?"

"A little. Not much of a pond," he said. "Some ducks might come down."

I turned to go. "You suit yourself," I said, "but you're going to do it alone."

"You have to try and understand, Gerald, I'm not trying to make it like it was before, when I was a kid or when you were growing up. It's impossible. I accept that. But I can make a reasonable facsimile. Like a photograph. A reasonable facsimile. That's all I can handle, Gerald. But you might try for more." He started the John Deere when I was halfway back to the car.

I drove to the house and went up the old wooden front steps. They always needed paint first because they stuck out past the eaves. What did he mean, you might try for more? The front door was open, the screen door unlatched. I went into the kitchen. There wasn't even a dirty cup; everything was as neat as if Greta were still there. I didn't touch anything. I went up the stairs. Into my old bedroom. I had a cardboard file box I was going to need, filled with papers: my birth certificate, résumés, things like that, and James's letters to me. I saw the package, wrapped in newspaper and tied with string, on the bed. I slid the string off and unwrapped the paper. It was my custom shotgun. Taken apart. The stock, front grip, the barrels. I had such plans then. I couldn't remember how it went together. I kept trying, but it was no use. I don't think I ever even used it before Elmo took it from me.

I carried the cardboard box and the pieces of the shotgun down the stairs. I could hear the motor of the tractor strain as another stump came up. I was breathing hard, as if I had just run a race. The stock kept slipping through my arm and it almost fell as I got to the front door. I wanted to get out of the house. Coming out onto the porch I was blinded by the sunlight. It had been dark inside. The stock fell and I had to set the box down to pick it up. It hadn't got scratched. Where was I going? I sat down on the top step, cradling the pieces of my shotgun in my arms, and waited for Elmo. He'd be coming in for coffee at three.

I folded the newspaper, an old front-page section of the *Chronicle*. Laid the string on top. And what about the ducks, my herd that I'd rescued from the sports? They hadn't been mine to keep—they were wild; they belonged to the place; I knew that—but I'd saved them and taken care of them. How was he going to give *them* back?